For Alice Marie Petersen Welling

CRYBABY RANCH

Tina Welling

NAL
ACCENT

NAL Accent
Published by New American Library, a division of
Penguin Group (USA) Inc., 375 Hudson Street,
New York, New York 10014, USA
Penguin Group (Canada), 90 Eglinton Avenue East, Suite 700, Toronto,
Ontario M4P 2Y3, Canada (a division of Pearson Penguin Canada Inc.)
Penguin Books Ltd., 80 Strand, London WC2R 0RL, England
Penguin Ireland, 25 St. Stephen's Green, Dublin 2,
Ireland (a division of Penguin Books Ltd.)
Penguin Group (Australia), 250 Camberwell Road, Camberwell, Victoria 3124,
Australia (a division of Pearson Australia Group Pty. Ltd.)
Penguin Books India Pvt. Ltd., 11 Community Centre, Panchsheel Park,
New Delhi - 110 017, India
Penguin Group (NZ), 67 Apollo Drive, Rosedale, North Shore 0632,
New Zealand (a division of Pearson New Zealand Ltd.)
Penguin Books (South Africa) (Pty.) Ltd., 24 Sturdee Avenue,
Rosebank, Johannesburg 2196, South Africa

Penguin Books Ltd., Registered Offices:
80 Strand, London WC2R 0RL, England

Published by NAL Accent, an imprint of New American Library, a division of Penguin Group (USA) Inc.
Previously published in a trade paperback edition by Ghost Road Press.

First NAL Accent Printing, January 2008
10 9 8 7 6 5 4 3 2 1

Copyright © Tina Welling, 2006
Conversation Guide copyright © Penguin Group (USA) Inc., 2008
All rights reserved

LIBRARY OF CONGRESS CATALOGING-IN-PUBLICATION DATA:
Welling, Tina.
    Crybaby Ranch / Tina Welling.
        p. cm.
    ISBN: 978-0-451-22287-9
    1. Self-realization—Fiction. 2. Women—Fiction. I. Title.
    PS3623.E4677C79 2008
813'.6—dc22   2007025969

Set in Adobe Garamond
Designed by Ginger Legato

Printed in the United States of America

Praise for
Crybaby Ranch

"*Crybaby Ranch* follows the up and down and all-around adventures of a brave woman who's willing to ask questions we've all asked ourselves. The writing is vivid and will hold you through to the end—bringing home fresh answers to old questions about strength and weakness."
   —Clyde Edgerton, author of *Solo: My Adventures in the Air*

"A more winning heroine than Suzannah . . . would be hard to imagine. From page one, we are in love with this wry, insightful, funny survivor of the Sandwich Generation, squeezed between her mother's Alzheimer's and her husband's detachment. In reflections both luminous and humorous, she charts her way to love and independence."
   —Sarah Bird, author of *The Flamenco Academy*

"Women and men are suddenly revealed in *Crybaby Ranch*, an illuminating arc-of-life writing that unfolds in a rich detail of simple and complex feelings."
   —Craig Johnson, author of *The Cold Dish* and
   Death Without Company

ACKNOWLEDGMENTS

This novel is about love—maybe everything is. The first part of my life, I learned about love from my parents, Alice and Bud Welling; in the second part of my life, I learned about love from my husband, John Buhler. I am grateful for their lessons.

The process of translating their lessons into a manuscript required support and guidance. For this, I thank Tim Sandlin, who has generously given both for the twenty-five years of our friendship. I thank my Jackson Hole writers group: Susan Marsh, Geneen Marie Haugen, Connie Wieneke, Kirsten Corbett, with an extra measure of gratitude to Susan for her extra measure of help.

For stories and humor, I thank my sons, Toby Buhler and Trevor Buhler; my brother, Tom Welling; and my sister, Gayle Caston.

Hedgebrook, a paradise for women writers on Whidbey Island in Washington State, nurtured the early seedlings of this manuscript during the first residency I enjoyed there, then helped me to wrap it up during my second residency. I offer wholehearted gratitude for an exceptional experience with remarkable women.

My gratitude also goes to the Jackson Hole Writers Conference and the Wyoming Arts Council.

To the publishers at Ghost Road Press, Matthew Davis and Sonya Unrein, and editor Tess Jones, I give abundant thanks for their professional care and attention, making the entire process one of comfort and pleasure. Judy Johnson, Susan Wasson, Judy Boss, and Eric Boss, through their generosity of spirit, created the pathway that allows me to do what I love every day. And every day I send them gratitude.

For laughter and lunches (often brought right to my desk), I especially thank my life mate, John. Without his love, care and encouragement, none of this would have been any fun.

BEAD BY BEAD

The shortest day of the year (December 21) has come and gone
with the severest winter weather still ahead,
but the shortest, dark days are behind.

For Everything There Is a Season
—Frank C. Craighead, Jr.

one

Saturday morning opens like a meadow in springtime, about to flare with bloom and birth. That's the way the beginning of each weekend feels, even this one in the middle of January, even when memory proves weekend after weekend turns out pretty much the same. Still, possibility nests in the tall grasses. And if I keep alert I will not step on any eggs.

A world of beads nestles in my palm. Chinese cloisonné, East Indian mosaics, African eye beads, Venetian fancies, Italian dream beads. My tongue curls in silence around their names while the saleswoman tallies another customer's selections. Outside the shop window my husband waits for me. I imagine lobbing one of these beads off his forehead, just to break routine.

Instead, my fingers smooth the rounds and my ears absorb the ting of beads knocking into one another, and, as always, I am infused with the happy expectation that for two full days I can lose myself in the meadow of time. Bracelets, earrings, yard-long beaded necklaces, I will create them all and drape them on my body and the lamp shade beside my work space, then sell them and pocket the money to buy more beads.

Erik begins walking as soon as I push through the shop door. I step up my pace. "Hope you've bought something as fun as I did," I say.

"Picked up a couple newspapers," he says. His usual purchase.

I give a little skip to keep up with him. "Beckett sounded good on the phone last night. I think he's happy," I enthuse to Erik, who napped on the sofa during the call from his son, my stepson, off to college far from our Findlay, Ohio, home. "He says Wyoming feels like a foreign country. People try to scare him with blizzard stories and wonder why he doesn't ride on the rodeo team. Can you imagine? This college supports a rodeo team."

Erik doesn't respond, just keeps his head turned away from me toward the traffic on Main Street. It's a quiet day in town, but that's usual when offices at the Marathon building are closed for the weekend. A light wind nips at the bare skin of my wrists and neck. The sky is a milky blue—what we call cloudless around here. "Beck says we wouldn't believe the color of the sky out there." I continue my report. In lieu of eye contact, I talk to the pale skin behind Erik's left ear as he advances toward the car. I insert another couple skips and a trot to keep up.

"He says he'd fit in better if all his jeans had worn circles in the back pocket from holding a can of Copenhagen. I made him promise he wouldn't take up chewing tobacco and he said. . . ."

Erik steps off the curb at the street corner, and before I catch up to him, a car making a right turn separates us. The light changes, traffic flows, and Erik is striding down the sidewalk farther and farther away. My smile and exhilaration boomerang back and embarrass me. I look around, trying to suggest to myself and anyone noticing that my smile and energy are just a general condition, not dependent on the husband who heads off without me. A man on the corner to my right catches my glance as it passes his way. A smile warms his eyes and seems to send a message to me: You deserve better treatment than that.

I pretend I don't need this message. I look away from him. I check how far Erik has walked; I look at my feet, then at the streetlight. I look back at the stranger, and he nods as if to encourage what I'm thinking. But I'm not thinking anything. I just want off this street corner. I just want to finish telling Erik about how Beck's friends served elk stew for dinner one night.

After Erik and I arrive home, the stranger's eyes and kind smile still pulse behind my forehead. Instead of a wise and elderly shaman, the man looked my age, middle to late thirties; he was dressed in khakis and a Windbreaker. Handsome, too. Why couldn't he have just flirted with me and made my day?

The urge to make the stranger on the street corner wrong overtakes the urge to spread my jewelry tools, beads, and fittings all over the kitchen table right away. A newspaper barricades Erik in a corner of the sofa. I ask him formally if I can talk to him.

"You have been talking to me. Thought you were finished." But he lays the paper aside when I ask him to. Erik is easy to get along with, I remind myself. This is a nice man. He has never deliberately hurt me. I explain how unimportant to him I felt when he left me standing on the street corner alone. I leave out the handsome man watching us.

"Suzannah," he sighs, impatience tinging the edges of my name, "don't take everything I do so personally."

It's true that I used to carry a personal burden of guilt for half the stories on the evening news when I hadn't even left the house, but I've grown out of that. And now I feel I know what belongs to me personally—that is, if a handsome stranger alerts me to my feelings first.

I feel dismissed on the street corner again, and this time anger rises in me.

"All right," I say, gathering my dignity. "I won't take everything you do so personally. In return, I'd like you to take everything I do personally." I get up steam. "Whatever I say to you, whatever I do to you—take it very personally." I swat at his newspaper draped open on his knees, rise from the sofa, and leave the room.

At the kitchen table I unpack everything from the slate blue overnight case I keep my bead work in. I lift out six fishing lure boxes, each divided into small squares that keep my beads separated, but the mounting anticipation I usually experience doing this feels diluted. Erik works like a sponge on my good spirits. He shields himself not only with the newspaper, but with obtuseness; he refuses to catch my wit or the real meaning of my words to him. With Beckett gone no one is left to laugh at my silly jokes or to color in the blank spots between Erik and me. The loneliness makes my days drab as those leafless trees outside my kitchen window.

Packed at the very bottom of this stained satin-lined case from my childhood sleepovers is a cigar box holding my tools. The paper cover on the box is designed to make it look like a wooden humidor. A gold label proclaims: BERING IMPERIALS, TWENTY-FIVE ALL TOBACCO CIGARS. I lift the lid. IMPORTED LONG FILLER, NATURAL LEAF BINDER, it says beneath a picture of Vitus Bering, the Danish navigator who discovered the Bering Strait. That's what I need, an imported long filler for my natural leaf binder, I joke to myself, picturing the handsome stranger on the street corner. I lay out my tools with the care of a surgeon. Three pliers—bending, round nose, chain nose—side cutter, tweezers, gauge. I should take a trip. Just up and go. I have never done anything rash. Never traveled alone. Never made any discoveries. Vitus Bering had all the fun. All the good clothes, too, by the looks of his red velvet cap and ermine draped robes.

Happy by nature, I can become manic trying to produce boughs of good cheer to wreathe the air between Erik and me. Manic like today in town. I square up my bead tray with the table edge. Acculon wire cable, head pins, jump rings, I finger it all, trusting my hands to show me what I'll work on first. I love Erik, and sometimes when I'm not with him, I feel such a passionate yearning for his company. But come to think of it, I often feel that way sitting right beside him on the sofa.

CRAFTED IN TAMPA, FLORIDA, BY THE SAME FINE FAMILY SINCE 1905. I close the cigar box and set it aside. My family lives on the other coast of Florida in Stuart, and my father probably emptied this box of its cigars. Reasons abound for our scant communication the past couple years. The main one being my mother's drunken phone calls at one in the morning. But if my father had raised a decent daughter, she would visit and set things straight.

I bring my thoughts back home and line up black Czechoslovakian satin beads with tiny pink rosebuds inside them, both ovals and rounds, between the ridges of the white velvet-lined beading tray. Erik and I are both right in our advice to each other. I should stop taking his sulks and unresponsiveness personally; it would be a relief to us both. And if he'd stop treating me like I was the general public, it would help a lot, too. I separate the beads with frilly silver spacers. Suddenly I feel a cold grip to my insides: If it doesn't have to do with me personally, I can't personally fix it.

I pull out memory coil that slips from my right palm to my left like a small-scale Slinky toy, count off three loops, and snip. As I bend one end of the coil to catch the beads I'll thread onto it, I remember how I first started beading. Four years ago I stood in the hallway at school and looked at the watch on my left wrist, knowing vaguely that I meant to get information from it. Rather than hold the watch to my ear to check whether it was still ticking, I slowly brought it to my nose. This so frightened me that I was forced to discover at least one thing that would perk an interest in life.

That first trip into a bead store set me on a path that now weekly engulfs me with joy. For five days a week, I am stuck teaching junior high schoolers English, but weekends are mine to make jewelry. In my classes the teacher joins the students cheering on the clock till it hits three fifteen and the bell rings, calling an end to the day. Sometimes I'm even first out the door.

I need more silver for this bracelet—those lacy bead caps. I root around my lure boxes.

Again, the strange man's smile slices into my thoughts like a crescent moon slipping from behind cloud cover, and I see a reality I have refused to see on my own: I've been trotting after Erik the whole seventeen years we've been married. How can a total stranger witness a single moment and uncover for me a thing hidden so long? He did not pass judgment, rush into action, say a word. He just saw the truth and mirrored it back to me.

My hands stop their work. What truth?

In the shine of that man's smile, I felt something deeper than embarrassment. I felt shame, a lack of power to choose against taking part in something wrong. Again now I feel the red curtain of it rise to cloak and confuse my thoughts. In that man's eyes I saw how I allowed myself to be treated by the person with the most power over me. Power I had given along with the intimacy I offered him.

Perhaps I need to take the power back. Learn the trick of just offering the intimacy.

I have come a long way in this marriage. From a teenager in high school with the afternoon job of babysitting a college professor's infant to that professor's wife and that infant's mother. But what did I give away in the process?

Once, Erik needed me for Beckett's care. I created a home and a life for them both. Time passed and Beckett grew, and I became free to return to school, choose a career, but I'd forgotten how to make choices for myself. I didn't even want to. By then I disliked leaving my house; small interruptions in routine disarmed me of coping skills; I was easily rattled and very dependent on Erik.

I pick up the memory coil again, feed it a large round Czech satin. When I purchased my first jewelry-making supplies and discovered I could create something beautiful, I became stronger bead by bead. It was my first experience of doing something just for me. I should pat myself on the back, because when it does have to do with me personally, I know how to personally fix it. I just need alerting first from life's little embarrassments. Like smelling my watch in the school hallway. Like almost getting hit by a car while entertaining my husband.

I even pushed past my fear and began trying to sell my work so I could buy more beads, keep making new pieces. Now two shops here in Findlay, one downtown, one in the mall, sell my necklaces, earrings, and bracelets.

Hours later, dissolved in contentment and forgetting that I'm mad, I holler to Erik still in the living room. "What should we have for dinner?"

Long pause. I wait, head cocked. Newspaper rustles. Another minute passes.

"I don't know."

Big investment on my part for this nonanswer. I try again. "What do you feel like eating?"

This time I continue choosing beads, guiding them onto a yard-long piece of Acculon. Three beads, four, five.

"What do you feel like?" he answers in an uninterested voice.

Conversation with Erik is like playing catch with someone who keeps all the balls.

"I feel like escargot at a four-star restaurant followed by beef Wellington. Okeydoke?"

As I finish the necklace, I slide into a daydream in which Erik and I laugh and whisper on a dinner date while sending smoky, low-lidded looks at each other across escargot and glimmering glasses of wine. I touch my tongue to my lips, then lift my eyes to spot the street-corner stranger witnessing our flirtations. He corrects his assumptions of me as a wimpy wife left in the debris of the curbside and tries to come on to me behind Erik's back.

I take a break and stretch. That won't happen. Erik and I don't date, and the stranger's assumptions, as I am reading them, are right on the money. My evening holds silence from Erik and tedious noise from the television. I scoot back my stool and walk into the living room.

"Erik, I'm leaving."

No reaction. "Would you answer me?"

"I don't believe you asked me a question." He continues reading.

I ask one now. "Erik, did you hear me? I'm leaving."

Erik lifts his flat eyes from the newspaper to my face.

I mean to say that I'm going to the grocery store to get things for dinner, but his lack of responsiveness works on me and I blurt, "I'm going to Florida. Back in a week."

two

"Is there something I'm supposed to take *personally* about this trip?" Erik asks on the drive to the Toledo airport. I shake my head no. Fifteen miles later he asks, "Do you realize you could have saved yourself a hell of a lot of money on your plane ticket by planning ahead?" I nod yes. Ten miles after that: "Don't you know that if you'd waited for spring break, you needn't have used all your personal days from work?" I tip my head side to side and add a shrug.

All good questions. But for once I have nothing to say in response to him. I think Erik likes it when I'm quiet and slightly miserable. He carries my suitcase to the end of the ticket line and looks me over the way a parent does before sending a child off on the school bus. I hope he likes how this turquoise cotton sweater makes my blue eyes stand out. He kisses me goodbye rather rousingly, and I give a little laugh of pleasure. He frowns down at me.

"Don't get sunburned," he says and leaves.

I watch him walk off. He's dressed as if he were teaching today instead of heading into a lazy Sunday on the sofa. He wears a blazer, pressed khakis, and one of his dry-cleaned shirts with a tie. Erik moves with authority. Women like to look at him. Me, too. He comes across as neat and clean, simple and straightforward. Actually, he's only neat and clean.

I turn sideways in line and stare out the glass walls of the terminal where gray concrete fades into gray sky. A sudden thrill twirls through me. I'm heading for Florida. Blue sky, seagulls, and salty breezes. Perhaps the beach is the place to talk to my mother about those late-night phone calls. We'll walk holding hands like we do and I'll just tell her they are hard for me.

Once I secure my ticket, I sit with coffee near the windows. So far I've made decisions about this trip the same way I do making jewelry: watch to see what my hands do next. But I'm not used to this method in real life. I prefer thinking in correct grammatical English, punctuated, footnoted, spell-checked. I'm a teacher, after all. This trip must account for more than a response to a strange man's smile or my familiar husband's lack of one.

Perhaps at last I understand that a few new beads each Saturday morning aren't going to hold my life together much longer.

In the early years of our marriage, the unity among the three of us—Erik, Beckett, and me—felt like the ideal of a loving family miraculously drawn from three unlikely sources. But that unity demanded a sacrifice from me. My Tampax was the single belonging not borrowed, displaced, or mutually used. Over time I became especially attached to my Tampax, and that sentiment extended to my periods; I drew into my body and its secret rhythms. Erik and I didn't make love during that week. Also I hid precious things in my Tampax boxes, collected the empty ones for that purpose. Eventually, I acquired fibroid tumors, not a serious problem, but one that ultimately extended my periods to fifteen days of slowed trickle.

I watch people juggle newspapers, briefcases, and coats, as they make temporary nests in their bolted-down plastic seats.

I have been buying space and time.

That's the way women in my family purchase their personal boundaries, with their bodies. My mother suffered a hysterectomy when my father retired from teaching law at the University of Cincinnati and began teaching her how to keep house instead. Aunt Anne lost her thyroid and a breast before Uncle Roy agreed to attend AA.

I must learn a better way.

Next to me a woman struggles with balancing her coffee while trying to unload her tote bag, jacket, and backpack. I set my coffee down, hold her cup for her, and with my free hand, help her shrug out of her ski jacket.

"Thanks."

"Going on a ski trip?"

"Going home. Where I live we wear ski jackets everywhere. Weddings, funerals." She takes a sip of coffee. "I've sure felt stupid wearing it here."

"Where's home?"

"Jackson Hole, Wyoming."

"That's my dream place," I say and scoot to the edge of my seat and face her. "We go every June for a week." I look out the window and nearly have to fight tears at the memory of that isolated valley and the mountains whose icy peaks surround it like a diamond-studded nimbus. "Someday I'll just up and—" I stop and smile.

She nods in understanding. "Half the population got there that way, just up and moved. Must be magnets in the mountain slopes for some of us. I was vacationing and didn't go home when I was supposed to. At work I hear stories all the time about people who saw the valley once, dropped everything, and moved there." She takes a sip of her coffee. "I mean doctors, lawyers. We have the most educated restaurant servers in the country."

"Where do you work?" I don't care where it is—I want her life. An announcement begins and we pause to listen. "That's my flight." Reluctantly I gather my coat and purse.

She says, "When you just up and move to Jackson, find me. I work at the bookstore." She grins. "I recognize your magnet." She offers her hand. "I'm Tessa."

I give her my hand. "Suzannah. I love bookstores."

I dispose of my cup with its dregs of thin coffee and wave goodbye to Tessa. In line for the airplane, I wonder why I don't just step over to the Delta counter and change my ticket for Wyoming. Tessa and I could talk about books all the way to Jackson Hole. I don't go anywhere without a novel tucked in my purse. Then I'll tell her about Beckett, who applied to the University of Wyoming in Laramie because he heard it was the number-one party school in the country and because he thought all of Wyoming looked like Jackson Hole.

Once in my window seat, I wish I'd shown Tessa the small stone I carry in my coat pocket. I found it along the Snake River; a lavender oval, smooth as the water flow that polished it. I've never loved a place more than Jackson Hole, or felt so immediately at one with the dry air, the wild peaks, the scream of the red-tailed hawks. A woman slides past the knees of the boy in the aisle seat and slips herself into the vacant slot between us. I gather my coat tighter around me to give the woman space while tugging on the leash of my purpose for making this trip.

I calculate how many years since my mother began drinking heavily. Six, seven years ago she'd drink her dinners. The late-night phone calls began a couple years after that. Effusively cheery the first thirty minutes, followed by tears the next thirty. My gift to her was sympathetic listening, my cost was trudging scratchy-eyed through the workdays that followed. The almost sickening need for sleep dulled the anger that began building toward her self-involvement, which, in time, turned me from friend into audience.

Two years more before I accepted the fact that if she didn't remember calling me in the night, she didn't remember the loving support I offered. Eventually, I pulled the phone jack before going to bed and doubled up on daytime calls to her. But more and more she sounded uninterested in conversation and was still forgetful about things I told her concerning my life—a punishment I probably deserved after refusing her late-night calls.

My failure to draw boundaries didn't begin with Erik and Beck; it began long ago with her. More than once Mom said to me as a child, "I wish you were the mother and me the daughter." Often over the years we both seemed to forget which of us was which. She taught me to make decisions for us both when I was three years old. But that can't be right. A three-year-old with ultimate responsibility?

My plane lays over forty minutes in Cincinnati. Murals I remember seeing as a child in the now defunct art deco train station were moved long ago to the airport, and I go looking for them. At a mosaic depicting a burly worker feeding a printing press, I abruptly veer off track at a pay phone and dial Aunt Anne's number. My father's sister and I haven't been close since Erik and I moved from Cincinnati to Findlay a dozen years ago, so I give her time to get over her surprise at hearing from me, and then I ask: Is it true that I helped my mother make up her mind when I was quite young?

"Oh, absolutely," Aunt Anne says. "Why, I remember telling your uncle Roy, 'Lizzie sure does lean on that little girl.' You weren't even in school yet."

Soon I have to hang up so I can rush to wait in another line, this time in the restroom. There I recall the rest of Aunt Anne's talk. "Honey, how's your mother doing? There isn't a thing in this world that's rougher. Roy's sister Mary suffers the same thing. I told your father about the place she got help, but he wouldn't hear of it."

Is Aunt Anne getting the phone calls now? Of course, somebody would be getting the calls once I refused them. Late-night drinkers develop dialer's finger along with the fierce need to tinkle ice cubes. Did I think I was my mother's only resource? Yes, I did. That's exactly why the burden has been so heavy.

As my plane arcs out over the Atlantic Ocean south of Palm Beach, preparing for an eastern approach to the landing strip, I pull out my comb and lip gloss. I've been pressed against this glass by an immense-bodied man since leaving Cincinnati. He tips toward me, looking out my window, and releases heavy exhalations in my face. I'm seconds away from a screaming fit, and feel claustrophobic against the close curve of metal above my seat. I fidget in my strap. The plane loops over the barrier islands that separate the Indian River from the ocean; then it dips inland. I assure myself that in minutes I'll be unbuckled and standing in the aisle.

West Palm Beach spreads out beneath the right wing of the plane. My father's car is part of the metallic strip I see flashing below me. He is always late and always rushing, cutting off people, maneuvering short cuts, making everyone around him wait. I spot the airport.

As I stare out the window, we fly past the usual approach, past the suburbs and out over orange groves again, then head toward open sea. This isn't right. I look around. No one else seems to notice. I know this isn't right.

Twenty minutes pass before the captain introduces himself over the intercom. "Well, folks, got a little glitch," he jocularly reports. "The landing gear indicator isn't lighting. Most likely there's just a short in the wiring, so our copilot will head back to the rear cabin, lift the carpet, and take a peek down an opening to see if our landing gear has dropped into place."

The captain does not use the word *malfunction*. I distinctly note this.

Around me people laugh. Not nervous titters—belly guffaws. I don't join them. I feel heat prickle between my breasts and climb upward to my scalp. I'm certain if I tip my head, perspiration will gather where my hair is parted, and dribble onto my lap.

In the aisle a few rows in front of me the copilot and two attendants lift the carpet, peer down an opening, and claim to see the landing gear in place. Cheers go up from the crowd. But I know they might be fooling us, and even if it is down, is it *locked* into place?

We don't circle around immediately toward the beach. Why not? Because we are emptying the tanks of fuel for a crash landing, of course. I'm dismayed at how poorly I'm handling my fear. My fellow travelers chatter gaily among themselves.

Thirty minutes later we head back for the coast, and half an hour after that, we are once again approaching the airport. I look down and see the flashing lights of emergency vehicles lining the airstrip. I knew it. And I'm not ready.

I'm hot again. So hot. And I can't remember my spiritual philosophy concerning death, or even life. Or how I meant to deal with either. I'm not out of control, but in fear of the fear gaining on me. I'm mushy inside. Formless. I just want to be out of this plane, waiting for my luggage to spit out of the plastic strips and chug along the conveyor belt to where I wait talking about this awful scare.

Another thirty minutes and that's where I am.

Dad asks, "So what was the holdup?"

I tell him, my voice quavering.

"I wondered why you landed way at the far end of the airfield," he says. "Keep alert here for your suitcase now."

"They kept us away from the terminal in case we blew up!"

Curiosity satisfied, Dad dismisses my near-death drama with statistics that make my itchy scalp and shaky legs prove I'm less evolved than I meant to be and am an alarmist to boot.

"You were safer in that airplane than you'll be driving up A1A in the car this afternoon."

With him driving that's probably true. But I want to entertain my father, so I begin to parade out the better lines I heard from the fearless jokesters around me. "Some guys fly by the seat of their pants, but I'll have to change mine when—"

Dad stops me. "I'll go get the car and save us some time. Mom's anxious to see you."

"Is she in the car?" Mom's the one who will kiss me hello, tell me how glad she and my dad are to see me.

"She's home. Get on up there closer," Dad says, pressing my back through the crowd at the luggage carousel. "We're running late, thanks to you."

I watch Dad zigzag around people and hurry toward the parking lot, a tall, skinny man with thick white-blond cowlicks sticking up like soda straws around his head. His knobby elbows and knees jut at odd angles from his body as he races to make up lost time. I pull in deep breaths of wonderfully humid air, grateful the West Palm Beach airport still has outdoor luggage pickup. Yet the Florida heat doesn't account for my prickly skin as I keep replaying the landing scare in my mind.

During the forty-minute drive up the coast to Stuart, I ask about Mom.

"She's doing great."

The quivering in my stomach begins again, but I press forward. "You know, Dad, I've been having some trouble with Mom's . . . drinking." I look at him for a reaction. His head darts around, checking the lanes for an opening so he can move up ahead. "Maybe you knew that," I say.

"Well, I took care of that. I don't give her any more alcohol." He swerves out, passes two cars, slips back into the same lane.

"What happened?" This is a big event in a drinker's life, yet he speaks as if it had more to do with him than her.

"Nothing happened. I have a drink before dinner—she gets juice."

"That's wonderful. Did she get some help?" I recall Aunt Anne's remark about telling Dad about someplace they sent Roy's sister.

"We don't need any help."

I look out the window and distractedly read the billboards. My mixed emotions about this trip, ever since I blurted out my words to Erik, resemble the airplane malfunction; I want to fly down here; I just don't want to land. I long for my parents' company, yet I fill with anxiety over the time I'll spend in it. My stomach feels almost as bad as it did on the airplane.

To keep a conversation going, I return to my drama. "They were *peeking* down *holes* to see if the landing gear dropped."

"Apparently, you were the only one that was worried."

"Me and the fire crew foaming the runaway." With my father I'm hardly ever quick enough to retort.

"They have to do that for the insurance company. I doubt you were in any danger."

I turn and face him directly. "But I *felt* in danger." It's also rare for me to acknowledge feelings in my father's presence. I'm usually numb to them.

"You should have just enjoyed the extra hour's ride. You got more than you paid for."

I let this one go, but I'm glad to find those two years since my last visit accomplished something. Though there's Mom to get through yet.

How could I have let two whole years go by? But then they never visited me in Ohio either. Somehow that thought never occurred before. I have the bad habit of taking up the duties of both sides of my relationships.

When we pull into the drive, Dad says, "I'll bring your suitcase. Go ahead and say hello to your mother."

I spring at the chance to greet her alone and dash through the garage door, into the laundry room, down the hall to surprise her, though I know she expects me. When I reach the kitchen, I see the back of her hair above the glider, where she is sitting on the porch.

"Mom." I come to a breathless stop beside her. I am five years old, knowing that when she lays her eyes on me, her face will open like an Easter lily.

She tips her head up toward me slowly. She smiles.

Oh my God, she's mad. She's not going to hug me.

"I'm so glad to see you." I stoop down to her level. Her petite prettiness is so familiar to me tears sting my eyes. Everyone has always remarked on Mom's natural vivid coloring, and it has not faded one bit. Perhaps her startling blue eyes are a shade or so paler, but still not a silver hair in her black curls, high cheek color the same, and she's wearing her trademark bright pink lipstick, the only makeup she's ever used.

"It's nice to see you, too," Mom says. I've seen this set-faced friendliness before with clerks and salespeople. Her fingers rub the ironed edge at the hem of her cotton dress over and over.

"Mom?"

I hear my dad coming and look toward him.

"We're back, Lizzie," he says in a hearty voice. He bends down and kisses her mouth and nuzzles her beneath an ear. "How's my best girl?"

I have never seen Dad do more than give Mom a parental peck on the cheek in front of me. She sometimes nuzzled him and teased him flirtingly, but Dad always pretended he wasn't involved. He straightens upright again, yet keeps his eyes on her.

Mom says to him, "She's pretty. Who is she?"

Horror slashes me wide-open. I swing around to face my father. "Dad . . ."

He refuses to look at me. "You know this ugly duckling. This is Suzannah. This is our little girl."

three

The first moment Mom leaves the room, I say, "Dad, my God, why didn't you tell me?"

"Don't get dramatic. You caught her on a bad day."

"She didn't know me."

"I think she was just teasing." He says Mom is depressed; she's on medication. He keeps his eye on the door while he talks. "She doesn't know. That's the one thing I can do for her. You are not to say a word." He moves away and hollers, "Lizzie, what are you doing in there?"

"She doesn't know what?" I follow Dad.

"Not now," he whispers and leaves the room.

I take a couple steps toward the closed door. "Please," I whisper. "I'm tired of being scared." I know they can't hear me and I'm embarrassed to act like a small child in need of the grown-ups' assurance, but I've exhausted my fortitude for crash landings today. I move away from their door and go to my own room on the other side of the house.

Somehow I slept straight through the night. Now this morning during breakfast I wonder if that's true about the bad day and the teasing, or whether Mom may still be drinking. Either Dad gave Mom a good talking to and she's trying to please him or she really knows me today. The sticky Florida heat is a rumor to my skin, I feel so chilled and afraid. My fingers try to draw warmth from my coffee mug. I hold the mug between my breasts to melt the ice crystals that inhibit my lungs from fully expanding.

"Look at you with your high neck and long sleeves," Mom says. "Why, I haven't seen a top like that for years." She talks to me as if we have breakfast together every morning. She turns to Dad. "Do I get my hair done today?"

"No, that's Friday."

"What day is this?"

"Monday." Dad scrapes his chair back. "See?" He goes to the rolltop desk in the corner of the kitchen and pulls out a calendar. "We wrote down *Andre* on Friday. Here we are on Monday, so we don't go for one, two, three, four more days, do we?"

Mom rolls her eyes to me behind his back, and I laugh right out loud, giving her away, I am so relieved. This is my mother. This is the old game we play, how we defend ourselves from Dad's bulldozing and ever-present focus on our lives. Mr. Buttinsky, she always calls him, when we're alone. Sometimes Mr. Butt for short.

"Same old Dad?" I ask, grinning. He could slip out of a conversation and into his professor mode in an eye blink. But this lecture on counting the days seems a bit patronizing, even for him.

"Worse." Mom tips her head back and smiles when Dad passes behind her chair. He ruffles her hair and bends to kiss her upside-down mouth before taking his seat again.

He acts like they're honeymooners. That's something new, but it's at least a positive change. For the first time, I take more than a tight and shallow breath. A full measure of air draws into my lungs. I push my long sleeves up past my elbows and reach for a piece of toast and the orange marmalade.

Dad points out a hummingbird. We watch it kiss the feeder that hangs from a scrub pine near the screen. When my grandparents owned this place, they called this porch across the back of the house the Florida room. Mom and Dad and I always eat breakfast here and sometimes nap on the cots in the afternoon. A pair of sandhill cranes squawk to each other over the toast Dad threw to them in the yard, and a squirrel taunts from a pine branch, hoping to discourage them from eating it all.

Dad says, "Girls, I'm off. We meet back here at five thirty to dress for dinner and watch a little news. Our reservation is at the Prawnbroker for seven. Suzannah, let me show you this." Dad walks to the end of the kitchen counter; I follow him. He holds a pad and pencil in his hand. "This is where we leave notes to each other." He looks at me sternly, with meaning. "Do not forget to leave a note here whenever you leave the house. Even for a walk outside, you leave a note. Understand?"

I nod, but I understand very little. Is Mom putting on some act here? The thought surprises me. But it's true that Mom has always pretended she didn't know what was going on to get our attention. I've never questioned her acting dumb. I've just repeated information or explained the obvious by habit. Or perhaps Dad is exaggerating a small memory problem into a large one, taking the opportunity to exercise more control over her. I follow Dad down the hall to the door, step outside with him.

"Are you two still seeing Dr. Mengele?"

"It's Dr. Meagher and you know it. Don't be disrespectful."

"He's arrogant and keeps his patients in the dark." Anger seeps into my voice. I'm tired of this fear and uncertainty.

Dad lowers his chin, raises his eyebrows. "Perhaps you'd like to take over the bills. Then you can choose whomever you like." He salutes me and steps into his car. He rolls down his window. "Remember, don't discuss your mother's trouble with her."

"But, Dad, I want to know how she feels."

"You're here seven days. I'm here every day, around the clock—and I mean around the clock. Sometimes we are awake all night."

"How come?"

"She gets upset. Sometimes she throws things." He starts the engine. "I can't talk about your mother behind her back. . . . Just be good to her."

"I have always been good to her. Dad, wait."

His car begins to ease out of the drive.

"Keep it that way. And wear something decent tonight for dinner. You look like a Cossack all bundled up like that."

I watch him follow the circle drive out to the road. I am costarring in one of those movies in which the plot is based on nobody knowing what any of the other players know. Where all the suspense comes from everybody saying, "Don't tell so and so." This movie begins with Dr. Meagher, who is probably withholding information from Dad, who in turn is withholding what he knows from Mom, who in turn is withholding from the other two. And nobody is telling me one damn thing.

I return inside and check on Mom.

She is playing solitaire on the coffee table and watching a game show. Smoke from a cigarette drifts across her cards. Looks pretty normal to me. Exactly what she's always done when left alone. I carry our breakfast dishes from the porch table to the sink. I'm glad Mom and I get time today away from Dad. I might discover things aren't too different from the way they've always been. It's just me. I've been gone two years. I've forgotten how it used to be around here. And besides, I've worked at becoming more alert to life. Somebody at my house needs to keep the dust stirring.

This is the first time I've thought of Erik since I arrived. I pause on the porch with two short towers of used juice glasses and coffee cups and watch an anhinga land on the bare branch of a snag leaning over the creek. I don't miss my husband one bit.

I start down the hall to change into cooler clothes, turn back, read Dad's note: *Gone library. Back 5:30.*

I tell Mom, "I'm going down to Bessie Creek after I change my clothes. Back in thirty minutes." And I also write that out in a note to her.

She says, "Okay, honey," takes a dainty puff off her cigarette, and lays a black ten on a red jack.

I walk down the hall to my room. I've slept in this bed since

I was a child visiting my grandparents. The window beside it catches the breezes off Bessie Creek. I remember Mom tucking me in at night. If I wasn't sleepy, I'd ask questions about God to stall her leaving.

Have I heard her use my name yet? Stop worrying, I remind myself. Get outside. The purple martins return this time every year. End of January they arrive by the thousands from South America, first sending scouts to check out their old nests. Dad said he hasn't seen one yet. Maybe I'll spot the first one and report the news to him at dinner. I dig around my suitcase for shorts. I hear a sound and look up to see Mom standing in the doorway. She holds my note in her hand.

"Did you think I'd forget?"

I am a toddler, caught in a lie. I don't know what to answer. Either yes or no will get me in trouble. "I wasn't sure you heard me. The television—"

"Hmm," she says, "sounds like your father's gotten to you." She raises her dark brows and leaves.

I collapse on the bed. I have insulted her. Betrayed her.

My dad is right: I'm here one week; then I go home to my life. He stays. Still, I carry my sandals down the hall to the family room, ready to spill all.

Mom stops shuffling her cards when she sees me. "Honey, what day is this? Do I get my hair done?"

four

Erik tosses my luggage into the backseat, gets into the car. Under the sound of the ignition starting, he announces that he has made an appointment at a marriage counselor for us. Tomorrow.

"Erik, I've had the worst week. I told you on the phone, I'm just wrecked." Bring on that boredom and routine I used to groan about. Bring it on now. "Can't this wait?"

"You've been after me to see someone for years. Well, now I'm ready."

"But I'm not ready." This reminds me of the times when Erik and I don't make love for a while. I finally woo him into the mood. Then he comes too fast and blames it on the fact that it's been so long since we've made love. I feel set up not to get the most out of this therapy appointment.

Still, at last Erik is taking some responsibility for our relationship; I should feel glad about that. But then I always think

I should feel glad we made love, too. I'm learning a thing or two there, finally. Part of my recent move toward independence includes taking charge of my own orgasms.

I say, "I'm just so worn-out right now." Tomorrow a week's worth of catch-up waits for me in the classroom, but it's hard to stir up sympathy while glowing with a Florida tan in the middle of a gray Ohio winter.

When Erik drives, he leans into the door and tips his left shoulder down. He glances my way. "Your hair lightened on top. Must have spent a lot of time at the beach."

"Mom and I went for a couple walks."

I told Erik on the phone how hard it was sorting out the truth about my mother's mental health. I tell him now, "I still don't know what's going on with Mom. It could be depression or she could be sneaking drinks, for all I know. Memory is affected by a lack of certain B vitamins, too. So is depression."

"To ask you, everybody is suffering from depression. Ever think you might have an opposite problem?"

"Like what? What's the opposite of depression, glee?"

"Maybe. If there's no good reason for it, that defines a problem."

That's Erik: taking a firm stand against irrational glee. I hope he catches me pursing my lips at him. I admire his profile as he drives. Good thing, too. I seem to spend a lot of time talking to the side of his face, even outside of the car. He has a good strong chin and a mouth I just want to kiss. I like Erik best from the nose down. His eyes make me mad; they seem like hard brown nuts. I'd like to crack them open, poke around until I find something juicy inside.

"Well," I say, continuing to prove what a hard time I had

in sunny Florida, "I can't get my dad to discuss even buying One-A-Day vitamins from Publix. He's intent on shutting me out of the problem, and I can't wiggle my way in." I look out the car window at faded red farm buildings and fields of brown stubble. A few hibiscus and bougainvillea bushes with their tropical neon blossoms could add a lot of zip to this January country.

"First part of the week I kept score, shifting Mom's points back and forth from the *healthy* column to the *not-so-healthy* column. Middle part of the week I created a new column and labeled it *uncertain*. By the time I left this morning, all the points were lined up there."

Erik doesn't say anything. "You know what I mean?" I ask. Erik lifts his chin a notch.

I look out the window. I can't tell Erik the whole story. That gives too much reality to it. Perhaps this is the way Dad feels when he claims he can't talk behind Mom's back. The farmland is so flat I can see sky between the wheels of a train traveling beside us a half mile across a field. I remember Tessa from Jackson Hole remarking at the airport about the lack of hills here, even gentle slopes.

I say to Erik, "This is hard on my dad. He feels like he's betraying a secret trust talking about what's going on with Mom." I angle toward him in my seat. "Like us," I say. "Married all these years and yet tomorrow we're going to bring someone else into our private world. It'll be hard talking about our problems."

"You wanted this."

What I wanted originally was for Erik to deal with his moodiness, get help with his depression. But honesty demands that I take a deep look into myself. I shift back around to face forward in my seat. These fields along the interstate with their narrow shelter belts of brush and bare trees look as depleted and forlorn as I feel.

Maybe I want Erik to deal with his stuff because . . . What is that word therapists use? Projection? I could be projecting a depression of my own onto Erik. After all, he isn't the one who tried to smell his watch, for God's sake. He isn't troubled with an alcoholic parent. He has never expressed dissatisfaction between the two of us. He even claims to like his job. Is this all my problem? Is my irrational glee a cover-up for a depression I keep attributing to Erik and my mother? I close my eyes and lay my head against the seat back. I'm too tired and confused to convince anyone, a therapist or even myself, that I'm a mentally stable person.

For a long thirty minutes, it looks bad for me in therapy as Erik talks, talks more than he has at any one time during our seventeen years together.

"She might be on something—drugs—I don't know. . . . She's real . . . high all the time. Forgets to sleep and works at the kitchen table late into the night. I get up for a drink of water and she's sitting there with four, five necklaces hanging around her neck and bracelets covering her arms. She's always gushing over some new enthusiasm."

Even I feel persuaded that a second, radically energized entity has taken over my body sometime in the past few years. As I listen to Erik's report to the therapist, I begin to interpret my elation while working with my beads as a prelude to a pendulum's swing into certifiable mania.

Dr. Whitely checks me for a reaction. I refuse to look at him. I shift my eyes to the rows of orchids lining glass shelves in the office window. It's going to be my turn to talk next, and I don't have my life explained in my own mind, so I can't set it to music and roll it out onstage for someone else.

"She's changed," Erik tells Dr. Whitely. "I don't know her. I don't like her this way."

It all started with Beckett. Erik's ex-wife, Delinda, filed for divorce and returned home to Los Angeles when Beckett was just five weeks old. I came to babysit him. Every day after high school during my senior year, I relieved the neighbor lady, who cared for both Erik's baby and her own crippled husband by parking them in their wheeled seats in front of the television. Soon Erik interested me much more than the high school boys I had been dating. The money earned that summer I spent on new clothes to entice Erik. I realize now I went to way more trouble than I needed to. I had figured I would find it difficult as an eighteen-year-old to arouse the interest of a thirty-five-year-old. As it turns out, I have never aroused Erik's interest, but I did lure him into marriage.

Erik leans forward on the sofa as if to speak confidentially. "She used to . . . well, she never used to have orgasms. Now she's quicker than me. I mean, that's not bad. It's just . . . I heard this doctor talking on the radio last week while she was visiting her parents. Here, I wrote it down."

Erik lifts his left hip up and extracts an old envelope folded into thirds. He reads from the outside of it. " 'Temporal Lobe Epilepsy.' " Erik looks up. "Ever hear of it? This fellow on the radio, this doctor, said to watch for personality changes, sexual-desire changes. That's when I started listening." Erik turns the envelope all around to collect his jottings. "He called it TLE. There's a tendency to carry on conversations longer than the other person wants."

Erik looks up at Dr. Whitely. "She's always done that—that's not different. But this other stuff: appears to experience spiritual awakening, an obsession to create—that's Suzannah right there. Panic attacks . . . I haven't seen that. But she gets wound up, you know? Goes around smiling at nothing. This fellow said van Gogh had it, maybe Poe." Erik turns his envelope. "Dostoevsky," Erik says in his English lecture tone. "That's the author of *The Brothers Karamazov*." He lowers his envelope. "That's all I could write down."

"She smiles a lot and has orgasms now?" Dr. Whitely asks.

"Every time," Erik says. He looks relieved to have this off his chest and into the hands of a professional.

"That right, Suzannah?" the therapist asks me.

"Yes."

Dr. Whitely says, "So you're happy, Suzannah? Love your beadwork? Feel enlivened?"

"All yeses," I answer dully. I feel betrayed by Erik and glare at him. How am I going to avoid the medication Dr. Whitely will prescribe for me?

Dr. Whitely says, "Congratulations, Suzannah."

I sit up straighter. I feel normal again, like the kids on the swing set just asked me to play. I smile. Erik leans back into his corner of the sofa, putting distance between us.

"Suzannah, let's hear a little history about your marriage to Erik. Start from the beginning." Dr. Whitely rests against his blue swivel chair and makes a steeple with his forefingers.

I tie on my tap shoes and begin, voice shaky from nervousness. I don't want to blow the congratulations I just received, even if, in part, it was for having orgasms.

"Beckett was a two-year-old at my wedding to his father." I clear my throat. "My marriage to Erik, I mean. He insisted I carry him in my arms to the altar."

"Erik?" Dr. Whitely asks with a grin on his face.

He and I laugh. Erik is looking at the shelves of books across the room; he's aching to pick up something to read, I can tell. I laugh again at the picture of me carrying Erik to the altar. Dr. Whitely might learn he is more perceptive than he thinks.

"First Erik hired you as a babysitter, right?" he asks.

"Right. When summer came and school let out, I stretched my duties to include housekeeping and cooking." The laughing has relaxed me. "And my hours to include shared meals and rented movies. Erik taught at the University of Cincinnati. That fall I enrolled in classes there, scheduling them all for mornings when the neighbor, Mrs. Dobson, could cover for me. Even so I attended a good share of them toting Beckett along in a backpack."

Where were my parents? I wonder now. They had begun to travel a lot, joined Clovernook Country Club and the Cincinnati Club, played bridge, and went to parties. Went to parties a lot. Good girl Suzannah maintained an A average and a steady babysitting job. What did they have to worry about? Yet all the while I was seducing a thirty-five-year-old man. My senior year in high school, I was voted prom queen and didn't even have a date until Erik provided one of his teaching assistants as an escort.

"Did you resent shouldering the responsibility of Erik's baby?"

"Oh, no. At the time I thought it was exciting. I juggled illicit sex with a professor and fishing baby toys out of the toilet." I forget Erik is present. He feels so removed, way over there at the end of the sofa, staring across the room.

"I wrote term papers with Beckett teething on my pencils. Erik and I married during the semester break in my sophomore year. After that, it was just fishing baby toys out of the toilet."

Without warning, a shocking thought strikes. Was Erik surprised I stayed around so long? What if he just married his babysitter intending she would get sick of the situation about the time his son entered full days at school? The idea pulls my jaw down.

"What is it, Suzannah?"

"Well, I don't know. It's just that . . . What if I forced this long-term marriage on Erik? What if my hanging on upset Erik worse than his first wife's sudden departure? Maybe *that's* what Erik never got over, what induced his depression—not Beckett's mother, Delinda, abandoning him and their son as I've always thought—but *me* staying on for years and years. Cheery, earnest, determined *to make that marriage work*." I have totally forgotten Erik is here. I look in shock at Dr. Whitely, as if he has the answer.

"First, no one other than Erik is responsible for his feelings. Not you, not Delena."

"Delinda." That's another thing. I was never regarded as Beckett's real mother. Always Delinda was expected back. I was just the caretaker day by day. Delinda was the real mother. Will we have time for this problem, too?

Dr. Whitely says, "Erik, just jump in here anytime. We'd like to hear from you."

"That's Suzannah. So busy being the good person, she never stops to find out if anybody wants her help or not."

I sound like the joke about the Boy Scout who forces the elderly lady into being helped across the wrong street. A lump forms in my throat. All those years . . . all that effort. But, really, isn't it just like me to inflict a good marriage on a reluctant husband? And I accuse Erik of shielding himself with obtuseness.

"So is that what you're saying?" Dr. Whitely asks Erik. "You didn't want her help?"

"I was glad to have it."

"And now?"

Erik shrugs. "I guess so."

Dr. Whitely scoots his swivel chair over to Erik's end of the sofa. "Erik, I think I can help you understand what's going on here. Shall we meet next week? Just you and me?"

Erik is no dummy. As soon as we leave the office, he pronounces Whitely a quack. I don't agree but keep quiet. My emotions wrestle over whether to soar with relief for my own mental health or sink into worry about Erik's. Most of all I want to flop on the car seat and sob for loving a man so indifferent to me and to life itself.

In the month since our appointment with Dr. Whitely, I have accrued a hefty debt to the therapist. Every day I meet an imagined appointment with him and discuss my concerns. I tell him about Erik's flatness, and Dr. Whitely leans away from his blue cushioned chair, runs his fingers through his sparse silver crew cut, and informs me that Erik is indeed clinically depressed, that Erik should attend to this matter and not take it out on the marriage. He says my mother has a bigger problem than depression and to prepare for the long haul. Beckett must be set straight about my role in his life and honor me as his mother. My dad could use a hobby and a lot of exercise to balance his hyperactive mind. And I should stop living everybody else's life and muster the courage to live my own.

Beads are a nice start, but, really, get a grip on it. Go to the movies, hike at Van Buren Lake, make new friends. I would, I tell Dr. Whitely, but Erik doesn't want to. Do you hear yourself? Grow up. Forget about that guy. Stop blaming him for your own fears. It's not his fault you haven't lived your life. This weekend, take yourself out, Dr. Whitely says. It's a dare.

If I paid eighty-five dollars an hour for each imagined appointment this month, I'd owe Dr. Whitely more than two thousand five hundred dollars. An imagination is a thrifty thing.

Saturday night I accept the dare. I go to the movies alone, then carry it one step further and stop at Dietche's for a chocolate ice-cream soda afterward. I'd like to hide behind sunglasses or a book. I keep my eyes cast downward and scrape off the crystals forming on the vanilla ice-cream scoops with my spoon and eat them. Sipping through the straw, I brave a look around. Nobody is snickering or pointing fingers at the lone lady dating herself. I relax.

It's a relief, enjoying my own good spirits, instead of parrying Erik's disapproval for the movie or the people around us or the food we're eating. I never realized what a great date I was. Next Saturday, dinner before the movie. If things work out, I'll shop for a promise ring. I smile at my joke and make a little noise sipping the last of my soda.

As for Erik, I fear his one pleasure in our marriage—that of being the authority figure, the senior partner with the most votes—has been undercut by Dr. Whitely's suggestion of a follow-up meeting with him alone. Erik's withholding of his affection used to mean—to both of us—that he was in charge of our togetherness. Now it appears to be understood—by both of us—that it means he is not entirely in charge of himself. Erik continues to refuse responsibility for this, so in his way, he is still in charge of our togetherness. Because I may not continue to live with him under those circumstances.

Though life has improved with my imaginary appointments with Dr. Whitely and my dress-up dates with myself, each morning as my consciousness awakens, I feel anger rise. By the time I'm brushing my teeth, I am livid. Sometimes the anger is directed at my mother for getting sick right when I was going to refuse to carry her end of our relationship any longer. Sometimes the anger is directed toward my father for succeeding at last in gaining control over my mother's entire life. Sometimes the anger is directed toward Erik innocently yawning, as if the yawn symbolizes his entire aspect of life.

Most mornings I lean against the kitchen counter and shove toast past a throat constricted with the words I've failed to speak to any of them.

By the time I head for work this morning, travel mug of coffee on the dashboard, I remember when Mom greeted me one afternoon as I came home from the eighth grade with a question harder than any I'd been challenged with at school that day. "I'm thinking of leaving your father. Should I?" I wanted to say, "Are there any Oreos left?" I'd carried one goal on the bus ride home: Pour milk, dunk cookies. Talk of her decision went on for weeks. Maybe she'd find a job, move to a new town. Maybe she'd stay, have a baby. In the end she took golf lessons. She was never strong enough to leave him and save herself. Even I saw that.

Perhaps that's what I did to save myself, left Dad for a premature marriage to Erik. And though my situation has assumed a different disguise, perhaps I have inherited my mother's same choice: Give my life to my husband or leave him in order to save it.

five

Spring break finally arrives. Erik and I plan to stay home for Beckett, but at the last minute Beck's ride falls through and he decides to hop a bus to visit Delinda in California. I try getting Erik to talk about a last-minute getaway.

"Let's do something wonderful together." I circle his waist with my arms.

Erik leans his upper body on me, inert as a drowning man weighing down his rescuer. Rain drums on the rooftop like bored fingers.

"Let's go somewhere."

Erik shrugs, begins to move away.

If he turns on the television or opens a newspaper, I may scream and never stop. I taste the scream in my mouth. A corroded metal flavor coats my tongue, as if I've eaten leftover tomatoes refrigerated in their can too long.

I grab his shoulder to halt him.

Abruptly, I slam my flattened palm against the hallway wall. "You're off to work." I slam the wall again. "You're home." I slam once more and cry, "I can't tell the difference."

Tears braid down my face. Sobs stretch my mouth open wide. The inner lining must be flashing red with distress signals, like a baby bird's in a plea: *Feed me, feed me.*

Erik looks calm and reasonable, his eyes brown and glassy, his mouth fixed into a vague smile. I am staring at a mask. Behind the mask Erik is emotionally comatose. This is what scaring someone out of his wits looks like.

I press my lips and muffle my sounds. I pat Erik on the shoulder. "Well," I begin, knowing instinctively that he needs the emergency first aid of ordinary words and simple actions, "why don't you go pick up a pizza for dinner?" My voice is half sob. My chest convulses with the control I force on myself.

"What kind should I get?"

I can't bear the weight of this question and leave for the bathroom without answering. When I hear his car pull away, my tears flow hot and thick. Knowledge travels through my body, rather than my head: I must leave now.

Is this true?

When Erik pulls into the drive, my blue bead case is already stashed in the car and I am lugging two plastic lawn bags full of clothes out the door. We pass on the sidewalk; he is carrying the pizza. He doesn't ask what I'm carrying. For once it's to my advantage that he has so little curiosity, because how am I going to explain? I just want out. I close the car door and return inside the house. Erik opens the pizza box on the coffee table.

The pizza smells funny. I lean over to take a look. I shoot my eyes to Erik.

"You got the Hawaiian?"

"Something different."

"You ordered this pizza deliberately, knowing that I would hate it."

Now I am ranting.

"So now you're going to take a pineapple pizza personally?"

"No. You take it personally. Take the whole pineapple pizza personally. Because it is the reason that I am leaving you and not coming back."

"You can pick the pineapple off."

"You pick the pineapple off." I sling my purse over my shoulder and grab a big suitcase loaded with books. Outside on the stoop, I nearly fall down the three concrete steps when the books all shift to one side and the suitcase heads off without me. I lurch my way down the sidewalk to the car, the suitcase banging against my leg. With the last of my breath, I say, "Pick the pineapple off and stick it—"

"Don't get crude," Erik says from the stoop in his most arrogant, reprimanding tone. "There are neighbors, you know." His chin juts toward a man digging weeds next door.

Loudly, I say, "And stick the pineapple up your ass."

CRY WOLF

APRIL 3–9

Ravens are laying their first eggs, elk are moving higher as snow recedes. Moose are congregating in the open to feed on bitterbrush twigs and leaves. Ground squirrels are emerging from hibernation to be preyed on by red-tailed hawks, whose numbers are increasing. The hawks are building large stick nests. The earliest nesting Canada geese are laying eggs.

For Everything There Is a Season
—Frank C. Craighead, Jr.

six

Some might say Jackson Hole, Wyoming, is no place to plant a woman independent for the first time in her late thirties. That as with thin-skinned tomatoes, the ruggedness of this mountain valley would nip any new growth. But it's the one place I believe I can thrive.

Two hours ago, I signed papers making me the owner of this small cabin. I look at my new home and feel so thrilled I could gnaw on a porch pillar. I look closer; the base of the left pillar looks as though some woodland creature has beaten me to it. I give the post a gentle push. I don't think the roof will cave in anytime soon, but the supports are sadly deteriorated. The front step sags on one side. I prop it with a flat-topped stone and stand back to admire my first home improvement.

A comedienne I once heard said she wanted a man in her life, just not in her house. I feel the opposite just now: I sure don't want a man in my life, but I'd feel more secure if I could install one in my house, because propping boards with a handy stone is the outer limit of my renovating skills. As I circle my small cabin, hands caressing the old stained logs, I realize more will be demanded of me.

I am a woman alone. I should buy health insurance, begin a pension plan, a savings account, prepare for the day the roof needs replacing or even a few of those shingles. But if I hurry back into town, I can get to Mountain House before they close. I know how to shop, my reasoning goes, and if I begin with a success there, perhaps others will follow.

I climb back into my Subaru and look at my new home framed by the windshield. Part of my plan is to fill my life so full that its demands will guide me through this transition, but I may have taken on too much. The logs need rechinking, the yard is overgrown with sagebrush, and the junk inside that old shed might be propping up the shed's walls.

I turn the ignition and shift into reverse. As if I'm a puppet whose strings are too short, my movements are stiff and jerky. I feel slightly estranged from myself. In less than a week, I've become single, jobless, a Westerner. Yet a subdued excitement spins up my spine at these same thoughts. This valley, these mountains choke me with their beauty. I've become a resident of paradise. I'm not the only happy person in my vicinity. People smile here when it isn't even payday.

I twist my head around and back out of my dirt drive. I can't escape the fact that I'm also a woman who's turned away from the role of caring for her aging parents—not that they would have allowed that caring, but it's the tradition for unmarried daughters. Perhaps I should have moved to Florida. I shift into drive, step on the gas. Why do I befriend misery so easily and suspect happiness? Like a Visa card credit limit, I have inflicted a happiness limit on myself—this much and no more.

Suddenly an immense dark creature steps from the trees, head and foreleg reaching out first. I brake, and my wheels slide on gravel. As if she were birthed from the willows, she stands awkwardly at the end of the narrow road, all legs and long, comical face. I meet my first neighbor, and it's a moose. We stare at each other in greeting. A brimming sense of vitality and pleasure in my aliveness pushes at my edges.

In town I purchase a mattress and down comforter at full price, to be delivered in three days. My budget gasps from shock, and I head for the Pamida Discount Store. There, I find an unfinished jelly cupboard for ninety-nine dollars. This is where I belong. A broom, a bucket, mop, and sponges. I buy an oil lamp and a dozen first-of-the-season geranium plants for a dollar each. Tomorrow, Saturday, I'll hit the yard sales.

I've saved a special treat for myself and now I collect. I look for a parking spot around the town square and go to the Valley Bookstore. I didn't want to contact Tessa without having a place to live, didn't want her to feel responsible for me as if I were some stray cat.

When I push through the store's door she spots me. "Hey, Ohio." She sets a stack of books on the counter and comes around to greet me.

"I can't believe you remember."

She leans over with both hands, gives my upper arms a squeeze, and I almost cry. "Sure, I remember. You're a couple months earlier than I expected though."

I joke, "I'm a couple lifetimes earlier than I expected."

Tessa nods. "Sometimes it takes a couple incarnations for us to get where we want." She speaks with a serious tone, then grins. "Congratulations. I'm impressed."

Business is light, and we talk undisturbed. I tell her about my shabby new home and meeting the moose.

"Moose symbolize self-esteem—did you know that? It just stepped out in front of you?"

I nod.

"Hmm. Good sign."

I feel like I just told her more about myself than I meant to. We talk a while. Then she says I've got a job here when the summer tourist season starts, if I'm interested. Tessa is manager of the bookstore. I might need work before then, depends on how fast Erik sells our house and settles up with me, but I'm pleased to be asked and tell her I'm definitely interested. I don't want to keep her from her work, so I move toward the door.

"How did that moose look to you?" she asks.

"Ragged and shaggy, like it's been through the worst winter ever." I cast my eyes to the left, remembering. "But shiny-eyed and its step was springy, ready for a new year." I smile. "I've never seen one so close. Why do you ask?"

"Just wondered. It's a tough time for the wildlife right now. But each day will get easier."

Tonight, I sit on the floor by my discount oil lamp and leaf through catalogs I found discarded at the post office today while signing the waiting list for a box.

Outside, a vehicle approaches, gunning upslope, crunching gravel, and I rush to a front window. I share the dirt road with the former owner of the cabin, whose ranch lies a quarter of a mile beyond me. I'm anxious to ask him about who used to live here and why he's sold the place so fast and cheap.

A long-bodied Suburban careens past with its headlights off. The night is dark and moonless. Imagine having lived in one place so long you could find your way home with your eyes closed. He must know every bump and curve.

Nope. Wrong. Branches screech along metal, a tire bounces hard once and shock absorbers thump. Rock scrapes the underside of the car frame. I hurry outside when the car begins skidding, but before I get any farther than the porch, the brake lights go off and the Suburban continues up the invisible road. I wait on the porch for any further sounds indicating trouble up the road; then I return inside the cabin.

I flip the light switch by habit in the bathroom, forgetting I won't be able to get the electricity hooked up until I call on Monday. To my surprise a dinky forty-watt above the sink comes on. I test all the switches and my oil-lit cabin blooms into a rusty glow. I feel suddenly industrious, as if the sun came up instead of the electricity on. Despite the late hour, I plug in the refrigerator, then fool with the hot-water heater. Soon the tick of metal expanding assures me the water heater is working, and I scrub down the bathroom, ceiling to curling linoleum floor. By the time I've finished, I have just enough hot water for a shallow bath.

With my sleeping bag unrolled on the musty square of thin gray carpet that lies before a mustier sofa of the same color, I fall asleep to spooky sounds inside and out: coyotes whooping like pirates, logs creaking, geese honking as they practice instrument flight in the dark and, nearer by, the tapping of toenails scuttling across hard surfaces—mice, I'll bet.

seven

've got a carload of furniture and household supplies I found at yard sales today. My best find is a kitchen table and chairs—only three chairs, but that's what made it affordable. Wood of some sort, pocked and scarred, but graced with curvy lines. My plan is to paint the table and chairs with Rit dye. Smeary, watery shades of coral, lime green, rose, turquoise. Every slat and leg a different color. I read about it once somewhere. If it looks like I think it will—like old milk paint rubbed on by happy Gypsies—I'll seal it with polyurethane and do something similar with the jelly cupboard.

Since I parked on the north side and came in the back door with my secondhand junk, I don't see the note tucked into a tear in my front door screen until I decide to strip the table and chairs on the front porch. I'm invited to a cookout. Tomorrow at four. *Please come so we can welcome you to the neighborhood.*

Chloe Hanes, Old Trace Ranch. Neighborhood? Old Trace is six miles away, though we do share an exit road off the highway.

I remember: This is Wyoming. Second-largest state in the lower forty-eight, with the least population of any. Six miles makes us neighbors. Going to a party alone in a strange place takes a lot more courage than going out to dinner alone back home, but if I go, I can imagine Dr. Whitely being proud.

If the wood is wet, I recall having read, and allowed to dry for fifteen minutes before applying the dye, the colors will be softer and the grain will show through. By the time I surface into awareness again, the sun is behind the tallest spruce, cooling the yard, and I am faint with hunger. While I wait for a Swanson's frozen chicken pot pie—the Hungry Man size—to bake in the oven, I get started cleaning the kitchen cupboards. By this time tomorrow I hope to have this room fully useful.

It helps to tire myself. I slept well last night. And the work allows my thoughts to catch up to where my body is, the way a long car trip prepares you for your destination.

Beckett was still in California when I pulled off I-80 into Cheyenne. I spent a couple days there anyway, getting familiar with his setting as a second choice to being with him personally. Walked around his campus, had coffee in the student union, ate dinner at the brew pub. There, between wine and dinner and dinner and dessert, I wrote Beck a long letter, explaining that I was divorcing his father, that I was moving to Jackson Hole, that I loved him and always would. I slipped it under his dormitory room door. Before leaving Cheyenne I asked for directions to Jackson at a gas station.

"Take this road to Rock Springs and make a right."

A four-hundred-fifty-mile trip with one turn?

It was that simple.

Now I read the directions for my new phone, untangle the wires and plug it into the phone jack. Just like the lights, this works, too. I dial Beckett's number, hoping he's back from visiting Delinda.

"Hey," he answers.

"It's me. How was your trip?"

"Rotten. She wasn't there."

Damn her. She has promised most of Beck's childhood away. Promised visits, gifts, phone calls, and only come through often enough to keep rumors from spreading that she was no longer among the living. Beck is like a laboratory mouse that gets food once in every ten lever pulls, and each promise has just increased his fervor to keep believing her.

"I want to tell you something, Beckett." I pause and ask, "You got my letter?"

"Yeah."

"All your life you and your father have called Delinda your 'real mother.' Delinda is your birth mother. I am your real mother. I have cared for you, fed you, watched you breathe at night, chased behind you on your two-wheeler, packed your school lunches . . . mothered you, Beckett. And I have loved every minute. I am your mother—do you hear me? I will no longer accept a diminished position in your life. I am your mother." I stop, exhausted. My heart revving. My hands shaking.

Long pause, no response. Has this stinker picked up his father's habit? Did I fail to insert a question in there?

"So . . . Mom, how's it hanging up there in old Jackson Hole?"

I laugh. Beck laughs. Then I begin crying and I hear Beck sniffling in the background. I wish I could hug him.

"Beckett, you are the best. If Delinda could stand still long enough for us to figure her out, we'd discover exactly how injured she is, but then . . . so would she. That's what she's running from, Beck, not you." While I talk, I mindlessly pace my three rooms—four if I count the mudroom. From there, I see out the back door that the shaggy remains of the winter's snow are shrinking farther into the shadowed areas, behind rocks, beneath the trees, the north side of the shed.

"This is not your fault, Beck. She does what she can, and that just doesn't happen to be very much where you're concerned."

"She's busy."

"She's afraid of you." I lift a stack of clean underwear from the dryer and carry it through the kitchen, into the living room a couple feet, turn left into the bedroom. Hold the phone with my chin, pull open the closet door, and set it on the top shelf. No bureau yet.

"Afraid? I don't think so."

"I do. I think so. Afraid."

"Producers don't have a lot of time. Even if it is a small film company. It's okay with me."

Beck needs to change the subject. I can tell he's close to overload. Before hanging up, I say, "I'll expect Mother's Day presents from now on. I like books and pajamas."

Cows and their nursing calves dot the fields far into the distance at Chloe Hanes's ranch, and the party spreads across the ranch yard into the fringe of Engelmann spruce that lace the base of the grassy butte. Mountains lasso the farthest perimeters of sight. And sky—blue as the gas flame on my water heater—cups us overhead. I stand listening to some old-timers tell tales on one another as a form of flirting with me, the new woman among them. Far, far across the yard is the Marlboro Man, cowboy hat propped on the buck-and-rail fence he leans against. He is lifting a can of Coors to his mouth. Eyes meet. Can jerks down from his face without one sip and jaw drops into a shocked and delighted smile. The act is clean, without blemish of self-consciousness or forethought. The reflex of a young boy. Without hesitation he starts across the yard toward me.

My smile grows as he nears, but keeps within boundaries of politeness in case any of these old-timers glance my way for an appropriate chuckle to their outrageous lies. I realize now I'm just a talking stick to be passed around their circle and used as a focus for stories they might not remember without me.

"Bark, here, was tossed so swift from that bronc, he landed straddling a fence rail and never knew he weren't still hanging on Young Major—just thought he'd tamed him to a standstill! We holler, 'You done it, Bark. That bronc ain't going nowhere.' Bark here just sits, holding tight. Had to *pry* you off that fence rail, Bark."

The man keeps walking toward me with his openmouthed smile, teeth glittering so brightly in the sunlight they flash silver for one moment like his belt buckle.

I am not so at ease as the Marlboro Man; my own can of half-empty Coors buckles once in my grip and pops back into shape with a loud noise. Part of me is taking inventory of my appearance, part putting on the necessary facade of appreciative audience for these storytelling Big Bellies, yet veiled over that is a wonder at this man's candid reflex at seeing me, his unshielded advance across the yard. It's all so simple for him. I am the new bike under the Christmas tree. I have his name on me.

A shadow falls across his chin; his eyes spend a moment longer with me before he drags his glance downward; my glance follows, and we both see the woman who earlier arrived at the party in a helicopter. She is Caroline Donnell, married to Dick Donnell, pilot of the helicopter locals say he uses like a Jeep, despite its burning twelve to fourteen gallons an hour of fuel. Their large spread is less than five miles away by road. The Donnells, too, are newcomers, but not as new as me. All this I learned earlier from the ranchers around me, as together we shielded our eyes from the dust and chaff that was rotor-whisked by the Donnells' landing.

The Marlboro Man glances once more toward me, and I adjust my position in order to appear as if I was expecting nothing. I laugh at another bucking-bronco tale, in which the rider is "so buggered up he can't walk nor talk till spring." I drop the sunglasses propped on my head onto my face so I can watch anybody I care to for long as I wish.

Possibilities for my life are suddenly endless. I could take on a cowboy lover. I smile at the cocky thought. I feel like someone I knew once—a potential version of myself. Someone who could actually be as confident as I am acting. I move to another gathering of people.

This group, I assume at first, is discussing breeding stock. "Smokey, he come out of Lucille by Chet, but Davy was out of Stella. Her daddy was once a banker back in Michigan someplace."

I see I have a long way to go before I'll fit in here. An hour later I am walked across the yard to be introduced by my hostess, Chloe, to the Marlboro Man and the Donnells.

Chloe says his name as she guides me over: Bo Garrett. Short, she says, for Bartholomew Owen Garrett.

I know this name.

We should have met Friday at the Jackson State Bank, but he sent his lawyer, Mick Farlow, for the closing instead. "Mr. Garrett is indisposed." He and the real estate agent, Myrna Loy MacKinder, exchanged smiles and familiar head shakes.

Once I signed all the papers and handed over my down payment, Myrna Loy joked, "You are now officially the owner of a one-acre parcel plus a run-down cabin and the odd shed or two." With a name like that—"My parents were *very* devoted fans"—and with the low price and fast paperwork, my ownership felt uncertain. It still does.

I'd walked into Myrna Loy's office last Wednesday just as she was taking the call from Bo Garrett. She had forty-eight hours to sell the cabin for cash.

"If Garrett wasn't in such a damn hurry for beer money, I could sell the place for twice that much," she said to herself, hanging up the phone. She swiveled around in her desk chair and spotted me just stepping inside her door.

"Sold," I said, joking.

Dad wired the cash to me so I could take my time setting up a mortgage when my share of the Findlay house came through.

Our hostess introduces me. "Our newest neighbor, Suzannah Perry."

He doesn't recognize my name. Chloe Hanes just assumes

we've met. "You know Bo, of course, and this is Caroline and Dick."

Bo doesn't get why I should know him, but he doesn't question Chloe; perhaps he is notorious enough in the valley to be accustomed to such assumed introductions; everybody at the bank knew his name. Myrna Loy says he has lived here all his life. Caroline Donnell, I notice, has not left Bo Garrett's side since she cast her shadow over our meeting-in-progress. Dick, her husband, comes and goes, but Caroline stays.

Chloe moves me on. We are to make the rounds of guests.

Later, after we've all eaten and only the tips of the tallest peaks of the Tetons luster pink and gold, with one shaft of last light beaming over a pass and into Cascade Canyon, I spot Bo, Caroline at his side, talking to the same group of old-timers I began the party with. I see Bo look surprised, then scan the crowd until he spots me. I know someone just told him: I am the person who bought his cabin on Friday. Since I have car keys jiggling in my hand, and I'm thanking my hostess Chloe for including me in today's gathering, I must follow through now and leave.

eight

n the morning I wake to sounds of homey stirrings coming from my kitchen. I swear I smell bacon, and I don't even have any in the cabin. Water runs in my sink. I lift my head from my pillow and ask myself why I'm not full of fright. Ready to arm myself with the stove poker, climb out a window, run. But what kind of threat can such domestic activity present? I scoot out of my sleeping bag and crawl across the carpet to peak around the sofa.

It's him. The Marlboro Man is in my kitchen. Cooking, I think. Dishes rattle. Then the side of his head flashes again across the space between the sofa back and doorway as he reaches for a paring knife by the sink. I flatten myself to the floor.

I try to figure what could account for this strange scene, but vanity surges to the forefront. I picture my sleepy face. My suitcase is in the bedroom, between me and the kitchen doorway. My robe is there. And my lip gloss. And I can't get to them without being seen.

No choice but to present myself as is, long rumpled nightgown and bare feet. I get off the floor and stand in the doorway.

Bo Garrett barely looks at me. "Go wash up. Breakfast in five. No shower." He's got the table set. He's moving quickly between the bacon and the oranges he's squeezing. Coffee sits on the back burner and something bakes in the oven.

I do as Bo says; I don't know why. On through the kitchen, I step into the bathroom and turn on the water and the exhaust fan so he doesn't hear me flush the toilet. I brush my teeth, wash my face. I smooth wrinkles out of my flannel gown. There doesn't seem to be a thing to do other than go back out there. I *am* hungry. I only nibbled at the party yesterday. I never eat well when I have to talk to strangers while doing it. Then I came home last night to empty cupboards. Bo must have brought groceries.

"So," he says when I reappear, "are you called Sue, Suzie, what?"

"Never," I say. "Suzannah."

"The whole deal? Su-zan-nah?"

"The whole deal."

"Juice. Su-zan-nah." He hands me a filled glass. "This used to be my grandma's place. I ate most my breakfasts here when I was a kid. I'd come over from the ranch house in my pajamas."

"Thanks for dressing this morning," I say.

He looks my face over real well, while I take a sip of juice. "You're prettier than Grandma."

"I don't cook much," I say, just to enhance the distinction between me and his grandma. Those blue glass Mason jars sitting on the countertop could fool a person. They look so good all lined up, holding dried lentils and peas, black turtle beans and pasta—but I don't plan on *cooking* those things. I plan on being a frozen-food thawer for a while. I did my stint of bread baking and stew making, roasting and toasting during my marriage.

Bo cocks his head toward a chair. I sit, and he serves eggs baked with herbs and Swiss cheese, brings over the bacon, toast, and coffee. Everything looks and smells wonderful. He pulls out a chair, sits, and smiles at me. Movie-star teeth. Slight cleft in his jaw. We unfold our napkins, and I wonder if this is what they mean by Western hospitality. Maybe somebody cooks breakfast for all newcomers in Wyoming. How would I know?

"Do you have salt and pepper?" I ask, stupidly forgetting he's the guest, not me in my nightgown. Or am I the guest in his grandmother's old kitchen, his old childhood haunt, bought by me for a song?

"Left it on the stove." He gets up again.

I take a bite of the baked eggs. Bo's a good cook, and I tell him so. He tells me that first his grandmother cooked for him; later, when she became frail with age and osteoporosis, he cooked for her.

We eat quietly for a few moments; then Bo says, "I can sand down this table and chairs when you're ready to refinish them. Got a sander." I tell him it took me five hours to paint it this way, and he says, "Oh, shit, I'm sorry."

"So you're friends of the helicopter people." I can't remember their last name, but we have to move on to a less-awkward topic of conversation.

"Caro and I spend time together."

His use of a nickname makes me think I have the wrong idea. "Oh, I thought she was married to Dick."

"Right. Dickie's her husband."

"He doesn't . . . ?" I don't know what I mean to ask.

"No," Bo says, "he doesn't." He smiles at my discomfort, takes a sip of coffee, then fills in the blanks. "Dickie travels a lot on business. I'm buying their stock for them—horses, some cattle."

I try too hard at conversations. Nobody is allowed to feel awkward in my presence. I won't allow it. Quickly I reply, "I hear they recently moved here."

"Right. Couple months ago."

It's eight thirty in the morning and I'm already worn-out. I rest my fork and my company manners. "Are you sorry you sold this place?" I fear his answer. I have rubbed my cheek along every square inch of log and chinking and have murmured endearments to the sagebrush surrounding it. All the while I have wondered if this man has sobered up and regretted the fast sale.

"Not anymore," Bo says.

"Then why are you here?" I wave to encompass our plates.

"Flirting with you." He looks surprised at my density.

"Look, I just got out of a marriage. I need . . . I can't . . ." I keep shaking my head no. It takes all I've got not to scrape the chair back and tear off.

Bo holds up an arresting hand. "Never mind the particulars. Just eat with me. I'll cook. You clean up. I've got a ham in the oven for dinner." He's trying to soothe me, I can tell.

"*My* oven?" I thought I'd smelled something I wasn't quite eating; the bacon fooled me.

"Sort of *your* oven. Appliances weren't included in the sale."

"They weren't?" My spirits plummet. There's nothing left over in the budget for new appliances.

"No, but I'll let you borrow them . . . when I'm not using them."

Right now, he tells me, he has to take off. He stands and fills his mug with coffee. He'll bring my cup back later. "Suz?"

I'm staring at my plate, hands on my lap. Who is this guy? What's he doing in my kitchen? Why am I watching to see if he leaves this last piece of bacon? I look up, disturbed.

He thinks I'm upset because he shortened my name, and he finishes it, "Zannah." He pauses, then says, "I'm a nice guy, you know?"

That's true according to Myrna Loy, but she also suggested Bo stopped off at a bar instead of the bank for the closing last Friday. His drive past my cabin that night with his headlights off backs up the idea. But that's no crime. So I nod and Bo reaches for the doorknob.

Before he leaves I ask, "About the ham, should I take it out of the oven in a couple hours?"

"No," he says. "I'm trying an experiment." He turned the oven to five hundred degrees for thirty minutes, then turned the oven off. If all goes well, the ham will be baked in five hours.

"But you *can't* open the oven door," he warns. "Not once." He says this sternly. Like I might sneak in there and brush a mustard glaze on his ham without permission.

*   *   *

In the late afternoon, Bo returns. He brings more groceries, three bags full. I'm showered and dressed and know to expect him, but all this works against me. I act so self-conscious it must be painful for him to watch. He's very attractive and offers his complete attention each time I speak. He rests his activity, turns his whole body, faces my way, and watches my eyes. I'm not used to this. I've picked up a halted rhythm to my talk, and seconds pass with us staring at each other. As a defense I begin to ask him questions while he unpacks the groceries.

"Does your, um, your family—" They should sell a contact lens the color of his eyes—or the many colors of his eyes. Blue and green with wedges of copper, outlined in black. I glance down at the bag of onions Bo holds. "Tell me about your family."

As he moves up and down the kitchen counter and between the stove and refrigerator, Bo tells me that his grandparents had two daughters, just one year apart. In order to save trips into town, both girls started school the same year and graduated from high school together, a common practice for ranching families. As a graduation present, his grandparents sent the two sisters to visit relatives in Ireland. A year later the girls returned home with a present for them: Bo.

"They wouldn't tell which one got into trouble," Bo says. "Still won't."

"They've never told *you*?"

"Nope." He sticks romaine lettuce, minus a few leaves, into the crisper, then tries to wedge in a bag of carrots and celery, too.

I ask, "But which one do you *call* mother?"

"Both. Neither. I call them my aunts, usually."

Maybe it's Bo's casual dismissal of the importance of his heritage, or maybe it's the dark side of my euphoric scrubbing binge of the past couple days, but I am so caught up in his story, I relax and even become argumentative. My next words imply he can't be in the best mental health with a family life based on a lie.

He falls right in with my familiar manner. He says, "Suzannah, *everybody* is messed up. It's a matter of degree. They were terrific mothers. They're nuts, but very loving. All during my childhood, I had *two* mothers telling me I was the best little guy in the world. That goes far."

He's right, of course. It was my own saving grace. My mother borrowed my mind, my ears, my patience from the time I was a toddler, yet she was always right there building me up. It wasn't entirely to strengthen me as a pillar for her own support. And even if it often was, I believed her and I grew to feel capable and loved. Still, the trouble I'm having suspecting she is not well-minded . . . everything has to be reevaluated.

I take over putting the groceries away, and Bo doctors up a can of black beans with lots of cumin, garlic, and red onion. We both work on the salad, then sit down to Bo's ham dinner.

"When you grew older and realized your mothers' unusualness, did you lose confidence in yourself?" I ask Bo, thinking about my own loss lately.

"They told me they were odd. Around my high school years, they said, 'Bartholomew, we think we're getting odd. We don't mind so much, sister and I, but we worry about your little friends.'" Bo and I laugh at his high-voiced rendition, but it's sad.

When the sisters were eighteen and nineteen and their adult lives just beginning, they stepped into "otherness." And I imagine to be "other" in a small isolated valley like Jackson Hole some forty years ago demanded toughness. But with Bo's help, I understand that to drift into oddness was for them easier than to fight it. The sisters' only choice was to follow their bold bid to differentness through to the end.

"My aunts have made a career out of being strange and they're quite successful at it," Bo says.

I smile. "You admire them." This is not an accusal—this is a compliment. Something about the way he says this makes the place between my eyes sting. He loves his aunts, I can tell. Makes me long to see my mother.

I also compliment his cooking. Bo's experiment turned out well. The ham is juicy and tender. When we're finished eating, I watch Bo knot his cloth napkin to the back of his chair. He did this same thing this morning. I wonder whether he plans on coming back *again* for breakfast. I worry that I have let him move into my life too far, too soon. As if the napkin drooping from his chair post resembles the plastic ribbons waving from the survey posts around my lone acre, marking off an acquisition. And I fear the paint of my newly won boundary lines is still fresh enough to be smeared, perhaps by any passing stranger.

Bo seems comfortable with the silence that's spread. He watches me eat and sips his coffee. Perhaps I don't have to entertain him to keep his company. Erik flipped on the television even in the middle of my well-rehearsed stories about his own baby boy. Bo seems easy with himself. Thank God he's got a major fault—drinking. Which reminds me, I didn't see him unpack any beer.

"Did you bring beer?"

"No, sorry. I didn't think of it. You like beer?"

"No. Thought you did." Now I've stepped into it. "I mean, I like it. . . . I just don't drink often."

Bo sets his mug down. "But you heard I did?"

"Umm. What? Like it?"

"Drink often."

I decide to come clean. "I saw you drive past Friday night."

"And you heard things." He tightens his jaw muscles and looks practically inside me. "Well, I deserve that talk. I used to drink quite a bit." He watches me a moment. "Friday night was the exception, not the rule. But that kind of talk takes a while to die down in the valley."

Especially when you break your own rule. I nod.

"Get rested up from your divorce. . . . Did you get a divorce?"

"It's, um, in the works."

Bo gets up and begins to carry away the used dishes. "When it's over, I think you should give me a whirl." He grins as if he's making fun of himself. I laugh and discard my nervousness for good. We got it all out in the open.

"For now," he says, rinsing his plate, "let's walk up Saddlestring Butte."

The early-spring forest surrounding Bo's Crossing Elk Ranch crackles beneath our feet as Bo leads the way up the path after dinner. New grasses poke through last year's brown flattened weeds.

Bo points out a warbler's nest that has fallen during the winter from a narrow-leafed cottonwood. Something about birds' nests intrigues me. The intentional gathering of supplies, for one. The deliberate downiness of its interior. I am reminded of my connectedness to other living things as I, too, prepare a home. I pack the nest along to place on a shelf beside my books.

The path leads down near a stream, which exposes mostly dry rocks this early in the season. Spring melt off won't begin until the nights warm up, according to Bo. The path forks and climbs uphill as it leaves the creek bed.

"To find my house, follow the trail south. I'll show you another time."

I don't say so, but I've seen his house already. From this slope, higher up behind my cabin, I spotted a good-sized clapboard house, painted gray many years back, one barn and three outbuildings, also a house trailer parked in the drive. Today, we are taking the north trail uphill to his favorite site for watching the sun set or the moon rise.

I wonder where his cattle graze, and I ask.

"I don't own any cattle."

By his tone of voice, I know I've touched a sore spot. He walks on ahead, increasing the distance between us. I figure the problem must involve money—a shortage of it—to guess by the quick sale of my cabin.

After a while Bo waits for me to catch up. He says, "Myrna Loy tells me you're a jeweler. Is that so?"

"I'm not a jeweler," I say, "I just like to make jewelry."

"That's what I used to say. I'm not a cattleman. I just like to have cows. But my reasons were the opposite of yours."

I don't understand what he means, but I counsel myself to allow Bo his own pace toward the subject of cows. We approach a bench of land on Saddlestring Butte where our trail levels off and we step out of the trees. The spread of valley lies to the east, north, and south. We'd have to climb higher, to the top where the snow is still deep, to watch the sun set. Tonight, Bo says, we'll view the alpenglow on the Gros Ventre Range across the valley floor. He pushes through sagebrush to a group of boulders and sets his butt against one, crossing his boots. He plucks off a piece of sage, rolls it between his hands, then brings his hands up to cup his nose.

"I keep thinking that someday I'll stuff a pillow with sage and sleep on it all winter."

I decide right here that I like this man. I feel impatient to know more about him. Against my better judgment, I introduce the touchy subject again. "But you don't have cows."

"Sold them. So I don't have to say my line anymore about having cows, but that I'm not a cattleman. I'm really a welder."

"Welder? Like at Wedco Manufacturing?" I drove around the place twice looking for the Pamida store.

"I weld metal sculpture." He looks away from me as he says this, over toward the pale cloud blossoms of lavender and rose drifting in an airy float across the eastern sky.

Sculpture. It takes me a second to put it together, I'm so stuck on picturing the fiery equipment and the face mask and heavy gloves. "Oh, you're a sculptor."

"No," he says, teasing me, "I'm not a sculptor. I just like to sculpt."

I laugh.

A gallery in town represents him, he tells me when I press for more information. They've given him two shows; one last winter, another scheduled for the fall. Recently a piece of his was purchased by a local hotel and is exhibited in the lobby.

But what kind of cowboy doesn't own cows? All this time I pictured a huge cattle herd grazing somewhere, soon to be trailed up Togwotee Pass for the summer. Beck and I used to be thrilled when traffic was stopped for cattle drives during our vacations here. "So you sold your cows."

"To help pay off a bank loan on the ranch. That sale and my hay last summer almost set me free."

"Selling the cabin fits in here, I bet."

"That, too. I'm going to give this a shot."

Dramatic life changes once furnished the main theme for my fantasies. Now the enthusiasm I feel for Bo's plans helps assure me I've done the right thing in making a big change in my own life.

We fall silent as the sundown flares on the stone headdress feathers of Sleeping Indian Mountain and the peaks of the Gros Ventre Range behind it. I picture the dozen or two galleries that line the boardwalks near the town square. Jackson Hole is becoming a major center for Western art. . . . Oh, *Western* art. God, he's probably one of those artists who sculpt little Sacajaweas and Sitting Bulls. Maybe bronc riders or mountain men.

"Welding exactly what?" I ask, trying to imagine his work.

"Found objects, lately. Parts from old ranching machines . . . plows, spring harrows, hay rakes."

This sounds promising, yet there's still a possibility of elk with massive antler racks—made, in this case, of hay-rake prongs. An outdoor man's delight. "Western realism dominates the market in Jackson," I say in order to get him pinned down better.

"That's true. My work leans more toward the abstract and contemporary, so I have to look farther for an audience. My roots are here though." Bo opens his palms, exposing the rumpled sage sprig. "I love those old machines abandoned in the sagebrush. And I like it that when I've begged some tightfisted rancher into letting me cart them off, that rancher can appreciate what's become of them. He sees my roots, and the people from the coasts who buy most of the sculptures see—"

"Your blossoms," I finish for him.

Both of us are loaded down with treasures I've found by the time we've returned to the cabin. Bo carries one fistful of tall dried weeds, beige blossoms down turned like little bells, seeds rattling inside them. In the other fist, slender, curvy pieces of wood, weathered smooth and twisted like driftwood, which I'll set by my door and use for walking sticks. I've filled the pockets of both our jackets with rocks I like the shapes or colors of. Sitting in Bo's upturned cowboy hat, crooked under one arm, is his barn cat, Tolly, who began stalking us on our way back. Bo has suggested I borrow her for that mouse I heard in the mudroom.

nine

I don't really like cats too much. They remind me of New Yorkers: They only acknowledge your presence if you can do something to specifically elevate their position in life. Two days with Tolly haven't altered that opinion. This afternoon, I'm fooling around with my beads at the kitchen table, and Bo stops by. I complain to him that Tolly is drinking out of my toilet, leaving tiny, muddy paw prints on the seat. And, worse, she used my bathroom sink as *her* toilet last night.

"How would *you* like to bend down to brush your teeth early in the morning and smell cat urine?" I ask him.

He picks up Tolly and smoothes her long tortoiseshell coat. "How would *you* like to have to drink out of your toilet?" he responds.

Reluctantly, I laugh.

Bo glances out the kitchen window, then crooks his head to see past the trees hiding a curve in the road.

I get up and look, too. Maybe the moose I saw my first day here has returned to the neighborhood. A flash of sleek metallic red slips between green pine boughs.

Bo sets Tolly on the floor. "Caro. She mentioned she wanted to get to know you better."

"You should have told me." I look around the kitchen, not feeling ready for company in my new home. Failed bead projects are strewn across the kitchen table, where I've flung them in disgust. Either I've lost my touch or my expectations have risen in response to all the time I've got to work on pieces now. I'll have to lower my standards, just to have some fun.

"I didn't know she was coming. Really," Bo says, "I've been discouraging this visit until you were more settled."

I start gathering up half-finished coil bracelets, multistrand necklaces, tools, and supplies. If she's accustomed to private helicopters, she's accustomed to classier jewelry than I'm capable of creating.

Caro's ruby Buick glides soundlessly into my side yard. Bo seems irked to see her here and doesn't go to the door to welcome her with me. Instead, he leans against the kitchen sink and watches Caro and me blunder through stiff greetings to each other. Caro is dressed in black English riding pants tucked into shiny boots with a silky man-styled shirt blousing from her belted waist. The purple shirt looks good with her long auburn hair and argent eyes. She is taller than I am but smaller-boned or maybe just thinner. I feel solid and grounded beside her, as if her bones were hollow, like a bird's.

I finish packing my beads to get it all out of sight quickly as I can, but she is asking the dreaded questions anyway: What are you making? Is this your hobby? She picks up my container of Balinese silver bead spacers.

"I never wear anything but gold. Do you?"

Because of the way she stands looking around my kitchen, at the black gummy spots rubbed through on the linoleum, and the way Bo observes the two of us as if he's bought a ticket for this show and has no responsibility for its success, I answer her question rudely.

"I don't like to support gold mines, like the one trying to destroy Yellowstone up in Cooke City." I've become an instant environmentalist. If she's read more than the single article I've read in the local weekly, I'm in big trouble.

I scoop up the last of my beads and watch Caro think how she'd like to tell me that I'm obviously too poor to buy gold. I know right off I'm outside the curve of Caro's lens. She is here because Bo is, and the refracted light rays of her focus do not converge on my image. Like Tolly the cat, she is merely wondering what use or hindrance I might be.

Behind a thumb pressing against his lower lip, Bo smiles at my answer, but doesn't look directly at either Caro or me.

I carry my bead case into the other room. I'm not usually bold enough to be rude. I have always needed approval too much. But something has shifted in me lately. As if I'm discovering some inner family of friends who will take the place of those lately dropped by the roadside: my mother; my husband; my stepson off at school; my father, whose narrow vision and dark negativity has become narrower and darker witnessing my mother's slow, unstoppable fade.

I pause before the woodstove, warm my hands, and realize that somewhere along the way I have inwardly acknowledged that my mother has indeed begun an irreversible decline, if for no other reason than once begun she has not the personal power or will to alter much of anything. Never has. To be honest, she began to back out of life years ago. That's what alcoholism is all about.

I return to the kitchen and see Caro sauntering around it. Several times she reaches out to touch things of mine, but repeatedly draws her hand back, as if she's fearful mites will jump out on her. The kitchen looks great, if you ask me. It's the one room I feel at home in. I sit at the table on a bench I found weathering behind my shed, and I read by the pin-up lamp on the wall, hung just below the shelf that holds my books and the bird's nest and a jar of wildflowers. I write in my journal at this table and sip my coffee.

But my contentment with this cozy log room isn't entrenched firmly enough to be safe from someone's disapproval. I struggle against the vision of this room flipping from my cocky celebration of color and the outdoors brought inside to the shabbiness Caro sees. It seems that if I key my look before me to the watery colors of the table and chairs and on toward the red geranium on the windowsill over the sink, it stays mine. If I focus on the bleak green coverings of the floor and the countertops or the once-white refrigerator now yellowing, the chrome flaking off the door handle, it becomes the room she sees.

"So"—Caro looks for a place to sit—"I guess I should have brought something to drink."

"Oh." I jump to action. "I've made some lemon bread. We can have tea." I dart around for the tea bags and cups, I reach for the bread, still cooling in the pan, leaping from one task before it's completed to the other. Tossing over my shoulder to Caroline that she should have a seat.

Bo takes the bread pan from me. "You fix the tea, Suz," he says. He misinterprets my look of panic. "—Zannah," he finishes.

Caroline brushes nonexistent crumbs or dust from a kitchen chair.

I calm myself while water runs into the kettle. I remember to be grateful that I have something to offer a guest. Bo cooks—he fixed scalloped potatoes and Mexican pea soup from the leftover ham—but says he never bakes, so I figured that could be my contribution. And I love baking breads and desserts. I take a deep breath. The kitchen aromas are a good mix of warm lemon bread and pine boughs from the open window.

Finally seated, Caroline says, "Tea?" As in "I don't think so."

I look. She is smiling benevolently. "Blackberry," I announce, trying to arouse interest.

"I'll just have . . . water, I guess."

I bring her a glass of water. "Ice cubes," she reminds me quietly, as if I'm a maid who has forgotten her training.

I don't have any ice cubes. Water comes out of the tap cold enough to hurt your teeth. I use the tiny freezer for Eskimo Bars and a bag of frozen baby limas.

"Bo?" Caro says.

Bo looks at me. "I'll just run to the house and get some Scotch for Caro. Be back before your water boils."

Oh God, he's leaving me alone with her. "No," I say, "I'll get the Scotch. You tell me where."

I'm acting silly. I've never even been to Bo's house. But Bo doesn't point that out. He simply says I'll find the liquor in the cupboard above the sink and thanks me, as if *I'm* saving *him* from an ordeal. On my way out the door, car keys in hand, I realize I may be painting a picture of neighborliness that will cause unease for him with Caroline. I'm beginning to wonder what exactly is going on between them. So I ask if he lives in the house I've seen from the hill or the trailer beside it.

"The house," he answers. He hands me a plastic bag. "Get some ice cubes, too."

On the short drive over, I have to admit more than the fear of being alone with Caroline propelled me out of the house. I feel off-balance wondering about their possible involvement. All she says is *Bo?* and he knows what she wants. I practice out loud in the car. "Bo?" Haughtier. "Bo?" And the really irksome part: He jumps to meet her desires.

I pull my Subaru into the drive and go in the back door. Bo's kitchen looks immaculate. I'm impressed. But then he's been busy the past few days making *mine* a mess, not his. The real test would be the bathroom, but I'm not going to snoop around. In situations like this, I act as though cameras are aimed at me, tape recorders are counting footfalls. I do exactly what I'm sent to do and barely let myself see anything between back door and liquor cupboard.

On the drive back to my cabin I reprimand myself for feeling threatened by Caroline. Maybe she stopped by to get to know me, just as Bo said. After all, she's new in the valley, too. Why did I get so defensive about my cabin and my jewelry? Why did I get as slitty eyed as a high school girl about a competitor for Bo's attentions?

The fact is I need to ease up on the time Bo and I spend together. Though I savor his attention and care, I'm sending the wrong signals by accepting both. I've lived here little more than a week, and we've eaten half our dinners together. It just happens without my noticing. We're also sharing his post-office box—he got a second key for me—because the waiting list is so long. Last night, as we walked up the butte again after dinner, I wondered out loud why Lower Valley Power and Light said I didn't need to make a deposit for electricity like everybody else does and learned from Bo that the cabin's electricity is included in his bill.

"It is? What's that mean?"

"It means I haven't gotten around to separating the two places into having their own meters."

"Hmm," I said. "I don't know about this."

"We're wired together," he joked. "And you can't get wired to any other man until I cut you loose first."

"You're flirting with me again," I warned.

"Damn right and I'm sorry as hell." He was grinning hugely.

"How come you don't ask me about my divorce?"

"How come you don't talk to me about it?"

"Not ready yet, I guess."

"That's why I don't ask."

And then there's that deal about Bo letting me borrow his appliances. Unless I've got that wrong and he's really borrowing mine. To make matters worse, his washer and dryer don't work, so he's bringing laundry over one of these days—at my invitation.

When I return with the Scotch, Caroline rises to get something from her car. Bo fixes her drink and one for himself. I stick with tea. Caroline returns with a fancy gift bag, silky ribbons streaming from its handles, and presents it to me.

"Welcome to the valley," she says. "I hope we can be friends."

I am awash with guilt for my suspicions and unfriendliness. I gush over the beautiful wrapping and hope Caroline is disclaiming her first impressions of me as fast as I am disclaiming my first impressions of her. Lime green and purple tissue paper whisper secrets as I rustle around inside the bag. I pull out a fat pillar candle with glittery glass beads and old rhinestone buttons embedded in the ivory wax, spiraled around the candle as if a many-stranded necklace were buried inside.

"Oh, it's beautiful." I pull out three balls of soap that match. "Thank you so much. My bathroom will cower in embarrassment at the sight of such elegance."

Caroline laughs. "Only an artist could picture a bathroom cowering."

No one has ever called me an artist before. I look to see if she's being sarcastic. There's a quality to her voice that lacks warmth, but her smile is a dazzle of beautiful teeth and friendliness. "I envy you, to tell the truth," she says.

"I can't imagine why. Unless it's because I have this beautiful candle and soap." I lift a ball of soap to my nose. I smell almonds and lilies and beneath that moss.

Bo hasn't joined us at the table. He's leaning against the sink, a spectator, sipping his drink.

Caroline says, "I'd love to move to a place of my own and do something creative . . . but I'd be afraid to."

"Well, I've just gotten out of a long, sad marriage, and I

needed a scary adventure to get me back into life. Moving here is as brave as I get."

I remember back in Ohio, thinking that if I dropped myself into the most exciting situation I could dream of, which to me was a cabin of my own in the Tetons, life would happen to me just as a result of what that act triggered. I look at Bo with this memory and think: fast start. There were a lot of reasons to believe that I would have been better off to move back to Cincinnati, where my family used to live and where Erik and I started out together. Yet I haven't been sorry so far.

I ask Caroline, "What part would make you afraid?"

"No money," she says immediately. Then adds, "No man. No . . . money," she says again. "I've gotten used to things I won't give up now."

Caro looks at Bo. "I'm trying to talk Bo into letting me make him rich." She turns to me. "Don't you think he's a wonderful artist?" I agree. I've seen some of his work now and I think Bo goes into the best of himself to produce it. His sculpture makes my heart pound with its earthy curves winging into space as if grasping at something in the clouds.

"I plan on making him famous and showing him how to invest his money properly. Not to mention digging into the gold mine he's sitting on."

"My sink?" I say. "Oh, good."

Bo laughs. "She means my ranch."

"I've told Bo not to let Dickie get his hands on it, but Dickie's idea to build an exclusive resort here is excellent. Bo should do it on his own."

"What do you think about that?" I ask Bo.

"I'll tell you," Caro breaks in, looking at Bo while she talks.

"He doesn't think much at all of my plan. He's got one of his own. But I'm with your grandfather there. Crybaby Ranch is right. Everybody poor, everybody crying."

"You've lost me," I say, wondering if that was the purpose.

Bo says, "Nothing is going to happen here for a while. Got to let the cow patties harden before traipsing a bunch of rich people through the pastures anyway."

Clearly, Bo does not want his ranch plans up for discussion. I trace beads on the candle with a finger and as my contribution toward changing the subject I say, "I can't imagine where you found such a lovely thing, Caro."

"The Wild Goose, right, Caro?" Bo says.

I can't decide if these two are showing off their knowledge of each other or including me in their friendship.

"Where's that?"

"It isn't any place," Caro says. "But I don't like people copying me, so I tell them I bought whatever they're asking about at the Wild Goose and I give them very thorough, very lengthy directions."

"Ah," I say, "you send them on a wild-goose chase."

"Exactly." Caro abruptly stands and says she can't stay any longer. She hasn't touched my lemon bread and she's left half her drink. I feel dismissed from the room even though Caro is the one heading for the door—with Bo in her wake. Even that snot Tolly is following them out.

Bo waves goodbye. Caro sticks her head back inside. "Creative people are the best to be around. Thanks for this afternoon." She blows me a kiss.

I say, "Thank you for coming." And I feel warmed by her.

I carry my cup of tea to the window and watch Bo and

Caro exchange a few words before getting into their separate cars. Some local history I'm reading pops into my head. A story about the Countess of Flat Creek. Back in the 1920s Cissy Patterson, a rich and powerful woman, recently divorced from a Polish count, came to Jackson Hole and bought the Flat Creek Ranch. I've read that Cissy, too, had reddish glints to her hair like those catching the sunlight in Caro's right now. Cissy hired Cal Carrington, a known outlaw who used to hide his stolen horses at that ranch, as her hunting guide, then as her foreman at the ranch. Photos show Cal was as tall, strong, and handsome as Bo. Stories say he was the only man Cissy ever really loved or respected, and the two of them carried on a torrid love affair that the whole valley whispered about.

I watch Bo's Suburban follow Caro's Buick out the drive, and I wonder if they will turn in opposite directions—Caro to town and Bo to his ranch—or will they both turn in the same direction. And which direction?

Just as I read about Cissy, Caro exhibits that same ability to offer a sudden and generous warmth that veils a typically chilly and distracted presence. Cissy's money and power and disregard for her reputation allowed her freedoms that made her a dangerous woman, even in Jackson Hole. Since her real home was Washington, D.C., Cissy didn't care what people thought of her here. Caro's real home is a small town in Arkansas.

Caro turns toward town.

The story says Cal stopped stealing horses, bathed regularly, and even accompanied Cissy to society parties back east and on trips abroad when Cissy got brave and invited him. Their love affair lasted decades.

Bo follows Caro toward town.

ten

t is a spineless way to create some distance with Bo, but I book airline tickets to Florida and don't tell him. I just leave. Every day another reason pops up for Bo and me to see each other. If he doesn't stop by to show me where the crawl space door is hidden (beneath the dryer), I call him to ask what metal thing just fell out of the pipe to my woodstove (the tin-can lid serving as a damper). We end up pooling our refrigerator contents for dinner, then sit on my front steps with coffee till dark.

My first flight is to Cheyenne to see Beckett. Though a week early, Beck surprises me with a Mother's Day celebration. Sunday morning I am his guest for a lavish buffet at Little America, Cheyenne's largest hotel.

"Beck, you're a student. This is too expensive." My eyes scan the white-cloth tabletops colorfully displayed with out-of-season fruits, lobster thermidor, platters of shrimp, roasts, frothy desserts.

He ignores me and orders champagne.

"Beck—"

"Su . . . Mom." He raises his eyebrows at me to be certain I'm impressed with his fast catch. "I've got extra money. I work part-time at the radio station. Mostly as a gofer, but I'm hoping to do some spots one of these days."

"Spots?"

"Commercials."

"Perfect. You have a great voice, smooth, warm, lots of tonal depths to it. You should sing more, too."

From beneath the jacket he has draped over his arm, Beck produces two gift-wrapped presents. My eyes tear even before I unwrap them.

Beck says, "I knew this was chancy. You've cried over every gift I've given you since day care." He checks the room to see who might be looking, then smiles at me.

Pajamas and a book. The pajamas are tailored in lavender silk; the book is an ancient leather-bound copy of Emily Dickinson poetry, corners rubbed nearly round, gilt lettering flaked and faded.

"It will probably fall apart if you open it," Beck says. "But it looks good. And she's your favorite."

I stare at this tall, handsome child with wonder that I raised him, while still a child myself, and that somehow we both came through it all to this moment of deep knowing and appreciation. I've said it many times before, but I have to say it again: "Beck, you are the best."

Tonight, Mom and I sit on the porch together, pushing back and forth on the cushioned glider. The fishing dory bounces against the dock as the brackish water of Bessie Creek laps rhythmically. Like me, Mom went straight from her father's home to her husband's. She has always been afraid to sleep alone in the house, and she worries so much about being widowed that she often plans how she'll survive if she is. This week she has repeated the same plan every evening that we've sat together.

She says, "I'll have to find a smaller place, one with more people and lights around."

Just in front of the long, low house, Bessie Creek joins a canal—part of the intercoastal waterway around Stuart—and off the side yard, the creek bleeds into a dark, swampy stretch that separates my parents' home from the golf course. Not one neighbor's porch light can be seen through the knotty growth of mangroves.

"Maybe one of those little apartments by the shopping center," she says. "I could sit on the balcony at night and watch cars go by on Monterey Boulevard."

About then we notice that Dad has wandered out to the porch. Embarrassed, Mom allows an awkward silence to settle, and Dad says, "You killing me off again, Lizzie?"

When Dad goes back inside and turns on the lamps and TV, Mom says, "Did Daddy tell you what the doctor said?"

Easy, easy, I warn myself and halt an urge to spill what I know about her depression. She lays these traps, remember. I don't believe in keeping bad news from people about their own health and have been longing to override Dad's orders and talk to her about it. But I say, "You tell me."

"Dr. Meagher says I have rheumatism in this thumb." She wiggles her left one in the dim light coming from the living room window. "I wish . . . you know, that he hadn't told me, just told Addie. I hate worrying."

Without noticing, I'd stopped the glider. I begin pushing with my foot again. She has always been cunning. Always flirted with truth—the way she just did, asking whether Dad told me—but has always scuttled from it before meeting it head-on. Her fears making her live a cat-and-mouse game, even with me.

"Now I know," I say, "so I'll do the worrying." What have I just done? The exact thing I hoped to correct in my relationship with her.

Suddenly, I get it. She has answered my question about whether I should tell her what I know. I glance at her in amazement over how well she has trained me. Telling me she wished she didn't have to know about her thumb is telling me—as directly as she ever addresses anything—that she does not wish to be responsible for *any* health issues.

I want out of these games. The trouble is that her diagnosis forbids me loading her down with more problems. I forget between visits how hard she is to be around.

Mom says, "Hear that music?"

A favorite old song of mine, "Stand by Me," is playing as background to a public service spot on television.

"I wish they wouldn't talk about that stuff," Mom says.

I listen a moment. It's a spot for Alzheimer's disease. Dad punches off the TV.

Mom says, "You know what we haven't done for a long time? Play beauty parlor."

I laugh. I'd forgotten our old game. But she'd remembered. Sometimes, I feel the issue is *my* memory, not hers. I try to recall if I'd ever gotten any turns as the customer or whether I always played the hair stylist.

"Let's do it now. Go get your brush and comb," I say.

"I don't know where I put them. You look."

She can act dumb as a doughnut when she wants.

In many ways I am like my mother. With Erik I acted powerless as a way of inviting notice, interacting with him, sharing myself with him—a form of generosity, an offer of friendship. I thought that was what my mother was teaching me: social skills. But I misunderstood; I assumed that to be accessible to others meant I had to invite them to help me in my own thinking processes. So, like Mom has always done, I, too, stood in front of an open refrigerator door and cozily asked, "What am I doing here?" or yelped in alarm, "Oh, no." My husband should then say, as I have done to my mother all these years, "You want a Coke." Or rush to see what's wrong, only to learn there are no olives for lunch.

Somewhere along the way Mom learned that helplessness was friendly and self-sufficiency was threatening and passed that information on to me. For a long time it glued my marriage together, even provided the conversation as I checked with Erik over every small decision.

Until this trip, I hadn't realized how manipulative Mom was all my life. Funny how I used to accept the most obvious behavior. She'd wonder out loud, "What's that noise?" when she didn't want to get up and answer the phone. "It's the phone," I'd shout on the run to grab it. Either Mom has lost skill or I have gained some, because I often catch her delivering some other message than the one she is actually putting words to. Dad says Dr. Meagher wants to schedule some tests.

*   *   *

The day after I get home, Bo calls. He's planned a cookout, invited the Donnells, a few other friends and his family. "Introduce you to everybody," he said. At last, I'll meet the aunts. I've bought an ankle-length gauzy cotton skirt, striped with buttons down the front, for half price because the waistband broke away from the gathered skirt and needs a few stitches. It's worn with stretchy white pants beneath it. A scooped-neck tee and my sandals, buttons on the skirt left mostly undone, and I'll look enough like the hostess/helper Bo asked me to be for this affair.

I think of my mother and her rules while I dress for the party: Never wear white after Labor Day or before Memorial Day. Same for straw purses and sandals. Officially, I'm on the edge of the good-taste plateau on two counts. I look in the cabinet mirror above the bathroom sink and worry whether Bo will think I'm pretty today. I heard my mother say to my father during my visit last week, "She's got nice . . . you know . . . these things." My mother poked herself gently in the eye, then blinked in surprise.

She seemed fine all day while Dad was gone or busy in his office, but from dinnertime on odd things occurred. Dad and I were involved in one of our impassioned discussions. This time about the absurdity of the golf course next door claiming they were a bird sanctuary. I maintained that the chemical runoff from the heavy use of fertilizers and weed killers poisoned the drainage ponds and made the idea a joke.

In a whisper and tugging Dad's sleeve, Mom interrupted, "Addie, Addie, who's that pretty girl?"

I turned to look at my mother, and she smiled formally to

me and pretended not to have said a thing. How does she remember her manners and not her child? She made no attempt
to join the conversation, yet repeatedly tried to distract Dad
from our talk. When I was little, three or four years old, she
used to scowl at me if I monopolized Dad's attention when he
came home from work.

Dad brushed off Mom's question and told a story about a
golfer claiming he scored a birdie when he killed a heron on
the green with one of his drives. Dad hated golfers and made
Mom quit taking lessons when they moved to Florida.

Mom asked who I was once again, and Dad, acting as if she
were merely a pesky six-year-old, wrote my name on a piece of
cardboard that came from his dry-cleaned shirts. Big letters in
blue ink: SUZANNAH. He propped it above the TV. I didn't
follow his reasoning at all. If she couldn't remember what she'd
named her only daughter, how was she supposed to remember
to look at the sign?

In fact, this worked against my father. Now my mother
had *two* repetitious questions to ask. "What's her name?" and
"What's that paper doing there?" Neither was Dad accepting
that perhaps Mom couldn't always read. When I found a way
to break the news to him later in the week, he promptly began
to teach her. "Ssss. Go, 'ssss.' Then, 'oooo-zannah.' Watch my
mouth. 'Ssss . . .' "

When Dad pulled that stunt, Mom slid her eyes over to me
and lifted her brows in the old family look of "Should I call
for the straitjacket or will you?" Once, we used to make a lot
of *crazy* jokes in my family. Now we pretend there isn't such a
word.

I roll my own eyes and lift my brows at myself in the

mirror. I grab my backpack and potluck dish and head for the party. Perfect for Bo's plans, the day has settled into a dazzling brightness, calm and warm. Earlier this morning, grasses on the butte were flattened into long, shiny streaks by the wind. They caught the flash of sun and shadow when clouds, like whipped mounds of meringue, slid across the sky as if on a cool blue plate. Now the temperature has covered its typical forty-degree span for late May and is holding at seventy-eight. By counting the number of cars passing my cabin, I time my arrival at Bo's so I don't have to meet too many strangers at once.

As soon as I pull up Bo's drive, two colorfully dressed woman pounce on my car door. One spreads her arms lightly around me in a hug, the other unburdens me of my backpack and potluck dish.

"We're Bo's aunts. I'm Maizie, this is Violet and you are Suzannah. We knew it right away, didn't we, sister?"

Violet agrees. "Bo said you had piles of curly light brown hair and was smiley as the Flying Nun."

The aunts lead me to the kitchen and present me to Bo as if I am their own special gift to him. Bo is relieved to see me. He's fallen behind schedule and sets me to work mashing avocados. Two by two, guests enter the kitchen and hand me their potluck dishes and introduce themselves. The last to arrive, Caro and Dickie, pick their way across the weedy side yard to Bo's grassy patch behind his house. I carry the guacamole outside and see that Caro's wearing strappy shoes with thin heels about three inches high, the dope. First thing, when she steps onto Bo's rough-board deck, her heels both sink into a gap between the boards, and when she pulls her shoes out, leaning on Dickie for support, the leather is scraped down to curls that wag off the ends of her heels.

She says, "Fucking shit." Not too loud, but everybody hears these first words of hers before she even gets introduced.

"What did she say, sister?" Bo's aunt Maizie asks.

" 'Fucking shit.' She said, 'Fucking shit,' dear." Aunt Violet answers in a tone slightly louder than her normal one, as if Maizie were hard of hearing, which she isn't.

Caro balances each foot to one board of decking and stands with legs not quite wide enough apart to look casual, not quite close enough to appear normal. In fact, she looks the way a horse does from behind while it's urinating. She says to me before even greeting any of the others, "Who's the designer of your skirt, Suzannah?" I don't know, of course. "Well . . . where did you get it? Was it on sale?" She wants to turn me around and read my label, which she instructs me—as if I don't know—is always sewn into the back of garments. But I distract her with introductions. I feel the aunts vibrating to get at Caro, so I start with them.

Violet says, "Now tell us all about *your* clothes, and you, too, Mr. Donnell."

"I'll bet they paid full price, sister," Aunt Maizie says.

Oh God, they're fun. And now I see they must like me.

Bo's head darts into view at the kitchen window, and he charges out the back door to intercept the roasting.

"Dickie, you drove." Bo wipes his hand on a dish towel before extending it to Dickie. "We were looking for you to drop down from the sky."

"Good to see you, Bo." Dickie accepts Bo's handshake. "But that word *drop* makes us chopper pilots nervous."

Behind the Donnells, the hiss of tobacco spit as it meets with burning coals introduces the presence of Bo's grandfather, whom I met earlier. Both Caro and Dickie abruptly spin around at the sound, as if their shirttails were sizzling.

Bo introduces his grandfather. "O. C. Garrett, initials for Owen Charles."

"A name I don't never use," Bo's grandfather warns. He spits another gob into the flames of the cooker, wipes his right hand across his mouth, then onto the thigh of his Wranglers, before offering it in a handshake with Dickie.

I watch to see if Dickie sneaks a chance to wipe his hand on his own pants afterward; he doesn't, but he holds the hand stiffly away from the rest of his body.

"Grandma always said O.C. stood for *Old Coot*," Bo tells us.

"Mr. Donnell," says Violet, "I believe you're wearing Lucchese boots."

"And I'll bet he paid just loads for them, sister," says Maizie.

Dickie stares at his feet undecided about how to react to the aunts. Finally, he just asks them to please call him Dickie and he moves away.

I look to see if Bo's sorry about this idea of a cookout yet, but he's fine, enjoying his own party. He appears not to be absorbing his family's antics as a reflection on himself.

The Garretts' old family doctor forms a circle with Bo's vet and both their wives over on the lawn. Mick Farlow, the lawyer who appeared at the bank for the closing of my cabin, joins them along with his date, a woman I've seen shopping at the bookstore, Tam Randall. She's a mental-health therapist, Tessa says. I've noticed she reads heavily from the women's studies section and new fiction, my own favorite areas.

Caro follows Bo into the kitchen to help carry out the pitcher of margaritas and the plates of nachos. I'm going to be hostess in name only, I see. I approach Tam, glad for the chance to get to know her better.

Some time later the aunts come out of the house carrying a large photo album between them. "You must let sister and me show all of you our pictures of little Bartholomew," Violet announces to the group. She turns to Maizie. "He was a darling child—wasn't he, sister?" The sisters become caught up in each other. I've noticed today that they begin addressing the group, then lose awareness of us. Signals bounce rhythmically between the two sisters as they trigger memories in each other, almost operating as a synaptosome, a nerve ending isolated from surrounding tissue. If they hold to pattern, it will be some time before they will recall the rest of us and again transmit messages to the body of the gathering here on Bo's deck.

Off to the edge of the mowed yard, another fire burns. This one, in a hole dug in the ground, is set up with a spit for meat. I trail over to join the crowd watching Bo paint a beef roast with red sauce.

"My favorites," says Maizie in a burst of delight, still holding half the photo album. "Suzannah!" she calls to me. "Come see darling Bartholomew."

The sisters and I meet halfway across the yard.

Even at four he was all masculinity. Stances of Bo, thumb and forefinger cocked low on each hip challenged the camera. Bo hanging beneath his pony at five, standing in the saddle about to shoot the photographer at seven. Bo with his first elk

at eight, driving a pickup at ten. Beside a baler at twelve, tossing that summer's straw cowboy hat into the final bale. Which,
the sisters tell me, is the custom at the end of haying season.
Flipping to the front of the album, Violet coos at a photo of Bo
as a newborn being bathed in a kitchen sink.

"He had large private parts, didn't he, sister?" Maizie says.

"Bartholomew was of good size." They agree with each
other that this is of importance to a man and again shut the
rest of us out. A few minutes later Violet speaks across the yard
to Bo. "Darling, are you still rather well-endowed? Sister and
I wondered because your feet also grew fast and then stopped
in your adolescence. Your feet are not of unusual size, though
adequate."

"My penis is of unusual size, Aunt Violet. My feet stopped
growing. My brain and penis just surged on to astounding di-
mensions." Bo paints more sauce on his beef, and his friends
laugh.

Caro likes the public talk about Bo's penis. From her private smile, I decide she is aching to report, but settles for looking knowingly as if she has an opinion she'll attempt to keep
to herself—but makes no promises. Dickie watches her. Poor
Dickie. He knows.

Poor me. Now I know, too. But maybe it's ending.

"Women like the large ones," Aunt Maizie offers to those of
us still listening. "But, oh, one can do nicely with any size."

By necessity, Bo would have had to move private territory far
inward, growing up around these two creatures. I could stand
to take a lesson from him, I think, while helping him and Caro
carry food to a long table on the deck. He has given his family
members back over to themselves. They cannot embarrass him;

they do not reflect on him. They are their own zany selves, and Bo figures everyone around has the job of dealing with this on their own. Unlike me, *he* doesn't have shoulder pains from the tenseness of making this gathering work for each person. Don't ask me why I feel responsible. Bo seems to feel his responsibility only includes offering palatable food and drink—not the weather, not the fact that his girlfriend's husband is present or that the owner of a New York gallery is joining us soon, or that his crazy aunts insist on monopolizing the talk with penis judgments. Though I could wonder if this would be different were the aunts to go on about the *smallness* of Bo's penis. Still, I doubt it would. Yep, Aunt Vi, Bo might say, so dinky I can't find it in the dark without lighting a match first.

To get everyone started in line, I fill my plate, then find a place to sit where I can further study the guests.

With the pain my imagination projects onto Dickie, I almost miss the quirk of a smile on his lips as he watches Caro smear a cracker with Brie and hand it to Bo.

I'm confused.

Dickie knows now they're having an affair or are about to—I'm certain of it—yet he appears to be . . . flattered. It's pride and pleasure I see on Dickie's face. You can lust after her, even meet her in motel rooms, but the woman is licensed to me. The smile of a man inviting another man—someone he really aches to impress—to drive his Lamborghini. See? She handles even better than she looks.

Aunt Violet and Aunt Maizie slide onto the bench where I'm speculating about the guests, one aunt to each side of me. We sit with our buffet plates on our laps, our glasses at our feet, juggling extra silverware and napkins.

"Now there's a man proud of his belongings," Violet says, tipping a speared melon ball toward Dickie.

"Is that it then?" I say with sudden surprise at having my inner musings confirmed.

"That," Aunt Maizie says, "and a fascination with Bartholomew that would make our little boy squirm in his sleep if he knew." Along with her silverware, napkin, glass, and plate, she has the added problem of finding a place to set the salt shaker she's brought. She solves this by passing it to me.

"*What?*" I say, accepting the salt.

"That's my take," says Maizie.

Violet says, "She's right."

The aunts sound more than sane just now—they strike me as extremely perceptive. Their words shock me. To keep myself from staring at Dickie, I scrutinize the aunts. The two have good taste in clothes, if you like expensive Western wear. Outfits straight out of the window of the Wild Turkey Saloon. Swingy skirts, woven vests, cowboy boots. Heavy Navajo jewelry in silver and turquoise parades around their necks and their wrists and dangles from their ears. Violet is pale in coloring, a bit taller than her sister and less effusive. Maizie, I would guess, took the lead in letting her hips and tummy soften and spread. Violet, perhaps once even lanky, has followed suit and settled into a comfort with her middle-aged padding. The aunts must be about sixty-three and sixty-four now. Violet, I know, is the older. They exhibit a certain glamour. They are definitely flirts. Much of that penis talk earlier was directed toward Mick Farlow's recently widowed father, I believe now. Jem Farlow has been targeted with saucy looks from them both.

"Mickey's got a nice girl," Maizie says about Bo's lawyer friend.

The two reminisce together about Mick's childhood, when he used to spend time with Bo here on the ranch. I hope for Mick's sake there are no nude pictures of him in the photo album.

Twenty years ago, when their mother died, the sisters followed Grandpa Garrett into town. Bo told me the two bought a duplex a few blocks away from their father's trailer; each of them live in one half. Bo says they have men friends, a pool of escorts they share and from which they select particular mates on occasion.

"So now there's Suzannah." Maizie turns to me conspiratorially. "We've been asking ourselves: 'Hmm. But where does Suzannah fit into the picture?' Oh, we have our silly hopes, don't we, sister?"

"But we know," Violet says, "that you have much on your mind these days and we'll have to be patient. We told Bartholomew."

"What, what did you tell Bo?" My head swings side to side, from one sister to the other, following their sudden inclusion of me in their talk.

"To be patient," says Maizie from my left.

"That you need to take your time grieving," Violet adds from the right.

"Grieving?"

"Your mother, your marriage." From the left.

"Lost youth." From the right again.

"Oh, now cut that out," Maizie says to me before I say or do a single thing. "Nobody's been talking about you. Bo just said *depression* and *divorce* and we understood."

"We're not stupid," Violet says.

"Sometimes we are," Maizie says.

"Oh, just for fun."

"Well, I don't know, sister—"

"She's been listening to O.C." Violet turns to me. "He says we're senile before our time."

I want to ask more questions, but I suspect the sisters can maintain attention on subjects outside themselves for only so long. Besides, we are being called to collect dessert, my contribution to the potluck. Chocolate cake, dark, sweet, and moist. The aunts brought Irish whiskey and two flavors of whipped cream, orange and almond, to accompany our coffee.

Later, it's me that sidles up to the aunts. They are talking about Dickie and let me listen.

"Attracted to Bo?" Violet asks herself in a search for words. "These matters are complex. More like . . ."

Maizie finishes, "If Dickie could, he'd *be* Bo. That is if he could still be wealthy and own things."

"That's it exactly!" Violet snaps her fingers in the air. "Dickie yearns to be a real rancher, instead of a pretend one with his fancy toys. Even more, he'd like to be as manly and handsome as our Bartholomew."

I wouldn't mind getting the talk back around to Bo and me and their silly hopes, but Bo is heading our way. He grins hugely as he joins us and flings his arm around my neck. Until today, we haven't seen each other since before I left for Florida. With his fist under my chin, he tips my face up and kisses me lightly on the mouth. "Welcome home," he says.

I'm surprised and dazzled. My ears heat up.

Bo and his aunts talk, and I miss the entire exchange while my mind replays the smile, the kiss, the happy look afterward. His smile swooping down to meet my smile. My lips sizzle and feel like they might be swelling. Turning neon pink. Glowing in the dark like the forgotten coals in the barbecue pit on the edge of the yard. I am sure these attentions are just for me. Bo is too straightforward to be using me for some message to Dickie or Caro. He never touches me at my house or anytime we're alone. I think he's afraid of scaring me off. He has a solid touch. Well-grounded, strong, and good souled.

After a while Bo releases me and moves aside to include Mitzi Beamer, the New York gallery owner, into our circle of talk. Mitzi is in the valley to fish. Bo was recommended to her as a guide by the sporting-goods store on the square because he could discuss contemporary art as well as fly fishing. All this comes out in Bo's introduction of Mitzi to the group.

A bit later I gather from their talk that Mitzi isn't offering Bo any gallery space even after seeing his work. Instead, she suggests to Bo that he produce brochures of his work, which she offers to mail to architects and interior designers in the East with her strong recommendations. To me this sounds like an opportunity to earn good money and create a steady following. Bo appears unenthusiastic.

When Mitzi finishes her sales pitch, Bo says, "I'm not a retailer, Mitzi. If I were, I'd rather sell popcorn."

This could be my answer to a question I've carried about whether Bo would court Caro for her financial ability to support his art career. If so, I'm left with the belief that Bo deals from his heart and doesn't do anything just for money, not even flirt with Caro. Kind of a good news/bad news deal.

Home again and getting out of my clothes, I think about the people at that party and wonder if natives of this valley have grown as strangely twisted as the junipers on the slope behind Bo's deck. Some of those trees hunker to the ground with low bushy growth, where the snows might bury them December through May. Others grow tall and spindly, all their lower branches nibbled clean by mule deer. Far to the south, in the drainage, trees have been severed by avalanches and only their spiky trunks remain. The trees with their branches all thrust out to one side, away from the harsh northern winds of winter, remind me of the aunts. This is how they have survived. They have grown all to one side, toward the safe shelter of the other.

Bo's grandfather, aside from actually being small and wiry in build, reminds me of the trees that hunker close to the ground, spreading tough branches horizontally rather than skyward in the expectation of winter's smothering snows. Bo told me once that the old coot is prejudicial and narrow-minded, and he's right. O.C. is a man who has lain dormant like the junipers half his seasons. Despite his bluster and grumble, he strikes me as full of unconscious fears, disguised as verbal barbs launched toward the rest of humanity.

At first, I enjoyed talking to him. He was funny and vibrant. Then, without warning, he injected a brutal swipe at homosexuals and Jewish men ("fags and kikes") and looked at me expectantly, as if waiting for my smirk of agreement. I was taken by surprise. As much as I hoped to be someone he liked, I excused myself during that pause and didn't wait around to hear the finish of his story. I imagine he's complaining to Bo right now that I'm a snippy, humorless "little gal," as he referred to me all night.

"Say, little gal, you keep an eye peeled, you're going to

find yourself some huckleberries along Singer's Creek. Bears don't need them, can't bake pies no better than they can tie shoestrings. They're just big, oversized rats—don't you think? Ought to shoot every one. The blessed Lord knows I blasted my share."

Honest to God, it's as if he's studied how to antagonize people. Yet I found him delightful, too, in his way. He attempted to charm me at times, went out of his way to introduce me as someone special to Dr. Goldy and the veterinarian, Gideon Haymaker. And the man could tell jokes—accents and all—like a pro. People huddled around him and howled so contagiously I could barely stand to keep away. But even from my safe distance, I could tell that half his jokes trailed abrasive punch lines.

I suspect O.C. was hard on Bo as a child. Hard on the aunts, too. Why else would the two women cling so tightly to each other? Been so afraid all these years to tell the truth about Bo's birth? Perhaps the sisters used Bo as a buffer between themselves and their father. But more often, I'll bet, they were buffers themselves protecting their son, Bo.

eleven

Middle of June and I'm still wearing fleece and flannel. Just as Bo predicted, the arrival of summer has stalled. The cold night air frosts the morning grass and delays the maturing of the tiny lime-colored leaves on the aspen and willow and cottonwood trees. The daffodil leaves are short stubs in the grass that border my cabin and the lilac bushes around the old shed out back may not bloom until the Fourth of July. Bo says it's happened before. I want to plant vegetables, but they need forty straight nights without frost and such an event has not occurred on the ranch in recorded history. "One year we only had nineteen nights without frost," Bo said. "This part of the valley is too high for gardens."

But tonight a chinook careens off the Tetons and the unexpected warm wind swats at the old Douglas fir in the side yard. It's nearly midnight, and I stand outside barefoot in my flannel nightshirt. The temperature has lurched up twenty degrees since sundown, and long ago I rolled up my nightshirt sleeves past my elbows and kicked off my slippers.

It's exciting out here, as if the elements are throwing a party and I am invited. I raise my nightshirt up past my bare hips, then stretch it over my head, exposing my entire body. My nightshirt is a sail between my arms that catches the wind and threatens to lift me into the migration of last year's dried leaves passing above me. I feel danger swirling in the blackness beyond the light cast from the kitchen door. I can't convince myself to move into the yard farther. I resort to a bribe: Three giant steps into the darkness and I can have another glass of wine when I go back inside. The brilliance of the light in Wyoming has made me wish I could paint, but I must learn to draw first and have spent the evening teaching myself. Sheets of paper and Magic Markers are strewn across my kitchen table, while the wine bottle stands guard against a judgment so critical that I might ruin my own fun.

Now legs lifted high, I leap once, twice, three times into the dark yard. A fierce blast of air slams against me and a shingle shears past my head. A cool shiver of fear spirals up my spine. This party has veered out of control. I turn toward the safety of my cabin. Before my eyes the lit doorway of my kitchen turns black. The power has gone out. Dense cloud cover allows no moon, no stars. As I drop my white nightshirt back over my body, it fades into a ghostly film around my knees.

Is my cabin really straight ahead or have I unconsciously turned around in search of light? What if I get lost in my own backyard and wander into the danger of the forest where I hear tree limbs breaking loose? I don't trust myself. Common sense knocks but I ignore it and feel stupidly immobilized in the spinning black night.

Maybe it isn't the wind that took out the lights. Maybe an escaped convict has found my breaker box and turned everything off. I don't belong in a Wyoming cabin all alone when I haven't stocked candles for a power outage or even bought a flashlight. And an escaped convict knows how to work my breaker box before I do.

When my eyes adjust to the dark, I wad my nightshirt hem in a sweaty fist and pick my way on tiptoe toward the black bulk of my cabin. My hair plasters my cheeks and grit blows into my eyes. With relief I reach the kitchen door, then remember Tolly. She's out in this weather, too.

"Tolly. Tolly."

I hear mewing and soon she is lacing my ankles with her soft body. I lift her up and hold her against me. The cabin is mouse-free thanks to her. We both go inside, and I begin the search in the dark for matches and that elegant candle Caro brought me. Each time I enter a room I forget and flip the light switch on.

Matches I find near the woodstove and the candle I find in my underwear drawer, where its scent seeps into my panties. I set the lighted candle on the kitchen counter. Then recall the oil lamp I bought when I first moved in and stuck away because it smoked.

I'm not happy about going back outside to the breaker box, but how else will I know whether it's just my house or an area outage? Already I've stalled a half hour or so. I can't see Bo's place from here and there's no use calling him; it's Saturday night and I heard him drive past hours ago on his way to town.

In fact, since his potluck, I haven't seen Bo much at all; he seems to have gotten my message about needing some distance and just stops by to leave my mail under the doormat. Without his cooking I've been on a dreary run of Stouffer's Lean Cuisine. Have these people never heard of herbs and spices?

The stiff, gummy wick of the lamp holds the flame I loan it from the candle and I go back out the kitchen door. On the driveway side of the house, I find the breaker box and open it. There's a line of square plastic buttons. I tip my head toward my left shoulder and read the block print labeled sideways on the buttons: ON, ON, ON. I tip my head toward my right shoulder and read them again: NO, NO, NO.

Which is it? ON or NO?

I stare at the labels. Should I push one of these buttons or should I just go to bed and worry about this in the morning?

Inside, the sound of trees thrashing, I hear a car chug up the road. Bo is coming back from town. Once again the night wind feels festive. I stand with my lamp raised high over my head like the Statue of Liberty as Bo's Suburban whips into my drive. Give me your handsome cowboy artists yearning to breathe free.

Bo cuts his engine and his headlights, climbs out and reaches behind his seat for a flashlight. He walks over to where I stand grinning and holding my nightshirt down.

"Doing okay?" He flicks his flashlight beam around me briefly.

"Sure," I answer, cocky now that he's here with me.

"Thought I'd check on you."

"You worried about me," I say in wonder. With Erik I had to produce a bleeding wound to stir his concern.

Bo moves in closer and leans over me to shine his flashlight at the opened breaker box. I smell beer and cigarette smoke on his clothes. He's been at the Cowboy Bar. Alone? With Caro? Oh, never mind.

"The whole valley's down." He closes the cover on the breaker box. He shines the beam of light on the ground in front of us and puts a hand on my back to direct me around the side of the cabin toward the kitchen door.

Once inside the cabin I blow out the smelly lamp and stick it back on a high shelf over the dryer. I'm afraid Bo might leave. "Have a beer?" I invite. While wanting to create distance, I have also stocked his brand of beer. Go figure.

"Sounds good," he says.

Tolly trots out at the sound of Bo's voice like the little tart she is, and he squats down and gives her body a loving massage, ears to end. I watch Bo's hands in the candlelight from the kitchen counter, mesmerized by the strength of his fingers and the care in his touch. I feel the warmth and pleasure all along the ladder of my own back muscles, and for a moment, I want to purr and lick Bo's face.

I turn away to screw the caps on my Magic Markers. Bo opens the refrigerator door and reaches for a beer. He halts after closing the door and shines his flashlight on the drawings I just made and stuck up with magnets. They are the only two drawings that really turned out well tonight. I followed the directions in a new book. I never could draw for Beckett when he asked as a toddler, not even simple rabbits and cats.

Bo looks first at the chair I drew as an exercise in perspective. I had jumped to the middle of the book, getting a bit over my head. He says, "These are great. Little kids draw things so funny." He laughs. "Look at this stubby leg shooting out the side of the chair seat."

I am silent.

He directs the beam of his flashlight to my other drawing. It's the wine bottle with my wineglass beside it.

"What the hell is this supposed . . . ?"

I remain silent.

"Uh-oh." Bo checks my face over his shoulder. He looks at the drawing again, then turns and scans the flashlight beam across my table, taking in the wine bottle, the wineglass, the papers strewn about, the Magic Markers. He turns off the flashlight and sets it on top of the refrigerator.

In the candlelight he says, "You took on some tough subjects here. Chairs and empty glasses are difficult to draw." He wrenches the bottle cap off his beer and tosses it onto the counter. "How many times did you have to empty that glass?"

"Three."

"Maybe four?"

"Maybe." I am twisting the cap on my black Magic Marker and standing like a flamingo—one leg bent beneath my nightshirt with my foot propped against my knee. I couldn't maintain balance if it wasn't for the table edge where my hip rests. My father claimed he knew I'd done something that wouldn't please him when I stood like this as a child. "Look at this kid, Lizzie," he'd say to my mother. "She doesn't have a leg to stand on." I catch myself and stand upright on both feet. Grown-ups in their own homes don't have to please anybody.

Bo says, "Did you know there is a law against drinking and drawing?" He tips his beer bottle up for a swig while watching me.

"You're rude." I step nearer him with my black Magic Marker and carefully draw a goatee on his chin.

Bo sets his beer bottle on the counter. He reaches toward the table for a purple marker and just as carefully draws cat whiskers around my mouth. I stand still and take my medicine. When he's finished, I give him a black mustache to go with his goatee. He watches me draw with eyelids lowered in a way I find sexy. Or is it the mustache?

Neither of us cracks a smile.

In a sudden move, Bo blows out the candle. He says in the dark, "I'm counting to ten. You better hide in a good spot, because when I find you, I'm going to draw over every inch of your body. One."

I let out a yelp, grab another marker off the table, and shoot out of the kitchen.

"Two, three."

Where to hide? I stand undecided in the living room. The wind has quieted and each breath of mine seems to announce my position in the stillness left in the wake of the chinook. "Four, five."

Under the coffee table? Behind my bedroom door? In my closet?

"Six, seven."

I hear a boot drop. Keep on the move, I decide.

"Eight, nine."

I can't see a thing and I'm afraid I'll bump into something and give myself away. I crouch low right where I am beside the kitchen door. Bo's other boot drops; it sounds ominous. At the last minute I grab a maroon serape draped on the back of the sofa and pull it around me to cover my white nightshirt.

"Ten."

I smash my mouth into the crook of my arm to keep from making a sound; I feel so tight with the tension of the game I'm afraid I'll give myself away with nervous giggling. I sense Bo as he passes through the doorway. I'm right at his feet, right where he doesn't expect me. Once he slips into the living room, I creep back into the kitchen. My body just fits under the bench. Now I've lost track of Bo. I listen with my whole self, skin and muscles and bones, trying to pick up a vibration. The tension makes me bristle with awareness. Every hair follicle on my arms stands at attention. I can't keep this silly grin off my face.

Bo moves through the dark house as smoothly as an elk in the forest, so at ease not even a rack of antlers impedes progress through close-growing trees. If I didn't know better, I'd think I was in the cabin alone. Bo is here, yet he's not. He has shifted his molecular structure; he is part of the log walls. I stay low. Once I suspect Bo has passed by me and is in the mudroom or bathroom, I scoot out from under the bench and belly crawl back into the living room.

In no time I feel him near . . . I think. That could be Tolly shifting on her pillow by the woodstove. My stomach trembles with the mounting tension and the buildup of laughter. Under cover of a blast of wind hurled at the cabin, I skitter across the open space and scuttle beneath the duvet hanging over the end of my bed.

I listen for Bo in the other room. I hear nothing. Then a breath—not mine. Is Bo in here, sitting against the wall beside my bed? Has he been in here all along just waiting for me?

Suddenly my bare foot is clenched. I shriek.

He doesn't say a word. He just pulls me over to him by my foot and begins scribbling up my ankle. I release pent-up anxiety and laughter, and he joins me in a low chuckle, but doesn't halt his work. He feels around and finds my other foot and pulls both legs across his lap, looping his Magic Marker up my left calf, then my right.

I sit up, shrug off the serape, and feel for Bo's face in the dark. When I find a cheek, I keep him steady with my hand beneath his ear and draw lightning marks like those on an Oglala warrior. He laughs and reaches for my wrist.

"This ink better not be permanent."

I giggle in blissful exhaustion.

"It's washable, right?" he checks.

"I didn't notice," I say. "I wasn't expecting to wear it." With my free hand, I add some polka dots in the same area of the zigzags. I stay low on his face so I don't poke out an eye. I hope that other marker I grabbed is a nice bright color. He releases my wrist, and I hold his head still and daub my marker on his other cheek.

Bo feels around until he finds my nose. "If it's not washable, we're stuck here for days, you know." He holds my chin with one hand and fills in color on the tip of my nose with his other.

"We are?"

"Can't go into town looking like trick-or-treaters."

"Hmm."

"Yep, no visitors," he says. "Just the two of us."

Out the window, cloud cover breaks up and moonlight flickers into the room. I sit with legs draped across Bo's lap, our faces inches apart. If he doesn't kiss me in the next second, I'll pop.

I don't wait. I kiss him.

Bo kisses me back; he touches my mouth lightly with his own. Then lifts me onto his lap and kisses me deeply. Like a startled bird, I do not stir, but lie in his arms motionless. I have not been kissed in two months. I have never been kissed with this enthusiasm and finesse. Bo's mouth roams slowly in and around mine, as if he were considering moving in permanently, as if he were approving of the arrangement of teeth and tongue.

I put my arms around him. I wonder at the many sensory transmitters collected in and about my mouth. All that mechanical activity of breakfast, lunch, and dinner, thank God these nerve fibers have not been dulled by the traffic of fork and spoon.

As earlier when caught outside in the chinook, I feel somewhat drunk, with a mixture of excitement and terror in the emotion of the storm. Once again I have lost my sense of direction and don't know if I'm heading for shelter or have turned in confusion toward danger. I let Bo lay me on the bed. I watch him take his clothes off in the dark.

"Bo?" I whisper. We don't know each other well enough for this. We are moving way too fast.

Bo lays his body alongside mine. "Suzannah," he whispers back. His hand moves to find the hem of my nightshirt. I don't want this pace to continue but I feel oddly passive about expressing this thought. In Bo's arms my body is, for once, more alert than my mind. Each new spot he touches on my skin sings its own tune and I long to hear the rest of this music.

Bo cups the bare curve of my waist and touches my bottom lip with the tip of his tongue. I believe any moment one of us is going to come to and set things right. I'm pretty sure, even, that I'll be the one to do it. I intend to.

And then, "Suzannah," Bo breathes, "you're ready for me."

I'm a cliché. While my body revolts against my mind, splitting me into two, my body itself splits and I feel my insides gush out, pumping fluids held in bondage too long. I open to Bo's weight and his hardness inside me. I welcome the smell of smoke in his hair and bath soap behind his ears and I burrow beneath his chin. Tears leak out of my eyes.

How are we ever going to work ourselves back into the positions in which we belong? I recall Bo's tanned arms cooking at my stove and how I dallied with mind photos of them contrasting someday against these pale sheets. But this is an event out of order, not as things should be. Porno slides mistakenly shuffled into family shots and shown to the good neighbors down the street.

Within moments of Bo whispering, "Zannah, oh God," I feel my uterus contract sickeningly. I know right away what this means.

"Let me up, Bo."

Bo nuzzles deeper into my neck. He glides a hand downward to between my legs and, there, presses a nerve bundle above and just to the left of my clitoris. I shudder with a flood of sensation. A long-held release of sexual pleasure segues into a surge of emotional disappointment in both of us.

I take a chance on heaping more indignity upon myself: I ask, "Caro?" I need to know about him and Caro. I need to know now.

"Caro?" Bo jerks out of me and rears up onto his knees. "Shit. You hear her car?"

Without even a hum or flicker to warn us, the power returns. In the bright overhead light I had flipped on earlier while looking for the candle, I see my blood smeared all over Bo as he kneels between my legs. All over him and my nightgown, me and the sheets. And I see the truth about Bo and Caro. He doesn't want her to know he's here with me.

I pull the pillow, pushed up against the wall behind my head, over my face and wail.

Bo says, "My God, Suzannah, are you okay?" He pries the pillow off my face. "What's going on, Zannah?"

I keep my eyes closed and cry, "Caro. You're having an affair with her."

"Never mind Caro. I need to know if you're okay."

I look at Bo's earnest face bent over me and burst into laughter. He looks like a cross between Dr. Freud and Chief Crazy Horse, with his black mustache and goatee and his red zigzags and polka dots. Then I start crying again.

Bo says, "You drank too much wine."

"And you took advantage of it," I sob.

I scoot out from under him and head for my bathrobe hanging behind my bedroom door. "In some cases that might be called date rape." I feel so embarrassed at the indignation of my menstrual blood smeared all over him and me and the bed that I welcome the rage that inserts itself as a crutch to help get me out of this room and away from his scrutiny. I push into my robe.

"You didn't answer me. Is this normal?"

"Normal? Not for me it isn't," I shoot back, deliberately stretching his meaning. "I don't sleep with friends' lovers." I yank the sash on my robe. My voice gets shrill as if I have squeezed the sash around my vocal cords instead of my waist. "I don't take advantage of people when they've been drinking either." I spin out of the room before my face cracks because Bo looks funny sitting on the edge of my bed wearing nothing but face paint and I don't know if I'm going to laugh again or sob. Hysteria must feel like this.

In the bathroom I step into the tub, then out again, and lock the bathroom door. I catch a glimpse of myself in the mirror. Purple whiskers and purple bulbous nose. How did Bo keep a straight face while I railed at him? My tear tracks catch the light.

Since the flare-up of fibroid tumors, my period, though back into a normal five-day run, often starts in an unexpected torrent. Anywhere from twenty-four days to thirty-two, unless my life undergoes a big change—like a divorce and a move to a new home. Then it can be weeks late, like this. Erik once suggested, as he followed me out of the movies with his jacket tied around my waist, that my ignorance was a negation of my femininity. "Suzannah, can't you catch some *clue* first?" As if he were so alert to life nothing ever got by him. His whole life got by him. All through our marriage I was so frequently setting fires beneath him, just to get him to react, I felt like a pyromaniac.

Bo is knocking on the door and I am ignoring him. The shower is running over my head, but I hear every word: "Suzannah, please, I'm scared. Just tell me if you're all right."

I stay silent and let hot water spill over me. Now I hear tools. I peek out of the shower curtain and see the tip of a knife sliding beneath the hook, lifting it purposefully from the eye.

"I have to know you're okay," Bo explains, once inside the

bathroom. "Please . . ." From behind the shower curtain, I hear he is restraining his anxiety to a subdued politeness.

I have a Tampax in now. My dignity is restored; it's time to reduce his. Let him worry.

"I'm going to take a look at you. It's okay." He's speaking as if a crazy person lurks behind this curtain. As if I have the knife, not him. "I can look at you in the shower," he says. "We did just make love."

Fury erupts. "We did *not* 'make love.' You took advantage of me." I stop short of accusing him of rape again. "You committed double adultery with me. You sleep with your friend's wife. Then you sleep with your"—I'm losing track of my thought—"with your friend's wife's . . . wife, I mean, friend." My body vibrates with anger at him, myself, the awful mess of all this, and I ignore the inner voice that accuses me of throwing false light on our encounter. I brought this scene on myself. Plus, it serves me right that my period, which I used for so long as a shield in my marriage, should impetuously flag my desire for this man.

"You have plenty of energy," Bo diagnoses from the other side of the curtain.

I continue to yell at him. "What kind of man does that?" I never yelled at Erik, my parents, Beckett. I have never yelled before. I don't dislike it. But I keep hoping he will correct me and say he is not sleeping with Caro, that I misunderstood his abrupt withdrawal from our lovemaking at the mention of her name and his silence on the subject since.

"Please tell me, do you always bleed like that or did I hurt you? Are you hurt internally?"

"I'm hurt e-ternally."

"It's okay, Suzannah," he soothes, as if he's giving up on me answering him rationally. "One peek—just to read your condition. Then I'll let you shower."

Lulled by his pleading, I still think I hold the right of consent and I slap his hand in surprise when he tugs the curtain aside. He doesn't flinch. He's pulled on his Levi's, but left the top buttons undone. No shirt and barefoot. Concern softens his eyes. Dr. Crazy Horse. I burst into a bark of laughter again like a nervous loon calling for its mate, then abruptly sober up.

He gives me a once-over. Appeased at the clean thighs and clear water flowing down the drain, he asks, "Is it your period?"

I turn my back.

"Got supplies?"

I don't answer.

He closes the curtain, and I hear him checking the cupboard under the sink to see for himself. "Yep. We're set there. I'm just going to wash up myself," he says. "Then I'll be out. One minute, I swear." And lullabies me with small talk about his bathing progress throughout his hurried splashings. Then, blessedly, he does leave.

Quite a while later, I turn off the shower and put on my bathrobe. The water pressure dropped midshower, and I see, as I leave the bathroom, it's because Bo has the washing machine going. He's still here. In the kitchen. And—I can't believe this—cooking.

He alternately stirs eggs in a bowl and grates cheese into it. A pile of chopped parsley and chives rests on the counter. He's dressed and turns to me when I enter the room. He says, "It's permanent."

For a crazy moment I think he means him cooking in my kitchen for the rest of my life. Then he gestures toward his face. My face threatens to break into a merrier response to him than I am really in the mood for, so I turn on my heel and go check myself in the bathroom mirror. My clown face has not faded one degree from washing in my shower. Again I rub soap on my washcloth and scrub and rinse and scrub and rinse. I end up with red blotches surrounding my purple whiskers and nose. I give up. I am wiped out. In the mirror I see one tired clown cat.

Back in the kitchen Bo scoops the parsley in his fist and dumps it into the bowl of eggs. Reaches over to stir potatoes frying in a pan, then turns the burner down low. "I'm sick about this, Suzannah. I don't know how to fix things."

I tip him off. "Leave."

"Then I don't know how I could ever come back."

I shrug.

He pulls out a chair for me at the table and brings a warmed plate of scrambled eggs and fried potatoes. Tea, toast, and jam. I may have acquaintances here—women I look forward to knowing better—but there isn't anyone I feel comfortable enough to share this ignominy with—except Bo himself. The complexity of this realization dulls my wits. I accept the offering of food and sit.

Bo doesn't join me; he goes into the mudroom and takes the laundry out of the washing machine and puts it into the dryer. He stays in there, even though the light is off, for a long time after I hear the dryer start.

I was about two and a half or three when I first heard the story of the little boy who cried wolf. I pretended one afternoon while crawling between the sofa and the living room wall to get stuck back there. "Help," I cried to my mother. "I can't get out." But my giggles erupted before she fell for the trick completely, and she squinted her eyes at me and told me the fate of the little boy who cried wolf. "Never again did anyone believe what that little boy said. Not even when a *real* wolf was trying to eat him."

The story left a deep impression on me. I became over-conscientious about telling the God's honest truth and never again cried wolf. Until tonight. Tonight I felt stuck between two places more ungiving than the wall and the sofa.

When Bo comes back into the kitchen, he announces that he has decided to stay the night. He'll sleep on the sofa, cook breakfast in the morning, help around the cabin tomorrow, and in this way hopes to earn my trust again. I can rest, make jewelry, go for walks. By the end of the day, he figures, we might feel comfortable with each other again. He doesn't know, he says, but this theory is the best he can come up with. I can go sleep now if I like. My bed has clean sheets on it. He'll use the ones in the dryer, when they're finished.

I tell him this isn't necessary. I tell him the story about the little boy who cried wolf. He's off the hook, I say. "I am as guilty as you are."

We argue a bit about who is guiltier, each of us campaigning for ourselves as winning candidate.

Then Bo concludes, "We are not in good shape with each other. I'm going with my first plan."

I can't budge him.

twelve

As I come out of the cabin, pale sunlight floats at the top of the valley like foam in a glass of dusky beer. It's been raining off and on all day and now, far to the north, dark clouds bed down for a late-afternoon nap.

Bo's homeopathic remedy seems successful. His theory is that we are building enough good history together in small, benign doses throughout the day to offset our "bad" episode last night. With Bo installed as cook and caretaker today, I'm living the life of an artist. I had trouble accepting his gift at first and squirmed with discomfort this morning till I realized it only made him feel unappreciated.

I asked Bo what I could do for him.

He said, "I've never married because I couldn't conceive of living in the same rooms with the same woman from breakfast on through dinner. You don't need to do a thing. You're a living revelation to me."

"Sounds like you're practicing for your future." I was going to add *With Caro,* but decided just because I was sporting cat whiskers didn't mean I had to act catty. Now faded from more scrubbing, my purple whiskers look in a certain light like the shadows of wrinkles pursed around my mouth. And my nose looks like that of an aging alcoholic. Not a glamorous sight. I'm at the stage in which I'd rather ink in the marks again so that it's clear I'm masquerading. Bo solved his problem by not shaving.

Bo may be practicing with me on another count. At lunch he disclosed an idea he's working on to turn Crossing Elk Ranch into an artists' retreat.

"I don't intend to cook," he said, nodding at my plate heaped with tuna casserole, "except for barbecues. We'd need to cook a cow once a week over flames tall as the Tetons for everybody to feel Western." Rather, each artist would be provided a one-room log cabin with its own small kitchen. Bo envisions five cabins all together, tucked into the trees on Saddlestring Butte. The artists will have solitude surrounded by natural beauty and a social life with elk, coyotes, and each other. Bo has been awarded residencies at three different artists' colonies in the past and now serves on the board at Ucross, so he knows exactly the kind of experience he wants to offer here.

As I pick up these bits of his artistic history, I have to readjust my idea of Bo as a casual artist. Since I've known him, I've never caught him in the process of sculpting, whereas he regularly catches me stringing beads. I look at everything in terms of beads—M&M'S, lima beans, moose droppings—I'm always designing art in my head. Bo never seems to be. Yet he has an enviable résumé and a show coming up. I thought I'd learn about living as an artist from him, but I think he's having trouble getting into his work this spring with all the free time he's created for himself.

Anyway, I decided to enjoy being the guinea pig for his new enterprise. I beaded at the kitchen table, until he started cooking and needed the work space. His solution to that was to sand and finish a wood door he had stored in his barn, which now rests across a couple saw horses in a corner of the living room waiting for Bo to make real legs for it. I have my own permanent work space now and never again have to pack up my beads and tools to free the kitchen table.

As the path I follow for my walk slips into the trees, darkness sloshes around my ankles and shadows rise to my shoulders. In an opening of the forest near the creek, I spot my cabin. Furry tufts of smoke from my chimney send signals of comfort. I built a fire before my walk; I mentally jot a reminder to keep up such small gestures of care to myself, such as a lamp lit for my homecoming and soup simmering on the stove.

All this seems hard work and I wonder if I shouldn't just lure Bo into my kitchen for keeps, because Tuesday I begin working at Valley Bookstore four days a week. Tessa said by July I could move into full-time if I wanted. I will work with nine women, and I like the idea of that. It's been a long time since I've had women friends in my life.

Before this rain the forest floor crunched underfoot; it was like walking on cornflakes. Now the grasses are springy, yet the rocky ground has already soaked up the moisture and the trail is firm, not muddy like it would be in Ohio.

I suspect Bo procrastinates about repairs around his own place. He complains his old clapboard house has rotted windowsills, and I've seen that the sheds lean north like the pine trees beside me on the path. So perhaps he procrastinates about his art, as well. He is scheduled for a two-man show at River Rock Gallery the middle of September, but seems busier making plans to guide the Donnells into Mosquito Creek for an elk hunt in November. Not to mention the repairs he's put on his list for my place.

I'm satisfied Bo is not working out retribution today. We talked about that. Still, I carry some guilt over my wildly dramatic accusation of rape. With the exception of this episode with Bo, my mother was successful teaching me not to indulge in the childish prank of crying wolf. Yet all my life she has been guilty of giving false alarm. She petitions for help way before necessary, as if she's afraid that she can't handle what may arise. She'd holler, "Quick, somebody." I'd drop my toys, run to her, find her reaching for the top shelf in her closet, and she'd say, "Oh, I thought maybe that shoe box was going to fall."

Before heading home I rest on deadfall beside the creek. Surveyors left one of their wooden stakes here. A neon pink plastic ribbon waves from it to signal a boundary line. Around this stake a muskrat has deposited small mounds of mud marking his own boundary line.

All at once I realize: My mother's need for help was actual. My mother never cried wolf. Because she was my parent I thought she was more capable than me. She was not, not ever, not even when I was young.

But my own acquisition of her helplessness is false.

I experience an eerie lifting of her thought patterns, which have overlaid my own for so long. Beneath the shroud rests a far less fearful and inhibited self. I realize with a jolt: Much of what I have taken to be my own thinking is merely a process I've mimicked from my mother.

I poke at the muddy deposits beside the survey post with a stick to see how long ago the muskrat was here. This morning is my guess, but with the day's rain it's hard to tell.

Was she sick long before any of us suspected? Or did her games eventually turn into reality? Whichever, I'm frightened about all those years we were in her mind together, because Dr. Meagher's diagnosis is that Mom has early-onset Alzheimer's disease. She is only fifty-nine years old. And this form of Alzheimer's is genetic.

Moistness descends with the evening chill, and to relax myself, I drink the air in deeply. Matted leaves, fast creek water, tree roots, and wet rocks brew a hearty ale. I rise and start back for my warm cabin.

Bo's hands are full. One holds a pan of mashed potatoes, the other a pan of gravy. He pulls out my chair with a boot hooked around a leg of it and cocks his head for me to sit. I can't believe all the food he's prepared today. He wouldn't let me help. Says he likes to cook, but it's no fun just for himself.

"Thank you," I say when he dollops potatoes on my plate.

"Kind of lumpy," he says. They disappear beneath a ladle full of gravy.

That's Bo and me, all day long ladling friendly talk over what we'd like to have disappear. But something needs to be aired. I try a sideways approach.

"What did your grandfather think of the Donnells at the

potluck?" I ask this while Bo's back is turned, arms in the oven, fetching the meat loaf.

"He thinks Dickie's a weasel." Bo straightens and puts a slice of meat loaf on my plate and one on his. "Changes the color of his demeanor according to the weather."

I have to say her name. "And . . . um . . . Caro?"

"He said—after she'd left, thank God—'Hmm, narrow nostrils. She kinda critical at you, son?' "

My tenseness dissolves in laughter.

Bo takes his seat and tells me his grandfather has a whole list of character attributes that match physical features. "He'd say you were generous because you have a full mouth."

Immediately, Bo drops his eyes to his plate and mine follow. Talking about lips embarrasses us. This is not part of our silently agreed upon household rules. We don't even know we have these unspoken rules, until now.

I quickly ask more questions about his grandparents. By mutual though unarticulated consent, we drag our conversation out until, question and answer alternately layered, we build ourselves another foundation of rapport. In the process, I learn that long ago my cabin housed the hired hand. Then one winter Bo's grandmother moved the hand into a house trailer and moved herself into the cabin.

"Pop was caught with a fancy lady is how the story came down to me," Bo says, adding that the phrasing might have something to do with him being only seven at the time. "My grandparents stayed mad that whole year. Then one morning I came over for breakfast and there was Grandpa sitting at the table in his long johns." Bo nodded to the end of the table beneath the shelf, where I've placed that old bench I found out back. My mind removes my stacks of books and places a younger version of O.C. on the bench, wearing his winter underwear, boots, and a cowboy hat.

Bo can't say for sure that this dalliance with the fancy lady was a single event, but he thinks so. And he thinks the woman was earlier married to a neighboring rancher, both now dead.

I ask Bo, "But your grandparents never lived together after that?"

"The aunts said Pop wouldn't say he was sorry. But Grandma told me she'd never lived alone before and found she liked it. Went from her daddy's house to O.C.'s. Also, she said his neatness improved when he became a visitor and so did his table manners."

"How about O.C.?" I ask. "Think he liked being a visitor?"

"Seemed to work," Bo says.

That's the only kind of marriage Bo has intimately witnessed, I think to myself in wonder: a kind in which the husband *visits* the wife.

Another thought: Bo was raised to feel comfortable with two women playing the single role of mother in his life. Perhaps Bo also feels comfortable with two women playing the role of girlfriend.

"Why are you messing around with her anyway?" I blurt.

"Grandma? She's dead."

"I mean, you seem like a nice guy, but here you are . . . in a married woman's bed."

Bo looks into my eyes. "I thought you realized how sorry I am for that. I'm not like my grandpa. I can say I'm sorry."

I feel embarrassed, but there is nowhere to go but on-ward here. "I mean Caro's bed . . . oh, God." This is not my business.

"You think I'm sleeping with Caro?"

"Even Caro seems to think that." I don't know what I mean exactly; she just exudes sexuality around Bo. "Never mind," I say. Though it would help knowing how much like his grandpa Bo really is, because Bo's apology—although he doesn't owe me one—was not straightforward but as indirect as his answer to my last question.

We each take a slow bite. I hear a log shift in the woodstove.

"That's happened with Caro," he says, as if it didn't involve him exactly or was an accident. A passive response for the kind of lover I experienced last night. "Though that was before . . . you know . . ." He gestures to the two of us.

I say, "Nothing is different."

Just because someone barges into my life some night doesn't mean I have to adjust my emotional timetable—I just moved here. I just divorced. My mother is going to die of Alzheimer's. Someday her mind will not only forget my name, but forget to instruct her organs how to operate. I feel angry and my mind searches for a way to punish Bo for cornering me.

"Caro's a married woman. I don't understand such ethics," I say.

"Caro's thinking about leaving him. Dickie's probably fool-ing around, too." Bo shrugs. "That's the way it is with them."

"And is that the way it is with you?"

Bo looks into my eyes. "It's not the way my marriage is going to go. No."

"Just your life." I hide behind my glass of water, taking a sip.

"If I heard you right, you don't want a stake in this."

"You heard me right."

I scrape my chair away from the table and begin to carry the used dishes to the sink. I don't clearly understand what message I've just imparted or if it truly represents the one I mean to give. How can I say, "Back off . . . but just for the time being, please." It isn't a fair request.

"Bo." I turn to face him. "Can't we just go on like we have?"

"How's that, Zannah? I sleep with Caro and cook for you?"

I can't answer him.

He says, "I don't have a choice here, do I?"

"What do you mean?"

"I mean that I care for you, but you'd prefer I continue to sleep with a married woman so you can hold it against me."

"That's ridiculous."

"I don't think so. I think I'm reading it exactly right."

"I want us to be friends. I'm sorry. That's all I can do now."

"Take it or leave it, right?" He tosses his knotted napkin onto the table. "You know what I think? I think if I hadn't been sleeping with Caro, you wouldn't even have let me get this close."

My throat closes the way it does when I hear unexpected truth. I drop my eyes from his angry stare and try not to cry. I don't want this to describe me.

Bo pushes away from the table and stands. I'm afraid he

will come to me. I turn my back and begin rinsing our plates. If I could explain the constrictions I feel binding me right now, I would. I want to give him Erik's old advice to me: *Don't take it personally.*

"You know how long I've waited for someone special? Long enough to have given up. Then you . . ." He stops. "You don't want to hear this, do you?"

"Bo, I can't even ask you to wait. There's so much I need to do . . . before I could be ready for you."

"You can ask me to wait."

"No. I can't. I'm sorry." I hope he understands. This could take years.

After a long silence, he releases a big breath and rolls up our place mats. He sets them on top of the refrigerator, goes out the back door. After a while, he returns and sounding resigned, he says, "Still want to go up?"

I nod.

He gathers into Baggies some brownies I baked earlier, and I pour coffee into a thermos. We continue with our plan to climb up the steep side of the butte directly behind my shed to have our dessert on a rocky ledge and watch the moon rise.

"More cold is coming," Bo says, "probably even freezing temperatures tonight." The wind lifts the hair over his eyes as he halts his climb to look south and east, as if he hears the footfalls of the weather echoing through the canyons, making its way toward us across the flats.

Clutching tufts of grass to pull myself up on the steep slope, I finally reach the outcropping behind Bo. He hauls me over the ledge with his solid grip, as if we were shaking hands and things got suddenly rowdy. I scramble on hands and knees with my butt in the air, until he has to grab my belt in back to secure me in place. Just being this high up makes me feel off balance.

Then I catch myself. It was my mother who was afraid of heights and suggested that we shared that fear. I test my own feelings up here and realize I am exhilarated by the beauty of the land spread before me. No urge to perform headstands on the rock ledge, but I'm not uneasy with the height. I take a big breath and settle myself. Without the burden of my mother's fears, I feel weightless, ungrounded in the new self I'm discovering.

Bo pours the coffee; I unwrap the brownies. I want to do my share toward making Bo and me comfortable with each other. I search my mind for a subject we can talk about.

"Were your aunts close to their mother?"

"Nah. Too close to each other. Siamese twins joined at the funny bone, Grandma used to say." He sounds cool, still unhappy with me, but willing to warm. He doesn't look at me, but off into the distant hills. He asks offhandedly, "Were you?"

"Pretty close. She has Alzheimer's." I didn't mean to say this. Why have I chosen tonight to tell him? It reminds me of when I used to argue with Erik, then stub my toe or get a splinter afterward to help mend us back together. Here I am: injured. In need of you.

"Oh, God. When did you find out?" Bo turns to me, sets his coffee on the ground, and gives me his full attention.

"Few days ago. But I've suspected for a while she had something more going on than the depression I mentioned to you. Last month during my visit, she put the lit end of a cigarette in her mouth."

I look off to the distance, remembering. She and I were alone that evening. She played solitaire and watched television; I read beside her on the sofa. She turned to me and said, "Look." She opened her mouth and showed me the ash on her tongue.

"Oh, my God." I held up an ashtray to her mouth. "Quick. Spit."

"Can you believe anyone would do something so stupid?" She laughed. "I'm telling you, you got to watch me every minute." I thought that was the message: Pay attention to her. So I set my book aside.

Now I tell Bo, "That's when I really became frightened."

"You didn't get tests?"

"Got lots of tests, but a clinical diagnosis for Alzheimer's disease consists only of ruling out every other possible explanation."

"You still hoped?" Bo sounds tentative with his questions, uncertain how to respect my privacy, while trying to understand my situation.

"I don't know. . . . I kept expecting Mom to wink and confide she'd finally found a way to get Dad to show some real affection for her." I feel guilty suspecting Mom's games might have extended to faking Alzheimer's.

Bo seems puzzled. "Did your mother lie about things?"

"She never lied. She just trained us, my dad and me, not to believe her behavior." I try to explain to Bo. "Nothing was the way it seemed. She was the center of the family's attention, yet she always accused us of ignoring her."

I am ambushed with the realization that I am talking about her in the past tense. I press grass with the flat of my hand a moment. Then I continue. "She is the most dependent member but, somehow, controls us all."

"The world works like that," Bo says. "The strong are in service to the weak."

A shaming anger rises in me. "It shouldn't work that way." Maybe I'm not as generous as I like to think.

"Sure it should," Bo says. "What better use can strength be put to?"

"Gaining greater strength."

"Then what? Tyranny?" Bo strips a tall weed of its husk, breaks it off, and sticks the tip in his mouth. His eyes lift for the long gaze across the valley. "Nah, got to bring everybody along best you can."

We're getting cold. Our calculations for the moonrise are based on vaguely remembering that last night the moon rose about nine. It's now past nine thirty and the temperature has dropped to thirty-eight degrees, according to the zipper-tag thermometer on Bo's jacket.

"I got in trouble trying 'to bring everybody along,'" I tell Bo. "I never learned to erect psychic walls. I just wallowed in the trenches with everybody, sharing their misery." I'm thinking of Erik, my mom, Beckett. These are the people whose emotions have made up life for me.

"You sure as hell got walls now."

"I know." I attempt to explain myself to us both. "Somehow finding I could create jewelry a couple years ago triggered a delayed sense of self. I became decisive and more and more independent. Finally, I wanted something just for me. I needed to protect that." But maybe I have carried the wall building too far.

My eyes spot a glow seeping from behind pine boughs high on a distant peak across the valley. Bo leans up from his backrest against a boulder. We watch the moon finally slide into place above the Gros Ventres. It's a fat, gold-tinged beach ball about to roll over this side of the mountain range. We watch in silence. Then scramble down off the butte, chased by a deepening chill. Bo helps me carry my potted geraniums to the frost protection of the front porch, up close against the cabin logs still holding the day's warmth. He checks his watch.

"Okay if I brush my teeth? Brought a toothbrush over this morning. Think I'll go into town from here."

"Sure."

When he comes out of the bathroom, I'm sitting on the kitchen bench, leaning against the wall beneath the shelf, the lamp shining on a new bead catalog that I'm pretending to read.

"You don't want to know this," Bo says, "but I'm telling you anyway. If her brother has left, I'm ending things with Caro right now. I'm doing it for me, not you."

He's taken me by surprise. I could have sworn he wouldn't have touched the subject of Caro again with me. Stalling, I ask, "What brother?"

"Benj. He visits a lot."

"What's he got to do with it?" I don't care about her stupid brother. I just don't know what else to say.

"He sticks pretty close to her. I don't like him much, and if he's still in town . . . I'll wait. I'm just telling you my intention."

I nod. Maybe this intention is just like the one about not drinking too much.

"And . . . I'll take you up on being friends." He waits for a response, but I feel unable to speak without my voice breaking, so I nod again. He nods back. "Good luck with your new job Tuesday."

Once the sound of gravel bouncing off the underside of Bo's Suburban fades, I pull all the shades down, turn on more lamps, and try to retrieve my sense of adventure in solitude. But I feel restless walking the tight trail of my own and Grandma Garrett's single experiment in living alone. It's just so . . . solitary.

RESPITE

Ducks and geese are moving south. Brown and brook trout are spawning in increasing numbers. Elk, moose, mule deer, and pronghorn are mating as narrow leaf cottonwoods continue dropping their leaves and fall colors generally fade. Bighorn sheep are grazing alpine meadows located close to cliff retreats, the rams and ewes still in separate bands.

For Everything There Is a Season
—Frank C. Craighead, Jr.

thirteen

Each day I am reminded that I am animal. Lately, my sense of smell has awakened. Outside, the aroma of sun on fallen aspen leaves, the freshness of the earth, and the mineral smell of wet creek stones fill me to overflowing. Inside, I smell wood smoke and ashes, the fragrance of ripening apples.

Whereas once I was mainly aware of taste, now food presents a double delight, and so does Bo. Besides enjoying the sight of him, lately I notice he smells like the outdoors and saddle soap. Bo alerts all my senses. Half an hour ago, confined in the cabin with him during a fleeting hailstorm, I abruptly left him doing his laundry with what's become our communal washer and dryer and grabbed a jacket and an old cowboy hat of O.C.'s as I passed through the mudroom on my way outside. The potency of Bo's effect on me felt almost stifling.

I headed for the creek. A surge of physical need compelled

me to step off the trail to smooth the glossy bark of a willow, then lick a cattail as if it were a fuzzy Popsicle. I scooped mud from the creek bottom and smeared it like a potion on my inner wrists and watched the slush of softening hail balls rinse it off.

While this icy rain tapers to mist, I sit in a dry spot beneath a cottonwood and try to see the aura around a chokecherry bush. Tessa claims all living things have auras. She warned me during the hectic summer whenever an angry tourist, aura throbbing, approached the register at the bookstore. The chokecherry's aura evades me entirely, but my attention to my surroundings is rewarded, anyway, with a faint rainbow slicing through the Gros Ventres.

Later, Bo and I are going into town to O.C.'s trailer to cook for him. Pork chops. "I'm a vegetarian only in my spare time," Bo has said to explain why he cooks meat so often. He claims it takes longer to prepare meals without meat. Of course, that's because he isn't familiar with such a diet, which is natural for a rancher. Trouble is, Bo keeps buying enormous quantities of food for our once-a-week dinners together, as if we were a large Mormon family who took seriously the pledge to keep stores for a full year's survival. He bought the "fiesta" size salsa today, a sixty-four-ounce jar that will take us half a year to use.

Though on Bo's good side, I should list his excellent bathroom habits. It's good to know what it takes to instill them in a man, and, apparently, it's two mothers. Bo refers to our weekly dinners as "neighborhood potlucks," as if the rest of the people didn't show up, just forgot we did this every Friday—his way of making me feel less threatened about planned time together.

I feel an uncanny delight wearing this old hat, smudged and stained, that I found discarded in the shed. Once I wouldn't have touched it with a stick, but I've changed. During the summer, I sometimes removed my boots and hiked barefoot. I don't wash my hands as many times as I used to each day. I wipe them on my khakis, instead. Maybe I'm going native the way British officers sometimes did in Africa when they let their hair grow and cast off their uniforms for native dress.

I rise from beneath the shelter of the cottonwood and move along the trail. I pick a handful of late-ripening Oregon grapes and, without washing them first, eat the berries while I walk, even though the notion flits through my mind that a moose could have urinated on this very bush.

The sun glides into a slot between gray clouds and warms my cheekbones. The atmosphere pulses so purely just now. The glance of a raven above me in the cottonwood cuts through the air like flame does smoke.

At work the other day, I told Tessa that weather for me has become an ongoing drama of greater meaning than merely how to dress for it. Lately, it determines my activities and my moods. And I described my feelings of deliciousness while falling asleep lately and then again when waking up. Tessa said, "Your chakras have been cleansed. They're like circular fans and pull energy from the universe into the body. Yours, girl, are spinning to beat the band."

It's true I don't remember feeling awake like this before. But I suppose it's simply that I've found my spot on earth and I have come home to my self. I spend many hours outside each day and the rest at an opened window, when once I could go a week without a breath of unprocessed air. Now I check the sky for the first snow clouds, search the butte for mule deer, trace the siren calls of red-tailed hawks. Through these acts I feel as if I am touching the beads of an invisible rosary that remind me where I am and who I am.

"Your trouble is that you're stuck in that cow town in Wyoming," my dad said shortly after I left Erik and sounded low one phone call. "You should have taken yourself to a big city in the East where you had more choices." But when I left Erik, I wasn't looking for the kind of choices my dad had in mind: entertainment and opportunities and careers. I was looking for life itself. Here, where the land thrusts upward and the wild animals bound, the world pulses with aliveness. I needed majestic doses to stun me into wakefulness after marriage to Erik.

But waking comes with its own demands. Since autumn began I have wanted to stock food and firewood and candles for winter. I have wanted more sleep, more fats, warm creamy drinks, and baked cakes. Mostly I have wanted to scratch out a den, circle three times, and lie down with my mate.

Whether my mind and emotions feel ready or not, my body is looking for a mate. But it's just winter coming, I remind myself. It's just Bo hanging around my kitchen.

Erik sold our house in Findlay, paid off the mortgage, and sent me my share of the profit, but he doesn't respond to my phone messages or notes. Beckett said that his dad moved into a new town house complex with its own gym and that he works out regularly with weights. I was glad to replace the image of Erik standing alone on the stoop as I pulled out the drive with the image of Erik working up a healthy sweat.

My eyes follow the curve of land rising high against the sky, some peaks frosty with fresh snow that fell as rain and hail down here on the valley floor, and I feel I have completed a cycle in my new life. I arrived as last winter's snowmelt first trickled, then crashed down this mountain stream. I have watched bison calves grow from ovals curled in the meadows like golden eggs into rusty creatures half the size of their mothers. And I myself have burst through a placenta of misconceptions and fears that had held me both protectively and restrictively balled into myself.

The picture of Erik framed by my rearview mirror, alone on the porch stoop, has kept me twisting in and out of the covers many nights, entangled by the concern that I sacrificed him for my own life. I hear him calling to me as I bump down the sidewalk with my suitcase full of books, "If you're going to Florida, keep to the expressway." At the time I didn't hear these words or respond to them. Now something sounds off to me as the memory replays once again. Why did he assume I was going to Florida? Did Erik intend for his behavior to prompt me into going away without him for spring break? Or for the rest of his life? This was how Erik accomplished what he wanted. He got me to feel the emotions and express them for both of us. He did nothing that could be traced.

Some men ended their marriages by bringing home floozies, expensive cars, drunken friends, empty pay envelopes. My husband brought home pineapple pizza. I feel both freshly enraged and suddenly relieved. I did not single-handedly end a long-term marriage. Erik, in his passive way, also carries responsibility. How many times before had he done similar things and I disappointed him by forgiving, swallowing my anger—choking down pineapple pizza?

The sun has dropped behind Saddlestring Butte and only the dark hulk of the butte is contoured against the late-afternoon sky. From this, the dark silhouettes of Canada geese fly out of shadow and split off in a jagged V, looking as if the side of the hill has exploded into pieces.

It's time to return home.

O.C. twisted his knee. Dr. Goldy prescribed that he stay off his feet, which is why Bo and I are having our weekly dinner there tonight. We'll stock groceries and cook for O.C. and exercise his new puppy—the cause of the accident. Five months old and Pet of the Week at the pound, she has the bad habit of tearing around in a frenzy of joy and, in passing, bumping full speed into the back of O.C.'s knee with her head. O.C.'s knee collapses and down he goes. This has happened twice, twisting the same leg.

"Look at this," Bo says now. He cuts the engine and dips his head to get the full view of O.C.'s trailer out the windshield. "Have you ever seen such mess?"

I laugh in relief that Bo has said something first. Decades' worth of orange Wyoming license plates with the bucking bronco and county number twenty-two stamped on them cover the short end of O.C.'s trailer, which faces the street. Dozens of moose, elk, and deer skulls are mounted on the front side of his trailer beneath the roof of the deck, which is supported by highly varnished burled pine posts. That's not all. The yard, which Bo and I enter through an archway constructed of stacked elk antlers, is the size of two large lots and is enclosed by a cement wall with pale river stones and brightly colored pieces of glass embedded in it.

"Oh," I say. I spread my arms. "Look at all these . . . sculptures."

"O.C. says they're totems. He doesn't like them called sculptures."

The totems are built from the same mix of stone, glass, and cement as the wall and are scattered about the lawn. There's a giant cowboy boot, a sunflower, a fishing dory, a moose with a pair of antlers rooted in the cement, a jackrabbit with antelope horns, and a prairie schooner. I turn around and see a tall glittering cactus, a windmill, and an unfinished project that may be a doghouse.

Suddenly, the trailer door flies open. I spin around in surprise, and to cover up being stupefied, I bubble extravagantly, "All this . . . creativity. It's just . . . amazing. Such profuse amounts of . . . artwork."

While I search for words, O.C. hobbles along the deck hanging on to the burled railing. Every foot or so a colorfully painted wooden whirligig spins in the breeze: a man saws wood; a rooster bobs at a corncob; a woman hangs laundry; a little boy . . . the little boy, I believe, is shaking his penis after peeing in some wooden tulips.

I can't stop jabbering. "I admire your work. I didn't know you were an artist."

"I'm not a goddamn *artist*." Now I become aware of O.C.'s grim expression. He squints at me, raises disgusted eyebrows at Bo, then spits over the railing. "So," he says accusingly to me, "I guess you're his first one." He cocks his head sharply toward Bo.

"I doubt *that*," I say before thinking.

Bo disguises a grin by stretching his neck upward to take a puckered surveillance of the gathering clouds, of which an assortment of shapes and colors holds council low over the valley, behind O.C.'s head.

"I hear this one's a crybaby," O.C. says.

A prickly warmth flushes my underarms. My glance floats in forced casualness to Bo. I plan on denying this accusation, so I can't express outrage just yet that Bo would talk about me to anyone.

"I don't know what . . . I am not a crybaby," I say to O.C. Mentally, I add, *Except for that one night you're probably talking about, but your grandson didn't act so damn mature either.* Then I pull myself together and realize O.C. must be referring to something entirely different. Still, he is rude.

"I don't like the way you're talking to me," I say to him.

O.C. says, "I'm not talking to you. I'm talking to my grandson." Then he turns toward Bo and says, "Snippy little gal."

I wonder if O.C. always talks to one person while he looks at the other when he feels mean. Perhaps that habit allows him comfort with his harsh language.

Bo, I notice, is looking at his grandfather as if he'd like to reach up and stuff one of those rag brown clouds down O.C.'s throat. He says to me, "He calls artists crybabies." To O.C. he says, "Don't start on her."

O.C. ignores his grandson. "The girls tell me you make some kind of baubles."

Every time O.C. refers to the aunts as *the girls*, which he often did at the barbecue last spring, I get thrown for a second. I picture teenage twins, for some reason. Could it be because that's the image stuck in O.C.'s mind and somehow gets projected with his words? His daughters when they last made sense to him? Say fourteen and fifteen, before adulthood, before driving rights, illegitimate baby boys? Since Violet was held back a year, both girls, like twins, would have been in the eighth grade then.

"Pop . . . not yet. Okay?" Bo sounds like he knows what's coming.

"Hell to hope, she's a crybaby or she ain't. Let's get it out." O.C. spreads his spindly short legs—the left with a removable plastic cast around the knee—one step apart and challenges me. "You one of them God-farting artsy whiners? Expect to get your food from the government because you like to daydream on paper and doodle in colored paints and nobody in their hardworking honest mind is going to pay you to do that crap instead of working like the rest of us?"

"What?" I say.

"She works, you old coot. Nobody in government *pays* her. She creates things for free," Bo says.

I look at Bo, unsure whether he's defending or insulting me.

"Haven't learned the ropes yet, have you, little missy? Let Bo tell you how to get government handouts for putting pretty pebbles on string just like he did for screwing rusty junk together."

"All right. Shit. Suzannah, get the hell in the car."

"What?"

"Move. That way." Bo tosses his head toward the gate and guides me with one hand on the back of my neck toward his car.

"*What?*" I have lost track of the emotion erupting, yet somehow feel responsible for it all. Clearly, I have stirred up *something*.

"Boohoo," O.C. catcalls after us. "Give me a handout. I'm an *artiste*." He stretches out the word to a snaky hiss.

Bo stuffs me into the car and swings himself behind the wheel. We make a murky cloud of our own in the dirt drive to match the clumpy clouds, darkening above us, as Bo wheels sharply to the left backing up, then wrenches the gear into first and spins around O.C.'s arc of a drive.

"Run on back to Crybaby Ranch," O.C. hollers after us as we circle behind the trailer. O.C. scrambles to the other side of the deck and yells, "Go ahead, skedaddle. Crybabies! Boohoo."

Bo alternately grips his eyes to the road in front of him and ducks his head to the lower left, glancing out his side window to his mirror, as if checking to see if O.C. is chasing us. Crybaby Ranch. What does O.C. mean? One thing: I won't inwardly cringe anymore whenever Bo calls his grandfather Old Coot. I wouldn't mind letting Bo know I think his grandfather is a sly stinker, hiding his cruelty behind a good ole boy persona.

I maintain my silence and let Bo flex his jaw muscles. We reach the north edge of town, about to pick up speed to head out on the highway toward home. I notice Bo's glance stick to the rearview mirror. He slackens his press on the gas and slows into the pullout that overlooks the elk refuge and he parks.

"We got his goddamn groceries in the backseat." Bo stares at a family of trumpeter swans, dazzling white parents and two dirty gray cygnets, floating in the near curve of Flat Creek. "Ought to let the old coot starve."

I think back to my first impression of O.C. at Bo's party. I was in the kitchen helping guests find room in the refrigerator and oven for their potluck dishes when I heard a man's irksome voice say, "We can see through that girl's skirt."

"I'm wearing stretch pants under my skirt," I said over my shoulder while bent half inside the oven door.

"Long underwear," the troublemaker said. "We can see that, too."

Before I could retort, Bo broke in and made introductions. "That's all he wanted," Bo said in an aside to me. To be introduced, I suppose he meant, and I thought then O.C. could have found a gentler way to accomplish that.

So what did O.C. want today? To cover up embarrassment for needing help? To discourage remarks about his crazy yard?

"We didn't get to see the puppy," I say. That was the part I was looking forward to. "Suppose he's butchered it by now for knocking him down twice?"

"Grandma used to say O.C. saved all his tenderness for his animals. She'd say, 'If I could grow an extra set of legs we'd pret near have a perfect marriage.'" Bo's hands rest on top of the steering wheel and he looks out over the refuge flats to the base of Miller Butte. He nods toward two small bands of elk that have come down out of the hills early.

"'Welfare elk,' O.C. calls them. On the government take." Bo shakes his head dismally. "He resents the elk getting government-paid alfalfa pellets almost as much as he does artists getting NEA grants. As you can tell, O.C. doesn't think much of artists."

"But he *is* one." I add, "Sort of."

"I wouldn't say that to his face again, if I were you." Bo sighs. "Shit, I guess we better go back. The bastard."

He asks if I mind. I say of course not, and we pull out

onto the road again toward town. "NEA grants?" I ask. "How would O.C. even know about those?" Then it dawns on me. "You were awarded an NEA?" National Endowment of the Arts grants are one of the highest honors an artist can receive; I can't believe Bo didn't mention being awarded one till now.

"This spring. O.C. says I could have gotten food stamps for less trouble." Bo dips his head down and to the side, checking the other lane for traffic, except there is no other lane. His chin puckers a second, or am I imagining that?

"Crybaby Ranch. What's he mean? Oh," I answer myself again. "Your retreat."

"Right, but Pop began calling the place that as soon as I sold off the cattle to work at my sculpture full-time."

Five minutes through the town square, and then we pull up to the trailer again and lug our bags of groceries to the deck. The door opens and out rushes a beautiful black-and-sandy pup, tail a blur of waving fur, front paws high prancing in place. Bo and I prop our bags on the picnic table outside the picture window and bend to pet the dog.

"Name's Hazer." O.C. stays inside the screen. "Seems that's what she's trying to do, haze me into place, knock me down, and tie me up. All in eight seconds like I'm some rodeo steer."

The old coot sounds downright friendly. I'm surprised and wonder if I dare push his mood toward an apology. I expressed my feelings to him once already today; better not make things harder. Still . . .

"You were rude to me." Damn, I impress myself sometimes.

"This old knee gives me a crossness." O.C. steps outside and pats my shoulder. "You're a fine little gal," he says as if I need reassurance.

Bo turns his mouth down and widens his eyes in mock surprise at me, letting his grandfather see his expression. He says, "Hey, Pop, you were rude to me, too."

"Ah, go give my pup a chase or two. That'll show me you're good for something." He pats Bo on the shoulder though, then reaches for a rubber ball lodged in a corner of the windowsill and tosses it into the yard.

Hazer dashes onto the grass, and Bo and I follow. Her hindquarters buck in enthusiasm when she brings the ball back to us.

In less than ten minutes, Hazer has plowed into the back of my left knee just as O.C. reported she had done to him. I plummet to the ground, half my support suddenly hacked off. I'm more shocked than hurt, in fact not really hurt at all. But I limp at first until my knee and ankle muscles spring back into place.

Once Bo sees I'm all right, he grabs Hazer and swiftly flips her to the ground on her back. Down on all fours on top of her, Bo and the puppy are nose to nose and Bo shouts into the dog's face, "No, no. You can't do that. No, no."

Hazer lies immobile; clearly she is having genetic flashbacks about an alpha-wolf experience. Then her tail, lying between Bo's knees, begins to wag. O.C. and I break into laughter. Bo looks over his shoulder to us and we show him the lack of fright he's inflicting on Hazer.

"Still," O.C. says congenially, "she's a smart girl. She's learned something. Come on in, you two."

We carry in our bags, and while we unpack groceries, O.C., now as gracious as a society hostess, opens three of the beers we brought him. Pretty soon, Violet and Maizie stop by to deliver their father's laundry. The aunts end up staying for dinner with us. Afterward, we get out a deck of cards and play hearts. We have such a good time slapping down cards, jocularly insulting one another's decisions, that Bo and I don't start home till nearly midnight.

"Families," Bo says on the drive home. "It's the contradictions that keep them together, not prayer, as the old saying goes."

He's right. My dad scrawls my name on a sign for Mom, but refuses to believe her memory is impaired. My mom can't remember my name, but never forgets how to trick me into answering the phone for her. And O.C. pretends to hate artists while filling his yard with stone totems and his porch with carved whirligigs.

I want to know why Bo would even think of telling O.C. about his artists' retreat before he absolutely had to, knowing what he does about his grandfather's prejudice. After a few miles pass, I ask.

Bo tells me, "A while back, Dickie wanted to buy Crossing Elk Ranch. Pop doesn't give a damn what I do with his share of the land, neither do the aunts, but I felt I had to let them know about Dickie's offer and why I turned it down."

"I didn't know Dickie was interested in your land. Why didn't he buy my cabin when you put it on the market?"

"I waited until he left town and put that low price on it so the job would be done by the time he came back."

Bo says Dickie Donnell wanted to financially back the artists' retreat. "I think he wanted a legal hold on the land I refused to sell him. I figure Dickie believed the enterprise would get into financial trouble eventually, or Dickie himself would guide it there. Then he'd bail me out of debt by taking some of my land. He likes the piece where I plan to build the cabins—the twenty-acre saddle where the aspens grow."

"Smack in the center of your ranch."

"Right. I don't trust Dickie. I don't want to be in business with him. Besides, Crybaby—I mean the artists' retreat—isn't meant to be a *business*, just good use of the land. A way for me to move away from ranching without moving away from the ranch." Bo says the word *business* with a kind of sneer in his voice, much the same way O.C. says *artiste*.

"But why did you sell my cabin? With the NEA grant and the sale of your cattle, you must be earning enough for groceries."

"Your cabin is buying the materials for the five other cabins. I'm doing the labor myself."

We both fall silent. The night sky is dappled with clouds, like giant soap bubbles clumped here and there in a black tub. The moon is two days past full, and it begins to rise from behind a tree-covered mountain. Every bough of every tree is outlined. Trees hang off this chipped golden ornament, instead of the other way around. The moon clears the peak and heads into the sudsy clouds. I roll down my window and inhale the clean night air.

"I don't know," Bo says. "Maybe Crybaby Ranch won't work, but when you turned out to be a jewelry maker, I figured it was a good sign."

fourteen

Bo says November is the perfect month to leave the valley. He'd trade a few weeks in Florida for this month's miserable weather any day. He's driving me to the airport; the Tetons fill my side window.

"You're not missing a thing, Zann, except gray skies, wind, and snow."

"I hate missing that."

The accumulation of the winter snowpack begins. I think of the drama of blizzards and power outages. I tattoo the image of the Tetons onto my inner eye for reference for the next three weeks. An irrational fear that I'll get stuck in Florida and won't ever again see these granite peaks makes me whiny. "There aren't any rocks in Florida," I complain. "Not many sticks either. Just shells and palm fronds."

"Poor baby."

He's as bad as the women at the bookstore who've called

me *lucky* all week because I'm going where it's warm and sandy. But Bo should know better; I've told him what faces me there: caring for my mother alone while my dad takes a break. Maybe Bo needs a stronger picture about what I'm headed for.

"My mother eats with her fingers now." She needs help in the bathroom, too, but I'll spare him that fact. "She's hiding money, and last week she mistook her diamond earring for a piece of candy. Dad got the earring out of her mouth in time, but can't find the money. What he's *really* worried about is that maybe he's getting forgetful, too, and just misplaces his bank draws."

"What are *you* really worried about?" Bo asks.

"I don't know. I'm not looking forward to going home, but I miss my mother and I want my father to have a rest." Our plan is to change the guard slowly, a week caring for my mother together. Then Dad leaves for a week, and then another week before I leave. The transition is more for my father than my mother; he has a hard time giving over her care. "It's been two months since I've seen her; I don't know if I can deal with these changes."

I begin to argue with myself out loud. "I *should* be able to deal with them. My father does and he's sixty-nine."

"You'll know what to do," Bo says.

Easy for him to say. I watch a coyote cruising the sagebrush a few hundred yards off the road.

"There's just no break. Every minute she's asking, 'Where's Addie?' In August, when my dad left on a fishing trip, she wouldn't stay in bed unless I lay in the dark with her and she goes to bed at *seven thirty*." I don't even go into the times she wanders about the house after I've fallen asleep. Once, I found her in the guest room and she asked me where that other person was. Scared me to death. I thought she'd heard a prowler. Turned out she was remembering me from when I'd slept in there before my father left.

"It'll be damn hard, Zann."

This trip, a friend at the library is letting me check out half a dozen books on tape for an extra two weeks so I can lie beside my mother in the other twin bed with the lights out and pretend to sleep, while listening to novels on my Walkman. Tessa's idea, and just knowing I can rely on this plan is saving my sanity.

Once Bo helps me carry my suitcases to the check-in counter, I tell him he should head home. It's beginning to snow, just lightly right now, but the radio warned us all day yesterday to expect a major storm today. Luckily, I'm scheduled on the first plane out of Jackson Hole this morning, because the way it looks, visibility will be zero once that deep mauve-colored front scoots clear of the Snake River Range south of us. The rest of the flights could be canceled.

Ahead of me in line is a woman with five large pieces of expensive luggage. She looks fussy. I figure she'll probably hold things up. Bo wraps his arms around me and holds me tight.

"I'll miss you, Zann," he says softly into my hair.

I love the good feel of him surrounding me. I want to say I'll miss him, too, but I know once I step into my parents' house the fullness of the misery there will absorb all my emotions and even my memory of the other parts of my life. Already, I feel myself detaching from Bo and the things I care about here. Bo accepts my silence and kisses my cheek before leaving.

The line moves up a notch and the Delta clerk requests the

fussy lady's ticket. "Atlanta?" he asks when he opens her travel folder.

"Yes," she says, "but I'd like this suitcase to go to Chicago." She loads the largest wardrobe onto the scale beside the counter. "This one I want to go to Seattle." She slides number two onto the scale, and I know it's no coffee for me before my plane leaves. I turn sideways and see Bo's Suburban begin to pull away from behind a Snow King Resort van unloading Delta pilots and attendants. Bo waves in my direction just in case I'm watching, and I wave back, though I know he can't see me.

"The third bag," the woman continues, "I'd like sent to Washington, D.C. And these other two"—she points to the small bags at my feet—"I'd like sent to San Diego."

"Lady . . ." the clerk begins, exasperation pulling sideways at the muscles of his face. His eyes skim the row of clerks next to him to see if any of his fellow workers can share in his misery. "Lady," he says again, "we *can't* do that."

"Why not?" she asks. "That's what happened to my luggage on my trip here."

She doesn't look the type for bold humor. The clerk and I look at each other and then at her. It takes us a couple seconds before we break into appreciative howls of surprise and pleasure.

The clerk glances at her ticket. "Mrs. Forrest," he says, "gee, I'm sorry."

"Oh," she says, grinning, "that's okay. You made a good straight man."

I sip a mocha latte and watch luggage being loaded into the waiting plane, parked right outside the windows. Through the lightly blowing snow, the Tetons rise abruptly from the landing strip beyond, the peaks still pink from the dawn light, the snowfields looking both forbidding and beckoning at once. To keep myself from imagining the plane crumpled up like a wad of used tin foil on Skillet Glacier, I time Bo's drive into town. About now he's stacking storm supplies into a grocery cart at Fred's Market. I mentally urge him to hurry. Once out of the store, he'll still have a forty-minute drive home, chased by high winds and a thickening snowfall.

What I didn't tell Bo is that dealing with my father produces more tension than dealing with my mother. Last night when I phoned to confirm my arrival time and my father confessed Mom wasn't using her silverware all the time, he'd said, "She tried to eat spaghetti at Marco Polo's Pasta House with her hands."

I said, "You ordered *spaghetti* for her?" He's been cutting her meat for months, so I couldn't understand why he was making life harder for himself. Instead of offering the sympathy he needed, I tried to convince him to simplify his life.

"I could *simplify* her into a nursing home. Don't come down here bringing a bunch of bad news with you."

Nearly every night Dad dresses Mom in panty hose and bra, wrestles her into dresses and heels, teases her hair and smudges her cheeks with blusher, then sets her on the toilet lid in the bathroom while he showers himself. Last visit, I heard him talking a mile a minute from the shower stall to keep her from wandering away.

"Stay on your throne, Queen Elizabeth. You hear me out there? We're going to your favorite restaurant. Out on a date. Me and Queen Elizabeth smooching in a booth. Lizzie? Are you still there? Lizzie? Hell."

Dad says now he needs to lock the bathroom door to keep her with him, but he can't get accustomed to using the toilet with an audience.

When I'm in charge, I dress my mother in cool cottons, loose and comfy, no hose, no bra, no makeup. "She can't go to Conchy Joe's looking like that. You want to embarrass her?" Dad accuses. He says she looks like a toddler. When he leaves town, we drop the fancy restaurants and get carryout instead.

But I understand my father's thinking. Every step backward is a permanent loss. Once he cut her meat for her, she lost the ability to do it herself forever.

Kettie Jefferson, once-a-week housekeeper for my parents, sits with Mom until Dad and I arrive home from the airport. It's late but Dad insists Mom needs to have a treat, so we all take Kettie home, then go to the Blue Moon Diner for a snack. They serve Coke in the old bottles and Mom used to like those. Dad thinks she still does and ignores my concern about caffeine this late in the evening. The two of them sit across from me and Dad takes Mom's hand.

He says, "Elizabeth Ann and the Raggedy Man. That's us."

Mom says, "Who's that?"

"The Raggedy Man? You used to read that poem to our little girl here."

"No," she says and points to her reflection in the black plate-glass window next to our booth. "What's that woman want?"

"Lizzie . . . you haven't talked to Suzannah here. After we've been waiting all this time for her. Lizzie, turn around now."

"She keeps looking at me. What?" my mother asks her own image rather sharply. She frowns with impatience. "I don't know what you want."

My father tries to lure my mother's attention with her Coke. He's tipping back her head and holding the bottle to her lips. I feel antsy watching this, as if he is about to politely drown her.

"It's all right, Dad. Let her go." Over his shoulder I spot the waitress and announce she's loaded down with a full tray and heading our way.

"Lizzie, here comes your food. Look here."

My mother again murmurs to herself, face up close to the window. She has not sustained so animated a conversation in months. This could be my privacy in the bathroom. Introduce her to herself in the mirror and quickly use the toilet. While the waitress sets out our plates, I take the opportunity to fill in Dad on family news.

"Beckett is doing well in school these days. He's thinking about transferring to the University of Wyoming for prelaw."

"Where is he going now?"

My father has never been much of a grandparent to Beckett. Didn't believe it was his role to be, since he wasn't related by blood to Erik's son.

"You know, Laramie County Community College. L Triple C? Or, as Beck calls it, Last Chance Cowboy College." Maybe Dad will chuckle. I'm always trying to make Beck seem appealing to my father. I want him to accept, if not approve, of the child I have loved and raised since he was an infant. Dad is engrossed with trying to get a French fry between Mom's lips and doesn't respond to me.

"Nice and salty, Lizzie, just the way you like."

My father doesn't allow me to help feed my mother. He can't admit the trouble he's going through. He can let me witness it in person though, and in a few days, when he leaves for the respite I'm here to offer him, he can let me experience it myself. Only recently have I moved past a strong sense of guilt over talking about my mother's illness to anyone. I think my father still feels this way.

I am reminded of the one admonishment I heard most frequently as a child: "This talk stays strictly within the family. Understand?"

The Florida sky looks tarry an hour before dawn. Coral hibiscus blooms beside the driveway; just above the highest blossom rests a paler coral moon. Creamy breezes fold my nightgown hem around my calves as my father loads suitcases and fishing poles into the trunk of his car. Then headlight beams hop from palmetto bush to oleander to bougainvillea to the mailbox at the end of the drive. I am alone with my sleeping mother.

I wonder why I felt compelled to wake at four thirty to wave my father off this morning, why Dad sneaked his suitcases out of the house last night and hid them in the bushes in case Mom woke before he left. She doesn't recognize the uses of anything inedible now. Like a toddler, she aims all items toward her mouth. As for me, I'm still engaged in an imaginary competition with my mother for title of Daddy's Best Little Girl.

Too late to go back to bed, too early to hope for the Sunday paper, so I sit with a cup of coffee in the screened porch and watch the sky lighten over Bessie Creek. How am I going to make it through the next seven days? Since my last visit, my mother has become a stranger, and caring for her all alone scares me. She has acquired a fear of moving air, fans, and breezes. Those picnics I've planned, those strolls along the river walk in old town Stuart, the beach—all of it would make Mom cower with fright. She won't allow an open window in the house and won't come out to the porch anymore. The first day looms unendingly ahead of me.

"Addie?" My mother is padding down the hallway. I can't tell, is she calling my father by name or calling him *Daddy*?

A Sunday movie matinee. The idea strikes me as brilliant. Mom has always loved movies. And popcorn and Coke.

Timing is the key. We can't arrive at the movies with extra minutes to fill or my mother will not stay in her seat. Neither can we get there after the lights go down, because she's edgy in the dark. If I can get her seated with a bag of popcorn in her lap less than five minutes before colored pictures flash on the screen, the venture will be a success. My muscles tense for the race against the clock.

I notice an easing of my mother's customary agitation as soon as we have gained a steady traveling speed across the Palm City bridge on our way to the Regency Theater. She likes riding in the car, I note. Of course, I have to keep the windows rolled up.

"Look." My mother leans forward and points out the windshield to the sky above the St. Lucie River. "I see those every time."

"What's that?" I ask.

"Those things up there. Every time we go out I see them."

"Clouds?" I ask.

Mom sits back in her seat satisfied that we've communicated. "Yes. Those are nice, I think."

"I think so, too," I say. "Clouds are one of my favorite things." She and I smile at each other. We're doing great. My father just doesn't know how to handle her; he never did. He makes everything harder than it needs to be. I'd just forgotten that. My sweaty grip loosens around the steering wheel.

I carry Mom's sweater, my shoulder bag, two popcorns, two Cokes, with my mother attached to my elbow. The usher has to fish around in my skirt pocket himself to collect our tickets.

Mom keeps saying, "What is this place? Where's Addie? I think we better leave now." But I know once I give her food, she'll be content.

My mother's seat won't stay down unless she sits in it. I can't get this idea across to her. My hands are full, so I try to hold the seat down with my left knee.

One of the Cokes slips out of my grasp. It splashes across my sandaled feet, runs between my toes, and on down the sloped floor toward the people in front of me.

"Shit," I hiss between my teeth.

At least I've freed one hand. I press down my own seat, sit, secure the two popcorns and remaining Coke between my legs and hold down Mom's seat for her.

I convince her to sit, finally, and hand over her popcorn. The lights partially dim, but before I can congratulate myself on the perfect timing, Mom, startled by the abrupt darkness, knocks her popcorn to the floor. She pats the air in front of her face as if she were blind. "Oh, dear God, dear Addie, help me."

"It's okay, Momma." I point to the concession stand advertisement on the screen. "Look. Pictures."

"Please, let me out of here."

Thank God she's whispering. I hold her hand and offer a piece of my popcorn to her lips. "Looky, your favorite, 'member?" I notice my speech is regressing and feel a momentary confusion about my position: I am pleading with my mother like a toddler might, while also pleading as a mother might to a toddler.

Loudly this time, my mother says, "I'll give you anything. Just let me go."

"Shh . . . it's okay, Momma." I put my arm around her. I show her the Coke.

In a commanding voice that sounds just like my real mother, she says, "I'll pay you any amount of money, but, please, let me go now."

Heads turn.

I smile at the strange faces in the half-light and wish the room would fall darker.

"I don't know you and I don't want you touching me." She shrinks from my arm.

No one would believe this woman is ill. She sounds sane and cultured. And wealthy and kidnapped.

"I demand that you release me."

"Momma . . . " I talk a bit loudly, too, just to assure everyone. "It's okay. I'll take care of you." I add righteously, "Like I always do."

"Let me out of here. Please let me out of here."

She sounds panicked and shrill. A little crazy, I'm relieved to notice. I hope the theater audience notices, too.

She continues her pleas. "I must go home." The lights have completely gone down. The movie is beginning, but all the pale faces are turned toward us.

At last, I understand the hopelessness of this and I say, "Okay, we'll leave, Momma." She stands when I do, her seat snaps up and grabs her butt. She jumps, clinging to my arm, and the other popcorn tumbles out of my grasp. I rest the second Coke on the floor while I gather Mom's sweater and my purse, then forget about it and kick it over. I think I hear a collective sign of impatience from the theater audience, though maybe it's just the Coke fizz, which I feel nibbling at my bare toes like tiny piranha.

Finally, unencumbered, I take my mother by the hand and we scoot out of the row of seats, slopping through spilled Coke, crushed ice, and soggy popcorn to the aisle.

Out the door of the theater, a blast of heat greets us and immediately bakes the Coke syrup inside my sandals. Every step sounds like paper tearing as my foot peels off the insole.

Without speaking, we walk across the parking lot, my mother meekly trotting to keep up with me. Once we're seated inside the car, I drop my head to the steering wheel.

Why didn't my father tell me it was this hard? I wish I could cry, but I'm bound too tightly with frustration and hopelessness.

I feel my mother touch my cheek, and I tip my head to look at her. She smiles softly at me, eyes clear. My real mother has returned again. She smoothes the back of my hair and tucks loose strands behind my ear.

"You're doing fine, honey," she assures me. "Really you are."

*   *   *

Normally, Mom spends her days contentedly sitting on the sofa beside my father as he studies law books, answers mail from a laptop, and confers on the phone with colleagues. To borrow a favorite joke of hers when I was growing up: I have created a monster. Since the movie fiasco she asks, "Can we go someplace now?" Over and over, ten, twenty times an hour.

So we go. To the grocery store, to the Elliot Museum on the island, to the mall. The moment we arrive she pleads with all the drama of the movie theater episode to be taken home.

She is happiest in the car. My father is going to be shocked at the gas charges I'm racking up. We fill the Lincoln's tank every day. We drive up the coast to Vero Beach, down the coast to Jupiter. Up to Indialantic, down to Hobe Sound.

And once in these other towns, we drive through all the newly built subdivisions. There seems to be a pattern to Florida developments: Kill off the predominate species of the area, then name the neighborhood after it. We drive through Cougar Creek, Sandhill Estates, Panther Lagoon—here commemorating both the demise of the panther and the filling in of the lagoon.

Home again, I pull into the garage. Since my mother has forgotten how to open a car door, I try to assure her, as I have done hopelessly all week, that I will come quickly around to her side and help her out.

Before I trot clear of the car's rear end, my mother is clawing at the side window and whimpering. Hurriedly, I fling open her door and she falls into my arms. "Oh, thank you. I thought I'd never get out!" Both of us are breathing hard with the struggle to keep her fear at bay.

Inside the house I help her take off her sweater. One arm is out. Mom smiles sweetly. "Oh, good," she says, "we're going someplace."

I begin to explain that no, we are taking the sweater off, not putting it on. We just got home. . . . But I give it up. There are still six more hours until bedtime, and I know she will ask me to go someplace many, many times between now and then. I put her arm back into the sweater and wonder where we can drive next.

Mindless driving gives me unexpected time to think about Bo, and a distance of two thousand miles makes thinking about him more comfortable. One thing becomes certain: A thread stretches between Bo and me—I feel it even here. Beside Bessie Creek in my parents' backyard, a strand of spider silk is spun between two scrub pines standing fifteen feet apart. The silk, like the connection I feel exists between Bo and me, is only visible when light strikes it a certain way. Yet the elasticity of the thread holds even when winds blow hard and rain pelts in a sheet.

At times I believe I've imagined this connection between us. That I am holding one end of the thread alone, while the other end flings blindly in an errant search for home. But then I catch his warmth, sent through a glance, a brief touch, a remark that spins the two of us into sudden laughter, and I am reassured.

I think of the aftermath of our laughing together when our eyes hold and the heated surge of energy from clenched stomach muscles and the mental slide into surprise diffuses throughout my body. This feels like moments past orgasm when two lie together, body parts still interlocked, waiting for pulses to subside and skin dampness to evaporate. I am convinced, then, we inhabit this uncertain place together.

If Bo and I are, indeed, having a romance at all, we are conducting it sideways. We are paralleling our emotional lives, assuming the two paths will meet in the infinite future. For now, I am content with a schedule based on a geometric supposition. But one day we will embark upon something huge and new to us both, something frightening and full of risk. Until then, I believe we need to grow strong within ourselves and be patient with each other.

Or maybe I'm making all this up. Maybe such fantasies support me as I heal from my divorce and the crushed ideals I once carried about love, the recent independence of my stepson, Beckett, the long goodbye with my mother. I am losing the connections of love that have defined my life.

Tonight, after my mother's steady breathing assures me she is fast asleep, I sneak out to the living room. I open a window and breathe in humid, fragrant air. I listen to crickets and night birds. Then turn on a reading lamp and get comfortable with my book and my solitude.

Ten minutes pass. Is that a doorknob turning? I decide that it isn't and return to my book. Suddenly, my mother appears in the living room. She is fully dressed. She has not dressed herself for half a year.

"Good morning," she says. She looks quite refreshed for having only fifteen minutes' sleep. And she looks beautiful. Intelligent and cheerful. She looks familiar. The dread I felt at having my time interrupted glides smoothly into pure delight at seeing her remembered face.

"Aw," I say, hating to disappoint her, "it's not morning. It's still nighttime."

"Hmm?"

"Oh, never mind. Come sit with me." I pat the cushion next to me.

She walks around the coffee table and sits on the sofa beside me. She looks at my face a long moment, then says, "You know, you are very pretty. There's just something about you . . . something special."

I say, "Thank you. You always make me feel special. That's why you are such a wonderful mother to me." At the word *mother*, I almost lose her. Her eyes slip focus a second, before she regains her composure. I warn myself not to ruin this time for us, to be careful of what I say. But I don't want to heed my warning. I am with my lifetime best friend and we are telling each other important things.

She notices my flowered nightgown and admires it.

"Daddy gave this to me for my birthday."

"Oh? Do you know Daddy?"

"Yes . . . I do." I stop myself from saying more.

"Well, imagine that!" She marvels over my knowing my own father, but I smooth that away in my mind. My whole being soaks up her presence. So many nights since I was a young girl she and I have sat like this—the sounds of Bessie Creek lapping at the dock, the occasional croak of the pig frog, the mottled duck squawk drifting in to us and mingling with our confidences. This is the gift of one more night. I don't want it to end.

My mother looks relaxed and happy. She notices the opened window. "Goodness, it's black out there. What's that say?" She points to the clock.

"Eight thirty."

"What in the world are we doing up?" With the expression familiar to me as a prelude to joking, my mother raises her eyebrows, gives me her impish look and says, "One of us is crazy."

fifteen

Three weeks' worth of mail towers on my kitchen table. From the doorway I turn to Bo, who's carrying my suitcases behind me. "Thanks for bringing over my mail while I was gone." Still waiting for one of the scarce post-office boxes to become available, still using Bo's. Then I notice one letter bobs from a string tied to a helium balloon, hovering over the kitchen sink.

"What's that?"

On the balloon, fireworks explode around the word CONGRATULATIONS.

Bo swings my suitcases into the mudroom. "Open it."

He grins and rests his hands halfway into his coat pockets. The man isn't wearing any gloves. It's only three or four degrees above zero tonight, yet when he cupped my face for his hello nose rub at the airport, those hands were warm as mugs of cocoa. Or maybe that heat was generated by my cheeks. I practically wiggled my hindquarters like Hazer at Bo's greeting.

I shrug out of my coat and reach for the envelope. The return address is Three Peaks, One River—a local fine-crafts gallery. All three gallery owners get together twice a year—November and April—and make decisions prior to each tourist season about the work they'll accept. I submitted Storytelling Necklaces, a takeoff of the Navajo Grandmother Necklaces. Beads strung on tiger tail with hand-carved stone fetishes to spur stories: buffalo, turtles, bears, rabbits. I love making them so much I can hardly get myself to bed at night. I've sold several just from wearing one to work at the bookstore.

"It could be a rejection," I say, warning us both. Bo raises knowing eyebrows and opens the refrigerator. He pulls out a bottle of Mumm's and digs into his Levi's pocket for his knife.

"Bo, really. They usually phone. Mail: bad news. Telephone: good news. That's what I heard."

"Maybe, since you haven't been home to answer your phone in three weeks, they had to use the mail." Bo doesn't take off his heavy jacket, a gold brown canvas with a sheepskin lining. He just continues to slice through the leaded foil around the top of the champagne bottle. He now reaches for a dish towel to hold over the cork.

"Bo, really . . ."

"Zann, you're in. I ran into Tom, one of the owners." He loosens the cork.

It rips through my thin garage-sale dish towel and hits the balloon—not the window, thank God. The balloon dips and weaves, suds foam out the bottle and into the sink. I find myself shrieking, "Yahoo!" as I pull an acceptance letter out of the envelope and read it. If my work sells well enough, they'll give me more space for the summer season. A gallery in Jackson Hole.

Bo sets the Mumm's on the counter. He crooks his arm and dips his knees in an exaggerated invitation to square dance. I accept, and we swing around, back up, change arms, and circle in the opposite direction. Bo pulls out of his coat, and we decide which sort of unmatched jelly glasses lining my cupboard shelf would best suit champagne. We settle on two stemmed dessert dishes.

We toast. It's so good to be back in Wyoming. And it's so good to be with Bo.

"I'll have to tell Kelly my good news," I say.

"Kelly?" Bo takes a sip of his champagne.

"My famous artist friend—I told you about him."

"You said you met him in the bookstore. I thought that meant you sold him a book or something."

"We go out for coffee, sometimes lunch. He critiques my pieces for me."

"I critique your pieces for you."

"You critique them, I revise them, and then I pass them on to Kelly." Bo seems slightly miffed. By the time I take another sip of champagne and look at him again, I decide maybe I imagined it. But I keep to myself that Kelly is gay.

In return for Bo picking me up at the airport, I've brought home Florida specialties for dinner. I told him about it over the phone last night because he had planned to cook for us. First I unpack the shrimp and a jar of cocktail sauce from my canvas carry-on bag. The main course will be yellowtail snapper, the most divine of ocean delicacies, drenched in a lemon-butter sauce. Bo carries the fish into the living room to complete the thawing near the woodstove, where he has kept a fire going for my houseplants while I was gone. When he returns, I parade fresh strawberries under his nose. I toss him a meaty red tomato and waggle a handful of pencil-thin asparagus.

"All from this morning's farmer's market on the way to the airport."

"Good God," he says, taking the asparagus. "Green. It'll be six months before we see that color here." The longing in his eyes reminds me of the hard, unknown winter stretching before me.

As I spray water over the Florida produce, I gaze out the window. Though it is dark as deep night at ten minutes to six, the evidence of winter's presence thickly pads my windowsill; icicles sparkle off the eaves. As I admire the downy beds of snow laid tidily on each bough, I realize abruptly that the pines by the drive are flooded with light. At first, I think my attention has lit up the outdoors; it takes a second to realize that a car has arrived outside my window. I'm not used to the way snow muffles the warning signals of someone's approach. Before I put it together that it's a car with delayed headlight dimmers, Caro stomps snow off her boots as she opens my back door.

"I know you two don't want any company for dinner tonight, but I want you to invite me anyway."

Caro has seen too many therapists. Express your needs clearly and assertively. People not only appreciate knowing your needs—they are eager to meet them. And the worst that can happen is they'll say no.

Wrong. The worst is that they'll *wish* they could say no, but they'll smilingly rush in with yes. That's what I do—rush in with yes. Bo provides the smiles.

We try to make her company seem more than welcome, even desirable. This is probably easier for Bo than it is for me. I'd like her to melt into the same rag rug her snowy boots are dripping on. We both blather cover-ups for not inviting her in the first place.

Caro waits until Bo and I run down. "What are you fixing?" she asks, swinging off her hip-length suede jacket like a runway model and tossing it onto my kitchen bench.

Bo explains I've brought home yellowtail snapper.

"It's thawing near the woodstove," I add, in the thrall of nervous chatter, "under a colander for protection against any mice that moved in since hearing I was away."

"Fish?" Caro's question hangs in the air. From her tone I think she's misunderstood, thinks we're having mice for dinner, and the snapper is merely a lure to catch them. I don't jump in and assure her. I give her a moment to change her mind and leave.

Or is another agenda emerging? Bo seems to think so and waits expectantly.

"Love," Caro says to Bo as she stuffs her leather driving gloves into her coat pockets, "I put those beautiful steaks in your freezer last week and forgot to pick them up again when I left. Why don't you run over and get them?"

Bo turns toward me, ready to back up my Florida treats.

Resignedly I say, "Go ahead. The snapper will keep." But my nasty thoughts begin tracing Caro's moves. It's too preposterous to think she plans such things: stops at store, buys steaks, leaves in Bo's freezer, waits one week, invites self for dinner, retrieves said steaks—nah.

Still, I ask, "How many steaks are there?"

Caro says, "Oh . . . I don't know."

"Three, aren't there?" Bo says before going out to his truck.

The door slams behind him, and Caro settles herself in a kitchen chair. I assume Bo's usual position against the counter with my arms folded.

"How were your parents?" she asks.

"Managing." I quickly search for another topic so I don't have to talk about my trip. "What have you been doing the last three weeks?"

"First, I want to tell you that I couldn't stop thinking about what a boring time you were having. Dickie and I made a quick trip to Sun Valley one weekend. This wonderful needlepoint shop, Isabel's, is located there—hand-painted screens, glorious Persian wools, a canary sings its heart out from an ornate cage at the entrance. I saw Mariel Hemingway there, and she said all the movie people worked needlepoint because it's so boring between takes. So I decided that's what you needed for your next visit home. Sick people are much more boring than movie sets."

I've never been able to tell anyone about the excruciating boredom of caring for my mother. How did Caro know this? I feel understood. "You amaze me," I say. I unfold my arms, lean over, and kiss her cheek.

"I picked out a design by Mariel's favorite artist. It looks just like you—feathers, bird's nests, and eggs. I'll bring it over and teach you how to do it."

Caro and I meet for lunch once a week in town when I'm

working. Since she does most of the talking, I have assumed that she doesn't know me as well as I know her. Every once in a while she startles me like this with her insight.

"When you're finished working the screen, I'll have a pillow made out of it for you. It will fit right into your pagan motif." Caro shifts a thistle in a jar of dried weeds on the table to emphasize her joke.

I laugh, then say, "I'll start working on it during that long flight next trip."

"That's how I got started, on an airplane. You know Dickie. Go, go, go. The little runt."

"Travel anywhere else while I was gone?" I'm used to her calling Dickie names.

"Mozambique. I'll tell you both later. I haven't seen Bo much either."

"Oh, really?" Pleasure lifts my voice. "Oh," I say again, correcting myself with a down-curved tone.

Caro rises from the kitchen chair and comes to hug me in a loose-armed way. "I know you care about him."

"I do. He's . . . a good neighbor," I say, sounding as insincere as an insurance-company ad. I laugh to cover up.

"You know what I mean. You're so generous. You don't let it come between us. That's what I like best about you." She gives me another small hug, then sits back down. "Another woman might hate me."

"I hate you sometimes," I say to prove how really generous I am. See? I hate you and still find room in my great big heart to be your friend. Which, confusing as that is, expresses how I actually feel—a situation for which Hallmark has failed to create a greeting card.

Caro shrugs. "Most women hate me. You're sweeter about it."

"Thank you," I say.

"Thank *you*," she says. "You and I remind me of an old joke Dickie told once."

It seems a wife is confronting her very rich husband at a party about a beautiful woman the wife caught him kissing earlier. The husband says, "That's my mistress. You have the choice of either accepting my mistress or leaving the marriage without a penny." Another beautiful woman enters the party, and the wife says, "Who is that?" The husband says, "That's Frank's mistress." After a moment, the wife says, "I like ours better."

Caro and I laugh. But I am struck by how 1950s the marriage arrangement sounds in this joke—and in Caro's life. It occurs to me that the rich are often undeveloped in the way of relationships. The money must hold them back.

Caro says, "I always picture the wife and the mistress having lunch together, like us."

I dislike the idea of playing either the role of the wife or the mistress in this joke. I turn my back to her and open the refrigerator, just to have my face to myself a moment.

"You could fix a salad," Caro suggests from behind me. "Use that raspberry vinegar I like."

This amazes me about Caro: how she turns her position of supplicant so swiftly into queen of the arena. Fifteen minutes ago she was apologizing for barging in uninvited. Now she's advising me how I can best please her. I should say, *We're planning strawberries and asparagus—no leafy greens tonight, doll.* But I pull out the romaine Bo has stocked for my return and reluctantly begin washing the leaves, my wrists lingering beneath the cool stream of water to lower my body heat. Around Caro, I often think I'm possibly entering premature menopause: I have hot flashes and radical turns of temperament.

"Caro? Are you and Bo still . . . lovers then?" I hate asking questions I don't want answered. I can't turn around to face her; she'll see that white line around my mouth that shows my fear.

"Tell you the truth, things are a little iffy." I glance over my shoulder. She's plucking the crispy edges off my weed arrangement. "He suddenly got morals or something last summer."

I turn to face her, cupping relief against my heart as if it were a captured bird in my palms. She looks up at me.

She says, "I need him in my life and I intend to keep him there on whatever terms are offered. So far that's worked."

I return to the sink. I long for the glow of Bo's headlights outside my window. At last I see them.

Bo hesitates slightly inside the storm door. It appears as though he's just waiting to buffer the slam with his heel, but he catches my eye momentarily. "I just brought one steak. We'll stick it under the broiler for Caro and it'll be done in a few minutes. She likes it rare."

Is it possible I adore this man more than I even let myself suspect in weaker moments of daydreaming? Suddenly, I'm ashamed of my pile of romaine leaves.

"Great." I smile hugely, but try not to let the smile linger on my face too long or look directly at anybody with it gleaming there. I gather up all the romaine, except one serving, and stuff the leaves into a plastic bag. I sprinkle sugar on the strawberries, slice the tomato, and steam the asparagus.

We sit with plates on our knees. A picnic. I am grateful to be eating yellowtail snapper, strawberries, and asparagus while sitting beside the woodstove, eleven inches of snowpack outside my window. Caro struggles at cutting bite-sized pieces of steak with her plate on her lap. She is not so pleased. Bo and I give her lots of attention to make up for our mutiny.

After I refuse their help, Bo and Caro leave and I cart our used dishes back to the kitchen. I consider how difficult it is to be Caro's friend. People are service modules to her; we play roles, fill slots. I am in her friend slot, Bo is in her lover slot—never mind the pun—Dickie is in her provider slot. She is real. We exist because of her. Except, of course, for those rare moments like earlier when she expresses such insight. Still, if she remembers to give me the needlepoint screen and yarns, I'll be surprised. Slowly, I eat the two remaining strawberries with my fingers before rinsing the bowl.

When Caro lavishes compliments about what a dear, close friend I am, I'm flooded with guilt that I haven't exerted myself more in developing this friendship. My mind zips around in search of how I can fulfill her statement and make it true, and it's never occurred to me before that I have no responsibility for her exaggerations. I drizzle the rest of the lemon sauce on the leftover asparagus in a storage bowl and stick it in the refrigerator.

I squirt Ivory into the dishpan and slip in the silverware. Caro is impossible to nail down about her past. All I get from requests for further information is a flip of her wrist. She never remembers or will tell me later. I fish around for the sponge, then decide I can do this job tomorrow. I pour the last two inches of champagne into my glass, or rather dish, and carry it to the living room. So far I've only heard a single reference to her father. "Pa," Caro called him, then remarked flippantly that this was, "Short for *faux pas*." But refused further discussion about her family.

I sit before my stove, fire door open to enjoy the flames, and I feel both relieved Caro is gone and lonesome because Bo left with her. I had been looking forward to tonight, which Bo said over the phone he especially cleared for my homecoming. Did he exhibit a shade of disappointment at Caro's intrusion, or was it just that my own disappointment swamped the room so fully everyone's feet got damp?

I rise from the sofa and wedge a short, chunky log into the woodstove and stoop before the opened door to watch it catch flame. Why is Caro clinging to Bo and why is he letting her?

Suddenly, a deep weariness floods my chest. I close the fire door and decide to undertake the task of finding my toothbrush, buried in my suitcase, so I can get ready for bed.

I rifle through fruit-colored shorts and tank tops, ridiculous clothes held up against the backdrop of log cabin walls. Even in the peak of a mountain summer these thin cottons are useless; one snag on a Wyoming bull thistle finishes them off. A pair of these shorts houses my toothbrush in its pocket, if I can only remember what I wore early this morning, in that other life, that other season and land.

"Once I was like you," my mother said as I tucked her into bed last night. "Now look at me."

I didn't shed a tear. In Florida, I seem to unconsciously assume an army nurse facade. Nothing shocks or dismays me. My mother put her used underwear in the dishwasher beside the silverware. The army nurse cheerfully sorted clothes from dishes and washed everything over. I should offer a name to this inner soldier of mine: Agatha, perhaps. Agatha, the army nurse. Even-tempered and nonjudgmental, Agatha absolutely loves her work.

When I find my toothbrush and carry it to the bathroom, I recall buying this toothbrush back in October and picking one up for Bo at the same time. The toothbrush he kept in my bathroom had begun looking worn. While hiking later that same day, I found the skeleton of an elk tangled in sagebrush and I dragged out the jawbone. Back home I dug around, elbow deep, in the trash can to retrieve one of the old toothbrushes I'd tossed and surfaced with Bo's red one. The elk teeth were caked with dirt.

Bo walked in the back door, noticed what I was doing, leaned sideways against the sink counter beside me, and folded his arms. I glanced at him, and he nodded down into the sink, where I was scrubbing away on the inch-wide elk teeth with his toothbrush.

He said, "Were you eventually going to tell me?"

I realized Bo didn't know about the new toothbrush and I followed his mind pictures of me sneaking his red one back into the medicine cabinet after I'd brushed the elk's encrusted teeth with it. I burst into laughter.

Now, as I undress for bed, I remember how Bo's face softened watching me laugh, how he seemed to absorb me, stripped to pure glee, into himself. I remember how I needed to dip my head to encourage my hair to fall alongside my face and hide my psychic nudity from his eyes. I smile now at how easily his wit can set me off. Bo knew that day I wouldn't actually sneak his toothbrush for such a job, and he knew that the mental picture he was pretending to carry could be transferred to me with one brief remark and trigger my laughter. To me, this is the utmost in intimacy. This is about as sexual as two people can get, with or without their clothes on.

I lift my comforter and check for the tiny black spiders that are wintering near my ceiling beams. Occasionally, one will travel down and chance sleeping with me. All is clear, and I slip between my flannel sheets and stretch out stomach down, grateful to be home in my own bed.

sixteen

t is taking me days to unpack my suitcases and move back into my life, into my feelings and body rhythms. I've been home a week, but after being housebound—or carbound—so long with my mother, I can't get back into my habit of spending time outside. When I ran into Caro at Fred's getting groceries this morning, she claimed I looked "like a goddamn marshmallow." So I dig around for my twelve-year-old blusher, cracked and orange, hoping it will lend some life to my face. Suddenly in the mirror my mother's cheeks come to mind, rouged by my father's heavy hand, and I burst into whole-body sobs.

"Zann, what's the matter?" Bo's voice, full of alarm, is punctuated by the slam of the back door.

"Nothing," I call, as if I'm farther away than two short steps into the bathroom. I wish I'd heard him drive up. I reach for a tissue from the box on the back of the toilet, but Bo is there first. Knees bent, he dabs at my face with the wadded-up tissue as if repairing a canvas marred by unsightly blobs of paint.

"Aw, Zannah, tell me what's the matter."

To my horror I begin bawling all over again. Bo puts one arm around my back and presses his cheek on top my head. "You've been so goddamn cheerful all week." He peers down at me and shakes his head like he'd never believed in that act all along. "You haven't said shit about it since you got home."

"About what?" I sound as much like a creaky door as I do a coy, weepy woman.

"Florida." Bo dabs at my face again. "I know it wasn't any picnic down there."

As my crying snuffles to an end, tears congest and words flow instead. "We did every little thing together, all three of us, once my dad got back from the Keys." I reach for Bo's Kleenex. "We went to Bay Harbor on Sewall's Point for Mom's hair appointment together, and my last night there, we all lined up in front of the bathroom mirror trying to remember how Andre said to back comb."

Bo reaches for my washcloth and holds it under the hot-water faucet. I recall the nose-stinging fragrance of hair spray filling my parents' large mirrored bathroom back in Florida. "You're a beauty, Elizabeth Arden. Look at that." Dad had teased Mom's dark hair until it stood on end like lightning-filled cumulus around her face. "The prettiest girl in town and I'm in her date book. Of course, we have to drag along this homely kid." Dad tipped his head my way. Mom rolled her eyes at me in the mirror, and for a moment, she was back again, sharing humor with us. "Next step," Dad said, hairbrush high in the air like a sickle, "we form this hay into a stack so we don't scare everybody at Gentleman Jim's Restaurant."

Now, in my own medicine cabinet mirror, my eyes sideways to watch Bo wash my face, I tell him that may have been our last shared joke. I never know what losses my mother will experience before my next visit. "She's moving through this so fast. The doctor doesn't know how to help her."

When Bo finishes, I see more color in my face. It's just in all the wrong places—my nose and my eyes. I feel better though or, if not better, more at home in myself. Coming alive once again, the birth each time I return home to myself no less painful than the last. But I tell Bo, "I'm getting faster. It was two weeks before I cried last time."

I haven't polished the knack of fully acknowledging my mother's symptoms while caring for her at the same time.

I watch Bo rinse my washcloth, vigorously twisting it one way then the other so it will never be square again.

My mother and I have seen the truth and horror in each other's eyes and have held on to it together. We have shared this. But work needs to be done and professionals know how to do it. So Agatha thinks up helpers like using baby wipes in the bathroom and hiding smashed pills in a spoonful of applesauce. Agatha doesn't fall apart when my mother doesn't recognize her daughter. And Agatha forgives herself for loss of patience when my mother repeats and repeats the same question or wanders the house throughout a long night. But, eventually, Agatha departs . . . and leaves me with a blotchy red face.

"Why don't you throw this stuff away?" Bo opens my compact and smells the musty caked powder. "You don't need it."

He's complimenting me because he doesn't know what else

to say, but I follow his advice and discard the blusher in the wastebasket.

Bo says, "How about if I fix some Irish Cream coffee?"

"Great."

Baileys Irish Cream in dark rich coffee was our favorite treat before I left for Florida.

Sitting in my familiar place on the bench beside my stacks of books, elbows on kitchen table, I realize this is the best spot to ease back into my psychic clothes. Here, I daydream. Here, I sketch out new jewelry designs. My famous artist friend says it's important to daydream. To daydream, Kelly says, is an artist's job.

The geranium blooms on the windowsill above the sink. I tell Bo thanks for watering it while I was gone.

With strong square hands, he reaches for coffee beans and mugs. I admire the way his forearms flare into muscle from beneath rolled-up flannel sleeves before tapering into surprisingly narrow wrists. Bo's fine denim-covered butt passes in front of the kitchen cupboards from sink to stove; I admire that, too.

"The geranium's getting leggy," he says.

"Leggy?" My eyes move down the backs of Bo's legs.

"We should cut it back."

His Levi's are tucked into unlaced Sorel Pacs, and he's leaving little puddles of melted snow on the floor, but the worst of it is probably drying in the bathroom, so I don't mention it.

"My mother planted red geraniums just like this one outside the screened porch in Florida several years ago and now they're big as bushes."

"So you all went out to dinner your last night there." Bo is determined to keep me talking.

"Dad sat across from Mom and me in a booth at Gentleman Jim's. He said to Mom, 'You and I are partners, aren't we?' "

"What did he mean?"

"I think he began the statement conversationally. His tone was a bit patronizing at first. Then the words seemed to shift the atmosphere between them, and he reached across the table and held Mom's hand."

That moment in the restaurant, waiting for dinner, I felt breathless at the sudden vision of my father's truth: My mother and he were partners. They were playing out a holy exchange of life lessons. I was humbled by their vast undertaking. At that moment, I believed I understood the purpose of life, and I believed with absoluteness that life extended beyond the brief span we attribute to it. And though I can't with dependable certainty draw forward either belief at will just now, I'll never forget the certainty I felt of both at that moment.

None of this I say to Bo, who has stopped his work and turned to me.

I say, "My father has never acknowledged emotions before. With this disease he's learning to interact with my mother on an emotional level, because nothing about her life is rational. When I was a teenager, he sent me to my room if I became teary-eyed and told me I could join the family again when I conducted myself with reason."

"What about your mother? What's she getting from the partnership?"

"I know she never got this loving attention from my dad before, or this acceptance. Mostly, I feel overwhelmed by the hard road her spirit has chosen, but occasionally I glimpse a kind of harmony emerge in her life."

"Goddamn big price to pay for some attention."

"It makes sense to me. In a way, we all give our lives for attention and acceptance."

Bo considers. "This partnership deal, are you talking about something unconscious here?"

"I suppose. But whatever explains the exchange I witnessed between my mother and my father defines what I want in my own life. I want to learn life through partnering. I saw love and its long meaning that moment. I witnessed its worth despite the pain." I sound formal, as if I've thought this out, yet I am surprising myself with this statement of intention.

Bo nods. Behind him the coffee drips through the filter into the pot.

I remind myself, or perhaps it's Agatha's reminder before she finally departs, there will be times I'll forget this vision. That with the rage of the powerless I'll wonder where to point the finger of blame for my mother's illness.

"My father's energy is like his hair—cowlicks spurting in all directions. I think he's finally found his match in tending Mom. He gives himself totally to her these days."

Bo brings our mugs to the table. As he pulls out a chair to sit, I scoot off the bench and go searching for cookies to have with our coffee.

"Much of Dad's early-retirement funds will be spent on Mom's care. There isn't an insurance company in the world that covers Alzheimer's disease," I say, stretching on my toes to reach deep into the high cupboard over the stove. "Thank God he's well set there." I sit back down with my loot, a half-empty tin of Piroulines, a cream-filled wafer so expensive and delicious I have to hide them from myself.

Bo stirs the Baileys into his coffee, then into mine. I feel all these words pushing the lump away in my throat. Bo's listening soothes like a deep massage. If I keep talking like this, Bo might wish he had voted for the muteness of my tears. I offer Bo the tin of wafers. There's an interesting survey question: Would men prefer to hear women talk out or cry out their sorrows? I bite off the tip of a wafer. In this survey no third choice would be offered, such as: Suffer in silence.

"Your dad sounds like an unusual guy."

"Oh, he is. The star of the family, the one Mom and I worked to impress." I dip my wafer into my coffee. "Events were not real to us until we reported them to him."

Anger toward my father rises up out of nowhere once again. It's so inappropriate I'm embarrassed inside my own head.

I chase the little piece of wafer floating on top of my coffee. I sigh. "I don't know. While my dad encouraged Mom's dependence, I badgered her to get a job, to volunteer, make more friends, learn birding, anything. We both should have left her alone."

I take a sip of my coffee. I feel a deep gratitude for Bo's company and care.

I say, "Tessa is having a potluck and scavenger hunt later this afternoon. Come with me."

Turns out Bo knows most everybody at the party and introduces me to more people than I do him, even though a lot of Tessa's guests are associated with the bookstore. After the scavenger hunt, we all sit around with paper plates on our laps, the guests' dogs dozing between rows of Sorel Pacs at the front door.

Bo tells how his scavenger hunt team of five men stopped in the driveway of a woman, known locally as an ice climber. While she was unloading groceries from her car, the men asked if she had any crampons they could borrow, one of the items on the team's list.

"She hurried into her house without answering us," Bo says. "I think she misunderstood and thought we asked for tampons."

Bo is good at parties. I am not so good. Erik wouldn't go to parties and I never went alone. In Findlay, Ohio, if you're not with your husband at a party, you're just looking for trouble— or so goes your reputation. I'm way out of practice and not back into my skin from my Florida trip enough to be entertaining in a crowd. Fortunately, Bo hangs close.

Too close for many people at the party to believe we're "just neighbors," as I keep explaining. One woman, whom I haven't met before, asked a few minutes ago if I was aware that Bo spent a lot of time out with some reddish-haired woman.

"Oh, that must be his mistress," I said, using Caro's joke. "Isn't she pretty?" That took care of her.

But perhaps the stress of trying to be sociable is getting to me. I'm beginning to sneeze and sniffle. I ask Tessa for a tissue and she returns loaded with herbal remedies. She hands them to Bo, rattles off the dosages to him and says, "Stop at Fred's for oranges on the way home. And take some of the echinacea yourself to bolster your immune system, Bo, or you'll get this cold next."

Bo reads the list of ingredients on one of the herb bottles,

"Deer antler, peony, tortoiseshell, placenta—of *what* they don't tell."

"Why don't we just swallow pond scum?" I say.

With these remarks, Tessa decides not to chance us following her directions. "Open up, both of you." She squirts a dropper of a foul-tasting tincture onto each of our tongues, and we both rush to the kitchen sink for water.

Tessa follows me to the bedroom. While I'm getting into my coat, she says, "Inner crying. Colds and grieving, same symptoms: watery eyes, filled sinuses. Take care of yourself and don't come to work tomorrow." As manager, Tessa has authority over schedules. I know she thinks I have not fully acknowledged my sadness over my mother, and of course, she is right, but I don't like to encourage her reading metaphors into my life, so I just thank her for the day off.

A snowfall began during our potluck, and the Suburban's windshield wipers work against heavy piles of wet snow as we pull away from Tessa's house. During the drive home, everything in sight—the road, the buck-and-rail fences, the rumps of cattle—is covered unevenly, as if the snow had dropped in clumps instead of flakes. By the time we reach my cabin I'm chilled and achy, eyes streaming and nose stuffed up.

Bo says he'll squeeze the orange juice while I get ready for bed. I wait for him under my comforter, propped against pillows, wearing my longest, fluffiest flannel nightgown. I discarded the notion of staging a scene with lacy straps against bare shoulders shyly peeking above my covers. I really don't feel good.

"Open up," Bo says, coming into my room. He sits on my bed and presents a dropper full of echinacea.

"No icky-natia. I've had enough."

"Open up," he says sternly.

I do and he squeezes the awful tonic into my mouth, while I curl my tongue way back out of reach. He quickly hands me the freshly squeezed juice. I hold a mouthful and bathe my tongue in it, trying to erase the stringent taste of the tonic. I shudder.

Bo smiles slightly with his eyes cast downward, screwing the top back on the brown bottle.

"You enjoyed that," I accuse him.

"I wish I could give you some more." He stretches crossways on the bed over my lower legs and plants his elbow, resting his head on his hand. "It has to do with having some noticeable effect on you—good or bad," he says.

I know exactly what he means, but I act obtuse. "Give some to Caro. In fact, give her the whole bottle." I pop out two red Sudafed pills from their foil and chase them with my juice. I'm only a faithful believer in natural medicine when I'm feeling good.

"It isn't easy to have an effect on Caro. You're more fun." He shakes the bottle menacingly.

"I think you're in love with Caro." My voice sounds querulous, as if I'm challenging him. Part of me wouldn't mind picking a fight. I'm kind of irked by that woman's remark about Bo spending a lot of time with Caro. Can't be work. How much stock do you buy in the dead of winter?

"Men aren't in love with Caro. They're obsessed by her."

"Are you obsessed?" I grab Tessa's cherry bark cough syrup from the bedside table and take a slug.

"Once I was, for the heck of it."

I feel like acting superior. "I don't believe you're that much in control," I say. It was irritating to take him to *my* friend's party and have him know more people there than I did. And all the way home, while I'm ripping into the Kleenex box catching my sneezes, he tells me everyone's story.

"Besides, I know you only went to the party because Caro has family visiting."

"Believe what you want, Suzannah." Now Bo sounds irked. He rises from the bed.

"Sit back down." I pat the covers and look apologetic. "Talk to me till my Sudafed kicks in." I don't want him leaving me alone here, sniffing and restless. "Tell me about Caro's visitor."

He sits on the edge of my bed. "This guy Caro's taking everywhere? His name's Benj? Her older brother?"

"You sound like an up talker." I pitch my voice high. "Like, you know, everything has to end in a question?"

"Well, something's going on." Bo holds up the tincture bottle and swings it by its rubber squeeze top. "Something icky."

"Now you sound like me—*icky*."

Bo shoots off my bed again. "Sick people are so goddamn self-absorbed. Zannah, I can't talk to you. I'm leaving."

"Talk to me. I'll behave. Please?" I know I can't sleep yet and my eyes are too watery to enjoy a book.

Bo stares down at me disgustedly, and I wonder if he can read my mind. He says, "Shit."

I hear him in the kitchen rinsing my juice glass before he slams out the back door. I try to imagine being married to Bo and complaining about him to my women friends. They would say, "He rinsed the glass before slamming out? My God, what a dreamboat."

After turning out my light, I snuggle deep into my comforter. I follow the sound of Bo's Suburban backing out the drive, straightening onto the road, accelerating toward his house. I try to roll over in my long flannel nightgown, but between the flannel bedsheet and the flannel duvet cover I feel stuck like one of those felt cutouts arranged on a cloth-covered board used in Sunday school lessons. I'm not going *anywhere* unless someone peels me off the sheet and moves me.

From my imagination I pull out my favorite sleep inducer, a fantasy from another biography I'm reading about the Countess Cissy Patterson. It involves Cal Carrington, her Wyoming outlaw hunting guide, and—some say—dark and feisty lover. Cal looks remarkably like Bo in my version of the story. Lately, I've been changing things around. Cissy's French maid does not rush back east in fright after her first day in Wyoming, as she did in reality. She leaves the dude ranch, all right, but only goes to town. There, she stays with Rose Crabtree at the Crabtree Hotel on the corner of the square, and learns English with a flirty accent. In my version she looks remarkably like me. With the help of the local cowpokes, she learns to ride, to dance the Western swing, to gamble at the Wort. Then, having become an accomplished Wyoming woman and having mastered Rose Crabtree's chokecherry pie recipe, the French maid goes after Cal Carrington. And most nights before I fall asleep, she gets him.

I wake up the next morning surprised to feel so good. I recall Bo leaving in a benign huff last night, which he will not hold against me. Still, I need to apologize. One of these days I hope I can ask him to a party without canceling out the invitation with a scene designed to turn him away. I decide to go into town for cappuccino and eggs Benedict at Shade's Café. I hear steady dripping from my eaves as I lie in bed, so I know the snow is melting and the roads will be safe. I shower and dress and stuff two books and my journal into my backpack.

Tessa claims she "manifests" parking spots by visualizing the exact empty space she wants. I picture the space right in front of Shade's, next to the alley, so I can easily pull in and out. While I'm at it, I visualize the table I want, too. The small, round one smack in the middle of the big window.

I don't get the parking spot, but I do get the window seat. I order my eggs with yolks hard as rocks. "Bounceable," I call around the corner to Kim, who is cooking today. While I'm spooning foam off my double cap and eating it like ice cream, I spot Caro with a man about to go into a gallery across the street. This must be her visiting brother. He halts Caro from behind with one hand on top of hers, grasping the doorknob, and his other hand holding her low on her abdomen. He says a few words in her ear; then they both disappear into the shop.

Thirty minutes later, I glance up from my reading and see the two of them dart across the wet street, clotted with snow that has fallen off passing cars. They don't see me until they boisterously push each other into Shade's. My table is too small for three, I gratefully realize, but other tables are available. They are as relieved as I am, I'll bet, because Caro immediately begins a case for not disturbing me and the books I've spread around.

"Don't move a thing, Suzannah. Benj and I have business

to discuss before I drive him to the airport. Oh, this is my brother. He's here from Oklahoma."

"Where in Oklahoma?" I ask, as if I could name a single town there. I'm like my family used to be about Wyoming when I first moved here, mix it up with all the other square Western states.

Benj says, "Pierce. Small place."

"Ah," I say knowingly, as if I'm about to ask if that little drugstore on the corner still serves those great cherry phosphates. I may be picturing Kansas for all I know. Around and around my head march Bo's words, *Something's going on. Something icky.*

Benj looks older than Caro, maybe by as much as eight years or so. Tall, slender build. The most arresting thing about him is the contrast of his light gray eyes against his long, slightly curling black hair. Caro, also, has gray eyes. Though they don't share the exact same shade, they look out of those eyes the exact same way. As if they had a parent who often recited, "Don't take any shit. Ever."

While Benj lists the places Caro has shown him, Caro eases toward the order counter. I pretend to listen to him while picturing a rough-talking father who kept his distance, maybe traveled a lot. "You take any shit, you'll just smell bad." Two sets of gray eyes listened carefully.

"Benj," Caro urges, "get in line."

"There is no line, Caro." Benj turns toward me and switches his smile on again. I begin to think about what happened when the rough father left town and the weak mother couldn't do a thing about how her children spent their time together.

The trouble with my new life since leaving the blandness

of marriage with Erik and teaching school is that my newly awakened imagination soars out of bounds. Once I overheard someone discussing artificial legs in a restaurant, and my mind set off into picturing a policeman shooting somebody over and over in that artificial leg, trying to stop them from escaping a crime scene. Emptied his gun and still the guy kept walking away.

Caro tries to overhear what Benj is saying to me while she gives her order. It's nice someone is listening to him. I just want out of here. I gather up my belongings, jabber some polite words to Benj, wiggle fingers at Caro, and pull the door behind me before both my arms are in my coat sleeves. On the sidewalk I wrestle with my books and clothes. "Please," I beg myself, "act normal." From the counter they can easily see me out here. My coat half dragging on the ground, backpack spilling its contents. Lips moving, giving directions to myself. But I'm unnerved: Benj is Caro's brother like Heathcliff was Catherine's.

seventeen

This morning I cross-country ski around the base of Saddlestring Butte and encounter the heart-shaped tracks of elk, left like valentines in the snow. The name of Bo's ranch, Crossing Elk, originated from this heavily used game trail, swagging down the butte to the creek bank below. Bo says by winter's end the snowy trail will be paved a foot and a half wide in elk droppings. Right now droppings are still sparse, but definitely scattered along this particular route as if a herd of Hansels and Gretels was marking their way home.

Alongside the creek I pole myself slowly, eyes on the ground looking for signs. I become hypnotized, puzzling out the prints and scat. By the time I turn back after one of these outings, I am filled with calm.

Earlier this week, when I told my father on the phone about my new hobby, he said, "Hobby? That's not how your mother and I thought of it when we caught you in your crib with your diapers off playing with your *scat,* as you like to call it."

"*Caught* me? You sound as if I'd been committing a criminal offense."

"It was pretty damn offensive to me," he said.

I bend low over a twist of coyote scat prickly with fur and hope I'll come across prints of the chase. Farther up the creek, I see dirt heaped over the snow and realize there was no chase. The coyote just dug underground for his dinner last night. Vole, most likely.

I'd meant to tell my father about my latest sighting: tiny paw prints in fresh snow that suddenly disappeared in a flutter of feathery wing impressions. The drama of a raptor capturing a small rodent. Sometimes, even though I may laugh at my father's remarks, I feel him sucking out my psychic energy till I am nearly flat. The image of a vampire comes to mind.

I was determined on the phone that night to be the one to end our call for a change. I said, "Dad, I have to go now, but I wanted to cheer you with the news that tracking has finally made something of a scientist of me." He has accused me of being the enemy of rational thought with a one-sided interest in the arts.

My father answered, "Yeah? You saying I should have been cheered about hosing down a baby scientist and her crib that Saturday morning?"

I gave up, because he never does. I bet my father has no memory of talking to my mother in just that exact way. Now my mother doesn't either.

I ski to an area tamped flat by the many webbed prints of Canada geese. From reading descriptions of autopsies done on

Alzheimer's patients, I picture areas of my mother's brain looking like this, pathways knotted into a tangle of webbed prints.

I ski across the frozen creek and up the other side to a spot where a warm spring keeps ice from forming. A dozen mallards and the dazzling black-and-white of the Barrow's goldeneye crowd the tiny pool. Once, I saw a family of four otters lunch on fish beside the creek here, crunching bones. Today, I notice the otters haven't used their slide on the bank since the tiny hard pellets of graupel snow fell a few days ago. No fresh scat either. I worry about this family of otters and I worry about my own family. We are separating from one another in our various ways. What will become of us? What will hold us together?

Excrement seems to be a family theme lately. I think of the adult diapers my dad has had to purchase recently for my mother. Perhaps this explains his inability to honor my interest in tracking. And Beckett, graduating midyear with his associate's degree from LCCC, alerted me that all his classmates were depositing moose pellets into the dean's palm when he shook their hands while passing out diplomas. By the end of the ceremony every pocket of Dean Coates' suit bulged. He must have smelled a bit odd, too.

Delinda promised to come but, typically, canceled at the last minute. Thinking now about Beck's distance during my weekend visit, I wonder if he wanted to punish me for being more attentive than Delinda, because years ago I may have confused the issue in his young mind. Whenever Delinda failed to show up or call as promised, I offered treats—ice cream or a movie—to help fill the blank space in his life as if I were the one responsible for it.

I ski back to the cabin and find Bo in the kitchen, fixing

food for our "neighborhood potluck," as he still calls it. "Been shit tracking again?" he asks by way of greeting.

"Yep. What are you cooking? Smells good in here."

"Potato soup."

"Yum."

I haven't talked to Bo since I saw Caro and her brother in town a couple days ago, except to phone with an apology for my bad behavior, which I blamed on my cold. As I strip off my gaiters and boots, the washer finishes its final spin cycle. I switch Bo's load from the washer to the dryer. He has begun adding my laundry to his to make up a full load. I have mixed feelings about this blurring of our belongings. Mostly, I am so wrapped up in my jewelry designs these days that to be spared brushing my own teeth would be welcome.

"Bo," I call into the kitchen, "thanks for washing the blue bathroom rug."

He turns off the kitchen faucet. "I didn't. I washed the white one."

I hear potato slices thud one by one as he slices them into the soup pot.

"What else did you wash with it?" I holler back.

"Flannel sheets. Your new blue plaid . . ." The hollow thumps of falling potato slices halt.

Bo appears in the laundry room doorway. "I do the laundry. How come you're in here?" Paring knife in hand, he defends his position in the household. My household.

I never say the obvious. I never say because it's *my* house, *my* laundry. It seems unfair to express the unequivocal in an argument.

Bo picks up the rug, holds it by its fringe, and aims it toward the lightbulb overhead. "That's not blue. That's practically white."

"It's blue. Once it was completely white."

"This is white with a shadow across it. The blue is a *pigment* of your imagination."

We never get any further than this. I laugh at his silly wit, marvel over his even, good nature—despite provoking him like I did the night of my cold—and it's over. But I never quite get to any points about my rights around here, his lack of them. Yet, too, from the kitchen, the aroma of diced onions sautéed in butter breezes past my nose. It's clouding up outside, the wood burning in the stove gives a wild whine, reminding me of the rough-legged hawk soaring earlier over the snowy butte. I don't have to eat dinner alone. I don't even have to think it up or cook it.

My laughter winds down into a smile that matches Bo's. We stand there and just grin. Really, I feel such contentment. Euphoria bubbles up, then simmers like Bo's soup will soon, and I place the shadowy blue laundry on the back burner of my mind.

Bo returns to slicing potatoes. I check the mail he brought and use his pocket knife to unwrap a box from Rishashay. Brand-new silver bead caps and fancy spacers. I carry them to my work table.

During my marriage it never occurred to Erik or me that anyone but me would handle the laundry. Traditions change. Now even my father is doing laundry. Dad said he found a box of cookies in the tub of the washing machine last week, washed, rinsed, and spun. "But that's okay," he assured me, deeply tucked into his denial. "We're doing fine."

I can't document this, but I believe there was a plateau in my life at which I made a choice whether I, too, would fall sick, give up, and roll downhill or gather myself together and trudge on up. I remember one winter in Findlay, wishing I could stay in bed forever. For several weeks I carried a low-grade fever, vaguely ached from head to toe, and was smeared with a faint rash, like strawberry jam on white bread. The doctor said, "Maybe scarlatina. Maybe nothing."

Then it was over. I had begun to make jewelry. As I grew stronger, beadwork took over my life, as if it were a fierce disease itself. I got healthier, happier, even sharper in my thinking—I swear, my IQ rose twenty points.

Tessa said that was my Saturn return. "How old were you?" she asked.

"Thirty-five," I told her.

Like a game-show host, she congratulated me for giving the right answer. "Exactly."

An ego crisis, she explained. We each get one. We reach the peak of our ego's arc—usually between thirty-five and forty—and decide there and then whether we rip through outer dressings and soar on upward or follow the curve back down to death.

Bo's soup pours into my bowl like ladles of ivory velvet. It's speckled with fresh dill and parsley. He bought baguettes from the Bunnery. Split, buttered, and toasted them beneath the broiler. Lettuce this time of year is not green; our salad looks more as if Bo just laundered the white leaves with a green sheet. For dessert, I baked lemon bars. Our dinner is monochromatic, like the view out my windows: all shades of white.

"I met Caro's brother the other day," I say, once I come

up for air from my potato soup. "You felt something wasn't right. . . ."

"Never mind," Bo says. "It wasn't anything."

He begins clearing our dishes off the table and carrying them to the sink. What's his rush? He didn't even finish his soup. I grab another piece of bread as the plate flies past. Bo has a heavy hand with butter, which I love.

"When Dickie's on these long trips, we usually see a lot more of—"

Bo interrupts. "Caro made reservations for the two of us at Chico Hot Springs this weekend." He crosses to the stove.

"I've never been to Montana." For one wild moment, I misunderstand. I think "the two of us" means Bo and me. Really, I need a fuller social life. Sometimes I lose my place in this odd triangle Caro and Bo and I have going.

"She wants to check out some cutting horses in Livingston." Bo stands with his back to me, spooning soup into his mouth. I knew he couldn't have eaten enough.

I keep picturing how Caro acted as if Benj were a daddy, safe to flirt with, yet looking at him worriedly for approval. Kind of flirty, kind of anxious. Perhaps I can offer Caro a wider cushion of tolerance now, knowing there's complications in her life. Still, reservations at a hot-springs resort just to buy horses?

I brush buttery toast crumbs from my fingers and tune into Bo, who is talking about O.C.'s upcoming knee surgery.

"Trouble is, O.C.'s surgery is scheduled this week and he won't be able to take care of Hazer. So I told O.C. I'd ask you how you felt about having a pup around a few days." Bo is pouring the leftover soup from the pot into a plastic storage bowl.

"Why doesn't O.C. ask me himself?" I knew O.C.'s knee was giving him trouble and surgery was a possibility. He never quite recovered from his pup knocking him down.

"You mean a direct one-on-one, face-to-face interaction?" Bo looks at me wide-eyed over his shoulder. "How the hell you think a family can keep any ties going that way? I'm a little worried about Pop not phoning one of the aunts first to ask me to ask you."

"Books call that *codependent behavior*." I walk to the sink with my soup bowl and silverware. Bo seems to feel he has to be chatty for a bit longer until he's certain I'm not going to break into the first available space with my version of things between Caro and Benj.

"Codependent behavior *defines* a family. You think Pop and I would have anything at all going on between us if we didn't take on each other's business? You think I'd *choose* to talk to the old coot for *fun*?" Bo scrapes the last of the soup from the sides of the pot with a spatula to get every last drop. When he's finished, the soup reaches the very top of the bowl; if there had been another spoonful, Bo would've had to eat it.

I start the water for tea and rinse the bowls.

"We make up stuff like this to keep us hanging together." Bo rummages in a drawer for a plastic lid. "See, you'll give me an answer, I'll pass it on to O.C., he'll have another message for you, maybe one for the aunts so I get to call them, too, then call O.C. again."

"*Triangling*, the books call that." Slow times at the bookstore I educate myself in the relationships section and try to figure out my life.

"You bet. The family that triangles together, hangs together." Bo snaps the lid on the plastic bowl. I admire his genius for finding the exact size bowl to fit leftovers. I usually have to dirty two because I've guessed wrong.

Bo brings over the salad bowl and dumps the leftovers in the sink. He pushes the lettuce down the drain, while I gather potato skins, left on the counter, and toss those into the sink.

The sink fills with murky water. Potato skins and lettuce begin to float.

"Well, shit," Bo says. "Look what we've done again."

"Oh, heck."

Bo uses the ladle to bail out water from the sink into the soup pan. Then grabs handfuls of lettuce and potato skins.

"I would love to have Hazer here, but I think O.C. should have asked me himself."

Bo runs to his car for his toolbox. I convince him when he returns to let the sink go until we finish dessert. "Our tea's ready."

We sit back down at the table. I relate Tessa's theory about Saturn returns and ask Bo what he thinks while I cut the lemon bars into generous squares.

"I think Tessa's one of the nicest nuts I've met."

"Really, there might be something to this. Right now you're in the process of deciding whether to go on as before or climb to a new level and live more intensely."

"I've already decided. That's what selling the cattle was all about," Bo says.

"I know, but . . ." I want to say *but you haven't acted on this new life much.* I'm thinking about his lack of artwork—he had to cancel his gallery show this fall because he wasn't ready—and his apparent increase in seeing Caro. In fact, he continues to use his ranching skills for her now instead of himself. It seems to me like Bo might be sliding downhill. Though it could be just me. I'm finally feeling ready for an increase in Bo's presence in my life and perhaps feeling threatened by a fear of not getting the man I've been expecting.

I say, "Maybe you're stalled in your creativity because you don't confront your grandfather about anything, even his dog's care. You are an artist. It's time to make O.C. honor that." I let the delicate crust of the lemon bar melt on my tongue and pick up a fallen crumb with a licked finger. "Of course, that's exactly what I need to demand from my father, who's spent his life managing me, rather than enjoying me." I add this just in case my personal remarks sound intrusive.

"That's the trouble with you, Suzannah. . . ."

"Oh, good. Let me get cozy here first, shoes off, tea poured." I slouch back in my chair dramatically and look at Bo. "Now tell me all about the *trouble* with me."

"Smart-ass." Bo gets up to see if the sink is draining yet. Then, leaning against the counter he crosses his arms and faces me. "I wasn't going to find fault with you."

"Then say *the* wonderful *thing about you, Suzannah* instead of *the trouble with*."

Bo releases a breath of exasperation, then jumps right in. "The wonderful thing about you, Suzannah, is your intent— no, determination—to reach the deepest inside yourself that you can imagine. Now the trouble"—he catches himself— "*other* people have is that you demand they, too, reach deep down and offer you their insides, knowing all the while that you're way more experienced in this. And whatever they can offer won't be good enough to interest you."

"Are you talking about yourself here?"

"Your father was the guy I had in mind. Why not back off? Relax a bit and stop demanding an intimacy from him that he doesn't know a damn thing about."

"You *are* talking about yourself."

"No." Bo pulls his kitchen chair out again and sits. He lifts his mug of hot tea and holds it with both hands under his chin. If he wore glasses they'd be all steamed up by now. He's not looking at me. His eyes study an area near his left elbow, propped on the table. "No. I'd actually like to try to follow you there."

My eyes fill instantly. My throat clogs fast as the gooseneck pipe beneath the kitchen sink. I pull my cup close and look into the depths of my tea. All my life I have wanted this. A companion diver. Someone not easily scared spelunking the watery abyss of togetherness. Two grown-ups, consciously in-dividual, each with his own headlamp and oxygen tank, hold-ing hands for the sheer love of sharing the adventure. Is this what Bo is offering?

Of course not, he just reported he and Caro are going off to Chico this weekend to slither around each other in the hot springs. I give the lump in my throat a minute to dissolve.

"You would not." I speak softly but even so my voice gives me away with its raspy vulnerability. I take a long sip of my hot tea. We do fine talking about my insides; we get to Bo's insides and he cloaks the topic with my father's feelings.

"Things don't happen overnight." Bo sets his mug down. "I'm just saying you ask a lot from people and that's okay, but . . . expect to twiddle your thumbs while everybody is catching up."

Everybody. Sure, I'll twiddle. You go to Chico.

I sip my tea and know I'll be awake half the night decipher-ing Bo's words. He's putting me off. When did this begin? I've been so busy barricading myself from him, I can't tell when the switch occurred. Because, no doubt about it, he is now barricad-ing himself from me. All these months I've let him see exactly who I am; I've held back nothing. And I've scared him off.

Bo gets up and checks the sink again. After a moment, I follow. Nothing there moves one bit. Kind of like my love life. Still, reading between Bo's lines, I suspect my best bet is to lighten up. We both just stare at the murky water.

I'm a naturally positive person; the upside of Bo's words abruptly cuts through the blockage that has descended to my chest. I think he is saying, *I'm coming, I'm coming.*

We stare at the water in the sink. I say, "I'm amazed water swirls down a drain in the same direction all over the world." I sound reverent at the idea of such universal unity.

"Except below the equator," he reminds me.

"Oh, right."

We know plunging isn't going to work with this much garbage.

"Need a bucket. Get the big black iron pot," Bo says.

"Eew. I don't want that garbage in my pot."

"Most of this garbage is the same stuff going through your own body's trap pipe."

"Yeah, but . . ."

"We'll boil disinfectant or something in it afterward."

I have some old habits yet to break. I notice that while my mind is objecting, my body is lifting the pot out of the cupboard. This was how I ran my whole life with Erik. Arguing with him with my mouth, abetting him with my hands. I swear, I never knew I was leaving Erik until the process reversed and my mind watched my body pack a bag and climb into the car.

"Now," Bo instructs, "you do the job. I'll just show you, so you can handle it if I'm not here."

"Where are you going?" I sound stupidly bereft.

"Nowhere. You said once you wanted to know how to take care of everything around your place here."

I think *Eew*, again. But he's right. Living way out here, I have to expect times when even Bo can't get through a blizzard to bail me out—so to speak.

"Come on down here," he says from under the sink.

I stoop down and stick my head in there with him. "It's dark." Since my sink sits out from the wall several inches, these lower cupboards are deeper than in newer houses.

"I got a flashlight." He flicks it on. "Now take this wrench and unscrew that plug."

"Which way do I turn? Left or right?"

"Zann," Bo says, "to *un*screw you turn left. To screw you turn right."

"You don't have to be such a grump." The damn thing won't budge. "I haven't taken a pipe plug off before, you know."

"It's universal: left loose, right tight."

I take a breather. "Everywhere? All over the world you loosen left?"

I have trouble believing the planet is that organized. Bo has trouble believing I'm that uninformed. He shines the flashlight on my face. "Everywhere on *this* side of the equator," he says, "below the equator it's the opposite."

I laugh hard. I don't know. I feel giddy. It's nice down here together. We could buy furniture and move in.

Bo has that melted look in his eyes as he watches me laugh. His eyes shift down to my mouth. I stop smiling. My eyes drop to Bo's mouth. The upper halves of our bodies are tucked deep into this silly space. Old linoleum remnants from the mudroom cover the floor, beneath our elbows. The black-bottomed sink with speckles of old white paint, looking like a starry night, looms above us. Bo reaches a hand around the U-shaped pipe swooping down between us to hold my cheek.

But his hand halts midair as we both hear a car door close with an expensive cushioned slam.

I whisper, "Caro?"

"Sounds like."

She comes in the back door after a "Knock, knock" called into the kitchen. The silence feels deep and throbbing to me. Outside the cupboard my legs and Bo's legs, hips to toes, point toward each other.

I deliberately tap the wrench three times against the U pipe. Our alibi.

I apply the wrench to the plug again.

Bo corrects, "*Un*screw, Zann." He raises his voice. "Hi, Caro."

"That's right," Caro sings out. "I'm here, Suzannah, time to *un*screw."

She thinks she's funny. Five minutes later she might have been saying that from my bedroom doorway.

Finally, I *un*screw. The pipe drains into the bucket and Bo says, "Hand us that clothes hanger, Caro." He jams it around the pipe to loosen anything stuck there and we are finished. Except it might help if Bo and I are forced to write *I will not push garbage down the drain* one hundred times on a blackboard. We both keep forgetting I don't have a garbage disposal.

We get involved in our talking and mindlessly push peelings, coffee grounds, egg shells right down the sink drain.

If this is a metaphor for our relationship, I don't want to hear about it.

eighteen

"Sister, don't you think Bartholomew looks peaked? Bartholomew, you look peaked to sister and me."

"I'm not getting enough sex." Bo tosses this out slouched down in an easy chair, his Sunday-best cowboy boots stretched toward the fireplace.

We are sitting in Violet's side of the sisters' duplex. Maizie's side, as I have seen during a previous visit, is too crammed full of furniture moved from the ranch house to allow family gatherings, such as this Christmas Day dinner. Maizie continues with her analysis of Bo's color.

"That'd do it—wouldn't it, sister? Violet and I always look peaked. Course that's attractive in a lady. Men see that and want to help."

With our wine, cheese, and crackers, we wait in Violet's living room for O.C. to arrive. Though still in a brace from his knee surgery and using a cane, he refused offers to pick him up.

Violet says, "In a man, howsomever, it appears suspicious. A lady has to ask herself: What's the problem here?" She pauses to study that question a moment. "I think body odor first."

"That's indelicate, Violet. And you know it's not true. We want to help just the same as men do. That's why we took in Mr. Pearson."

Violet clinks her wineglass down hard on the coffee table. "Maizie."

"Bartholomew knows about our boarders."

"Suzannah doesn't."

"Suzannah knows what Bartholomew knows. Suzannah, you look peaked yourself." The boarders the aunts refer to are their live-in male friends, a relationship only Violet is engaged in at the moment. Mr. Pearson is off visiting his daughters in Tucson for the holiday.

Luckily for me, O.C. opens the door before I have to respond to Maizie's remark, and Hazer crashes into the living room. She jumps at each person individually in greeting. Luckily again, her paws are mostly snow-free by my turn. Butt wriggling, high prancing, she gets all pigeon-toed with friendliness as she makes her way toward me. I longed to keep her forever when I cared for her, and I begged O.C. for an extra week. Now she collapses tummy up at my feet, and I'm enchanted that she remembers my rubs.

Violet is peeking down the front of her dress, as she waits for O.C. to remove his coat so she can hang it. He says to her, "They still there, Violet?"

Violet scrunches around. "Cracker crumbs," she says.

"Aw, they're bigger than that." O.C. hobbles over to join

Bo on the men's side of the room. We three women are lined up on the sofa.

We all laugh at O.C. I like to get my giggles in loud and early before the more offensive jokes are paraded out and I get targeted by O.C. for being no fun. Violet complains about the scratchiness of the crumbs inside her clothes and that spurs Bo to recall an occasion of scratchiness outside her clothes. He tells about hugging her goodbye when the bus arrived on school mornings and feeling crusty little knobs of dried bird droppings on her bathrobe.

"Pop got his fingers bitten so often by Aunt Vi's parrot he used to call it the little rottweiler," Bo tells me. Violet defends her deceased parrot and suggests that Hazer, who is nosing all the ornaments in reach on the Christmas tree, is less than the perfect pet, especially for a brittled-boned old man.

"I might could have got me a more lethargic dog," O.C. allows. "The silly pupper races circles around me. She'll turn to butter one of these days."

We watch the tree boughs sway and anticipate the tinkles turning to plunks. I wish Beckett were here, though I am pleased that Erik has his company for Christmas. Next week Beck is flying out to stay with me until time for him to enroll at the University of Wyoming in Laramie mid-January. He'll get a good dose of all these characters then.

Bo says, "Hazer's a good mutt." He calls her over and gets down on the floor to wrestle with her. He tells Hazer she has a serious psychological problem with her need to win all their games. Two small bunches of muscle along each side of Bo's jaw intrigue me as he talks. Thin blue afternoon light, like skimmed milk, hangs in the window. And just as this kind of light often enhances the ridges and valleys on a mountain face, it also enhances the planes of Bo's face. I especially notice the slight indentation in his chin. Just a hint of cleft in the center. Makes me remember my attempts at creating a cleft of my own as a thirteen-year-old. I walked around my bedroom for hours with a bobby pin pinching my chin, hoping the impression would become permanent.

The memory makes me miss my parents as I sit here with Bo's. I think of my visit home last month and realize I never once sat in such relaxed comfort as I am sitting now, happy with myself. I didn't personally go to Florida. I sent my secretary of state. To negotiate peace, to promise aid, to fly over the catastrophe and report the findings to myself once I was safely home. I look around at the people in this room. I have to spackle the cracks in each personality just to get the meaning of their remarks, yet I wonder: Who's to say what is crazy? I close the bathroom door before I use the toilet when alone in the house. I've caught myself thinking it's because the phone might ring—as if the ringing represents the intrusion of another being.

"Christmas already." O. C. shakes his head. "I get up in the morning with nothing to do and by nighttime I'm only half done. I wonder some days how I ever had time for work before I retired."

"Hmm," I say, sitting deep into the sofa, an aunt on each side of me. "Every time I smell the turkey, I salivate like . . . what's his name's dog."

Bo says, "Does Pavlov ring a bell?"

I read once that catecholamine is released when a person laughs. The hormone speeds blood flow and healing. I probably have very speedy blood these days; I laugh a lot around Bo.

Before, I often felt that I was missing life, that life was happening in some other place and I couldn't get there in time for it. And if by some quirk I was in the right place at the right time, I still felt I was not included. Lately, wherever I find myself feels like the center of the universe.

The one difference is that I've learned how to be on my own, and the more comfortable I am alone, the more comfortable I am with others. Wherever I am—hiking or skiing in the hills, shelving at the bookstore, watching old movies on the sofa with Bo—I am convinced nowhere else is better. Even sitting here in lazy silence watching Bo caress Hazer into a swoon, with this family.

Scrawny, bow-legged O.C. hunches alertly on his chair as if he were sitting his horse in a hailstorm. He's got Bo's smile— all teeth and cheek creases—though not his grandson's larger build. A word like *cayuse* pops to mind when I look at O.C. Then there are the aunts. Once I ran into the two of them shopping on the square. We stood on the sidewalk talking and a man stopped to ask where to find the nearest barber. Maizie said, "At Shari's, for only fifteen dollars, you can get a haircut and a blow job."

"Oh?" The gentleman looked surprised . . . and interested.

Violet leaned over and said, "She means a blow dry."

"Oh," he said, his voice dropping as the full realization of his loss occurred to him.

Violet is not so with it herself. I followed the two of them into the drugstore that day to cast my vote for which pair of sunglasses looked better on Violet. She wondered if the glasses were designed for men or women and hollered over to the lady behind the cash register, "These sunglasses are bisexual, aren't they?"

In a very short time I've come to care about all of them and I'm pleased to be included in their holiday gathering. Caro and Dickie are spending the holidays at another of their homes near Charlotte Amalie in the Virgin Islands. I was invited there, too, but I've made the right choice.

We all talk a while longer as the fire spangles the tree ornaments. Then the aunts rise from the sofa to carry in the food, and I follow to help them; the men wait to be called.

During dinner I learn new things about Bo. For one, he takes a flashlight when he visits New York City, realizing the only thing he couldn't handle on his own would be a city-wide power outage. That kind of thinking—a Swiss army knife response to life—comes perhaps from being raised in Wyoming, where, self-sufficiency determines survival and happiness. Also, I learn that Bo shovels his backyard free of snow in early spring; he can't wait throughout the long melt to see the first blades of grass. And as a child Bo sculpted armies of small snowmen in the pasture and played ongoing games of war for days, sometimes weeks.

Then O.C. teaches me helpful hints about people's personalities and their body parts. Small ears on a person means they are ungenerous, tend to be selfish. A space between the teeth means they are: "Uh, what would you say . . . kind of pushy, tend to be sociable, and hard to pin down. That fellow Dickie—he's got small ears and a space, both. Watch out for him." I remember Bo warned me about this philosophy of O.C.'s a while back, but to believe it I had to hear it with my own ears—and hope they aren't too small.

Meanwhile, the bronzed turkey diminishes to half a carcass and the mountainous bowls of mashed potatoes, dressing and sweet potatoes, scalloped corn and fruit salad are scooped into shallow valleys.

After dinner, the aunts begin to carry out the used plates and I help them. Bo and his grandfather head for the living room to play gin rummy on the coffee table and listen to CNN. Before leaving the room Bo begins to apologize to me for the segregated routine.

O.C. interrupts. "It's Christmas, by God. For two thousand years, it's been celebrated the same way: Women do their work and men do theirs. And we won't be changing it this year."

"Oh," I say, thinking I should have known, "you two shot the turkey yourselves." Of course, wild Teton turkey. I have a big congratulatory smile on my face.

O.C. looks at Bo. "You bring us a fresh mouth into the family? Your aunts pick her out for you?" He cocks his head hard in my direction and says to Bo, "Tell her how we do it here, son."

Bo recites in a monotone, "The women get up early. The men sleep in. The women slave over hot stoves. The men read newspapers. The women—"

"Ah, hell to you all," O.C. says. He turns to me. "Guess you noticed who fixed the tacos last night?" I nod, recalling both men steaming up Bo's kitchen for an hour while the aunts reminisced to me in the sparsely furnished living room ("Remember when we taught Bartholomew how to sprinkle in the toilet, sister?"). "Right," O.C. says now. "And we cleaned up afterward, too. Tonight it's your turn. Stop your griping and hurry up in here, because next we play hearts back in the dining room."

"Do the women have to lose," I ask, "and let the men win?" The aunts cheer in the background. "Also, like in the last two thousand years," I finish.

"Ah, she's okay," O.C. says with a half grin as he directs Bo out to the living room with a hand on his shoulder.

I glow from O.C.'s benign acceptance of me and my contrary ways.

Maizie washes, I dry, and Violet divides up leftovers and sneaks Hazer, who lies under the table resting her chin on Violet's shoes, pieces of turkey.

"We told Bartholomew that this was a circumstance appropriate for putting the cart before the horse." Maizie sets a rinsed plate in the rack for me to dry. The two have a way of starting in the middle of a conversation, and I always feel I've been daydreaming and missed the beginning.

"We did," Violet agrees. "We said, 'There's your answer for Suzannah.'" Violet digs out every last trace of stuffing from the turkey and heaps it into three plastic bags: one for O.C., one for her and Maizie, and another for Bo and me.

I wonder what they know about Bo and me and, more particularly, what they are talking about right now. "Answer to what? What did Bo ask you?"

"You know men. They don't come out and ask anything," Violet says. "We just told Bo, 'You act like it already is, then pretty soon it will be.' And here you are." She smiles exultantly at me and directs a greasy fling of her fingers my way as if she were a magician and I were a flock of purple doves she manifested from the turkey cavity.

"That's how Bartholomew learns. Begins at the end, works to the beginning."

If anybody put the cart before the horse, I guess Bo and I did from the start. I picture Bo's face surrounded by the folds of my shower curtain last spring as he checked my bare thighs for blood before we hardly knew each other. And if the aunts are offering a metaphor for tearing his ranch apart before readying himself to live as an artist, that works, too.

"Nowadays," I say, "they'd call that *behavioral dyslexia* or something." Bo's family is such a mess, I notice terms from psychology 101 just freely leap to my tongue whenever I am discussing one member with another.

Violet picks up on my theme. "And fund a special school for the *directionally disadvantaged*."

Maizie tosses a handful of silverware into the rack. "We'd get government aid and special parking for the *spatially impaired*. The *invertedly challenged*."

"Born feet-first—just what you'd expect," says Violet.

About the time I decide Maizie is Bo's birth mother, because she seems perhaps a bit more nutty, and I reason that is accounted for by her actually giving birth and carrying the full load of the secret rather than just being an accomplice, Violet offers a mother's particular perspective, and I switch sides.

"The *sequentially disabled*," Maizie says.

"*Serially afflicted. Consecutively dysfunctional. Successively dis . . .*" I can't think of any more.

Bo pops his head in to check on how well I'm coping with the segregation of chores; hearing our laughter, he rests a shoulder against the doorjamb. "This hilarity has to do with me, doesn't it?"

Bo leans into the steering wheel. We are inching along the highway in whiteout conditions. Once we left Violet's house in town and hit open road, wind complicated the heavy snowfall that began just as we were packing up our Christmas-dinner leftovers. No other tire tracks are visible on the snowy pavement, no lights ahead or behind us. Since this is the only road north out of town, it feels eerie, as if everybody got word the world was coming to an end, except us.

"But, Bo, didn't you ever see your aunts naked?" I ask this as if the private mystery solving inside my head has involved him all along. "Ever look for stretch marks? Maybe one of them nursed you."

"They both tell stories about nursing, and they both have white, stretchy tracings across their hips. Violet has saggier breasts, but Maizie has small gathers around her navel. I know, because when I was little, we'd soak nude in the Boiling River. Drive the few hours up to Yellowstone at four in the morning with breakfast in our picnic basket."

I see by the dashboard lights that he's smiling at the memory. Clearly, his childhood was rich and loving. Listening to Bo makes me believe we should all have two mothers. Rather than being a hotbed for psychic disorder, for him the maternal duality evoked a double umbilical cord of nourishment and security.

Those two. Are they crazy, eccentric old ladies? Or just having fun? Sporting their silly selves like they once sported on the rocks inside the steamy breezes of the hot springs in Yellowstone? Or perhaps it is like the theory I carry about my own mother: seemingly harmless personality traits that have exaggerated over the decades into a form of insanity. Bo said once that calling each other *sister* began when the aunts were making fun of a family in town who referred to one another by their titles instead of their names: Tell brother we're ready for dinner, and get sister in here, too. The aunts thought it was hokey and very funny to emulate. Along the way that part got forgotten, and now they sound quite serious calling each other sister, just as serious as they sound calling each other Bo's mother.

"Why won't they *tell* you?" I ask Bo, frustrated by the secret.

"They probably would."

"What?" I'm stunned. My curiosity has peaked to a knife point inside my skull; I assumed his curiosity was a longtime festering wound.

"They said to ask when I got older."

"And you never have?" I can't believe this.

"How can I do that? The older I get, the more I become aware of what they have done for each other and for me. I cannot devalue one of them because of what is now a technicality. What's nine months compared to almost forty years?"

"You're right." I sigh with the effort of raising my viewpoint to match Bo's loving perspective. Then get pricked by the mystery of it all again and add, "I guess."

Finally we have company on the road; up ahead two sets of pink dots stain the dense snowfall, one set above another; the two cars must be approaching a hill.

I think of my friend in Findlay who was adopted as an

infant and the fact was kept from her until recently. She feels her entire foundation, as she knew it, has shifted beneath her. But I acknowledge a difference here. We are not talking about a different culture, family history, genetic makeup. Bo knows his mother. Was, in fact, mothered by her.

"Since I was a kid, I've told most people that I do know, but have sworn never to tell." Bo laughs beside me in the dark. "Because I've never told, everybody trusts me with their secrets. I know the damnedest stuff."

"What?" I grin with encouragement.

"Can't tell." Bo doesn't even smirk; he's easy with his dark burdens. "Glad to see we have a couple cars to follow now. This stuff is getting serious."

I watch the two sets of taillights and try to remember such a long incline on the way home. These streams of snowfall shining into the cones of our headlights, like prisms, unsettle me. I feel transfixed staring into them.

Bo hunches up closer to the windshield. Visibility grows worse as the snowfall thickens. "I don't get it. One car disappeared. Watch for it down off the road."

This, I remind myself, is why we load Sorel Pacs and shovels into the car even for a drive around the ranch. You never know when you might meet unexpected trouble. And the peanut butter and blankets are because you don't know how long you might have to wait out that trouble.

"Shit," Bo says and at the same time I gasp.

In a momentary clearing of the snowfall, we see that we are smack up against the backside of a truck. We have not been following two sets of taillights on two different cars climbing uphill, but two sets, one above the other, on a truck. The lower set of lights disappeared beneath clumps of snow—the car we thought had gone off the road. Only the higher set above the truck's loading doors—the car we thought was farther up the hill—is visible. We are close enough to the truck to lock bumpers.

My heart thuds so hard I swear the seat is bouncing.

"Hold on, Zann. Hold on."

Bo touches the brakes. The car swims viciously. Rear tires skitter across white glaze. I know Bo is determining our chances of going off the road without rolling. I know they are slim. The greatest percentage of road deaths across Wyoming are caused by rollovers. In these scant moments my future is reduced to becoming part of the lettering on this semi's backside . . . or not. Bo taps the brakes once again. The Suburban fishtails. He controls the swerves, and taps again. We fishtail, but gain distance from the truck. Another tap and we breathe easier. We have space.

"Goddamn stupid," Bo says.

"Who could have guessed?"

"The hill. There's no hill until farther up the road. Shit, my joints feel like fast-melting Jell-O."

I know what he means. I would be incapable of driving. The shock of that pale truck looming suddenly in front of us makes me suspicious of all my senses.

"Talk," Bo says.

What an innovative suggestion from a man. "About what?"

"I don't care . . . your kid . . . Beckett. He's got two mothers himself, doesn't he?"

"Oh, I guess he does." Too unhinged to organize my

thoughts, I babble the story of becoming Beck's second mother. Eventually, my stomach muscles stop quivering, and my breathing smoothes. "How are you doing?" I ask Bo.

"Fine."

As dramatically as the whiteout began, it now ends. The road still feels treacherously slick, but visibility is excellent. The sky prickles with stars, except for a line of small round clouds rising from Sleeping Indian Mountain, right behind the feathers of the headdress, as if the Indian had a hidden pipe and took covert puffs when I looked away.

When Bo pulls up to my cabin, he keeps the engine running while he helps me carry the aunts' food packages to my kitchen table. I follow him back out the door. On the stoop, I say, "Merry Christmas." And I reach up on my toes and kiss him, right on the mouth. Reflexively, Bo's arms come around me. Then I feel him correct himself, and he turns the act into a casual pat on my back as if he is matching my own casual manner. Casual, hah! My deodorant is so sudsed up I fear bubbles will waft out from under my arms.

"Merry Christmas to you," he says.

Back in my warm cabin, I nibble on leftover turkey and gaudy Christmas cookies as I put them away. I feel so sleepy I can hardly take myself to bed.

Yet now that I am lying here, I can't sleep. Maybe it's the adrenaline surge from the frightful drive in the storm or the kiss under the stars. Insomnia is unusual for me, though it's Caro's drug of choice. She sleeps an average of three to four hours a night and jokes that it keeps her thin. She stays up late and reads hardcover trash, usually falling asleep at six when Dickie wakes up. Small families could live on the resale of the books Caro purchases from the bookstore each week.

A close call with death may blur such things, but I can't remember, just now, how I meant to experience life. I can't remember what else there is besides achievement. If I'm not accomplishing something I can report to another, how do I know I've lived the moments of my day? I give up falling asleep and scoot upright and prop my knees. Lamplight syphons amber beads from the old log walls, and I feel high and full of something . . . myself, I think.

The effortless awareness I experience might be exactly what I'm after. Then again it is so effortless, so flowing, I almost seem to miss it. This question plagues me tonight: Am I living my life fully or sleeping through it soundly?

Once, Erik and I made love during a long Sunday afternoon while Beckett napped in his crib. Afterward Erik said to me, "I love you." Those words, at that moment, served to separate him and me. I remember the wash of cool thought that rippled between our oneness, as when one lover moves his warm body at a distance from the other's. His profession of love was discordant, inappropriate for the intensity of union I was experiencing. He threw us back into separation, built a bridge of words where no gulf of space had existed—until his sentiment created one.

So I wonder now if I need to separate myself from the flow of time in order to experience it safely in the same way Erik needed to refrain from submerging himself in the flow of intimacy with me. When I'm caring for Mom, each repetitive question of hers nails me to the clock and its agonizing creep through the day. I never need to evaluate how I used my time at the end of it. I fall with relief and exhaustion to my pillow.

I grew up justifying to my father how I spent my allowance each week, wore through the toes of my socks, used my free time. I might remember I am venturing into a different realm of values by pursuing a creative field and choosing to live in the place I do.

nineteen

n February North American biologists monitor hibernating bears. They crawl into the dens and stick rectal thermometers into the sleeping bears to get a quick reading on their metabolism. Quick, because bears rouse easily this time of year, and they are not happy about the waking or the method used.

Bo reads the bear story out loud from the Sunday *Casper Star* while sitting on the other end of the sofa from me. Out the window snow is falling again. This was fun in November, but by February it's getting old.

"There's a grizzly job," he says.

I laugh and tell him about the hotel owner in Bear Claw, Wyoming, from the section I'm reading. Photographs show walls and walls covered with mounted animals from all over the planet.

Bo says, "I know that guy, Gardiner Finch. He's a serial killer."

"What?"

"He's got more dead animals in that hotel than I can stomach. You should try to eat in his restaurant with all that carnage on the walls." Bo turns the page and refolds his section of newspaper. "He should be stopped."

Interesting words from a hunting guide. Bo has been in the business off and on for most his adult life. He took Dickie and Caro and some of their wealthy friends out last fall. Dickie hung the mounted elk head in his foyer and had salami made to send as business gifts. "What makes the hotel owner different than you?"

"Not a thing, other than the size of our egos."

I look out the window over the top of my paper, and I swear there are times when the snow doesn't fall in Wyoming—it just goes blowing by. Right now thick lines of snow are streaming past my window, as horizontally as the lines of print I'm reading. It's thickening by the second and suddenly the butte outside my window disappears. Still, this is a good sign. The earth here is warming. No more forty-below-zero days. This kind of snowfall doesn't occur during frigid temperatures. We have a long time to go before winter's end, but the worst is over.

As I watch the storm blow in, I feel as if I met a challenge in surviving January in Jackson Hole. Bitterly cold short days, deeply frozen long nights. During January it snowed without a cloud in the sky—orographic snow. The cold temperature pulled moisture upward to become fog, which crystallized and fell in flakes. When my own breathing produced snowfall, I worried I had chosen the wrong place to call home.

I alert Bo to the storm. Then I say, "My first joke as a child was about winter. A play on words. My mother huddled into her red wool coat as we waited for a bus in downtown Cincinnati and said, 'Brrr.' I said, 'It's burry cold, isn't it, Momma?' I was three."

"You were an adorable child." Bo gets up and heads toward the kitchen.

"That was my point," I call after him.

We're a bit dopey. We skied all day and are stupidly tired. I'm more tired than Bo—I fall often. It takes incredible energy to be a poor skier. Today I skied slopes at the ski village I'd normally be afraid to scoot down on my butt. Following close behind Bo, I felt I was inside the magnetic circle of his expertise and somehow had more courage and skill than on my own. We had fun, but Bo has seemed out of sorts all day.

He hollers now from the kitchen, "You never have any goddamn ketchup."

"I don't like ketchup," I holler back.

"Yeah, well, I do and I'd appreciate some around here once in a while."

I get up and answer from the kitchen doorway. "So divorce me."

"Go to hell."

"Go yourself."

Bo tosses his eyes sideways like stones and they land on my face. "I'm a jerk. Sorry."

"What's up?"

"Caro's brother is back in town."

"Again?"

"Again." He looks at me as if hoping I'll name his difficulty.

"Counting her money?"

"Snowmobiling. I lent them a couple of mine." He wipes a hand down his face. "I'm heading home, Zann. I'm taking this bologna to go with my ketchup, okay? I'll come over in the morning and we'll get that garbage disposal installed."

A Cowboy Junkies tape blares in the kitchen. Bo and I have our heads stuck beneath the kitchen sink—Bo, holding the flashlight once again, me, unscrewing the slip nut once again. At our feet lies the new garbage disposal I've been saving for since Christmas.

Suddenly, "Blue Moon" slashes to silence and Caro's voice says, "Is this a special ritual with you two? Honestly, if you'd just come out of the closet with your sexual interest in each other, Suzannah wouldn't need to stuff banana peels down the drain and, Bo, you could just buy a bottle of Drāno to fix this sink like everybody else does."

"Hello, Caro," I say, a deliberate yawn in my voice to cover up my share of the guilt she so aptly describes. My pleasure at lying shoulder to shoulder with Bo in the semidark, "Blue Moon" weeping in the background, thrives on being a secret thing, and I hate her a little bit right now for dragging it through her eutrophic pond of a mind. Sometimes Caro's intuitiveness is irksome.

Bo stays put, grabs the retainer ring, locknut, and washers before they fall on top of me. "How the hell can we do that, Caro, with you popping in unannounced all the time?" He responds with real venom in his voice. "Just about the time we zip out of our snowmobile suits and head for the bedroom, dropping our underwear behind us, you come walking in and catch us."

What? My head swivels toward Bo. What? From where I'm lying, I can see the ceiling through the drain hole; I wish Caro would bend over the sink so I could see her reaction to Bo's words. Bo scrapes off old sealant around the drain with a screwdriver as intently as any plumber taking refuge under a sink to announce his forty-dollar hourly wage.

"I'm leaving," Caro says.

"Do that, Caro. Leave. Get yourself some help."

"I don't need any *help*, thank you."

"No, wait," I butt in. "I'll leave." I scoot out from inside the cupboard, knocking over the flashlight. I set it back upright to shine a small moon on the black painted sink bottom. Bo chips away at old putty. I get to my feet.

"I need you down here, Suzannah." Bo sounds like somebody's father.

"Caro can help."

"Caro can't do anything but fuck people."

"Bo," I warn, "don't do this."

He says, "I'm dealing with this stinking mess right now."

I'm talking about addressing Caro like this in front of me, but he must think I'm talking about the garbage disposal. I start to explain, but he overrides my attempt.

"Caro, you fuck your brother. I think you should see a therapist."

"I saw a therapist. I fucked him, too."

"Caro . . . I can't manage this." Bo's arms drop; he crawls out from beneath the sink. "I just want to hurt you, and that's not right."

I lean over and take the screwdriver out of Bo's loose grip even though he looks fully defeated, not at all ready to hurt someone. He sits on the floor with his back against the center board, where the cupboard doors latch.

"You can get help with this," he says, but doesn't look up at Caro, just down between his propped knees to where his empty hands dangle.

"You walked in on us," Caro says.

"Yes."

A long, shapeless pause spreads. I am as immobile as either of them. I feel sick to my stomach and my legs shake. I can't imagine how Bo and Caro can possibly discuss this. Like hiking across the slope of a boulder field during earth tremors, each footfall might dislodge crushing rock and hurl the two of them downhill.

Still keeping his eyes cast down, Bo says, "I came over to drop off a new windscreen for the older snow machine and to adjust the throttles for you. I thought you were waiting till the afternoon to go out. I came in from the garage. When I saw the machines were snowy already, I opened the door to holler hello. Your helmets and gloves were strewn on the hallway floor. . . . I don't know. I—"

"You snuck up on us."

"I just didn't move away right off. Something has seemed so wrong all along."

"And you've decided I'm fucking my brother."

"That's what I heard." Bo looks up at Caro now, full of sorrow.

"You jerk. You fucking *crybaby* jerk." Caro dips low to borrow this insult from O.C.

"I don't have a right to be angry," Bo says. "I should feel worried for you."

"Oh, you have a right to be angry," Caro sneers. She folds her arms and glares accusingly at Bo, still on the floor.

I counsel myself: About now, you should move out of here. It's not like you are required to be in the room. Stalling, I argue back: But surely I am not expected to leave the house. The wind is up; whiteouts are brewing. I urge myself: At least go into the other room.

I walk out of the kitchen and into the living room and stand at the far window, looking out. I feel as if I'm at the scene of a terrible accident and, though splattered by blood, have decided not to get involved. I feel sorry for everybody—Bo, Caro, Caro's brother. I want to overhear what is said, hoping they will discover a familiar sign along the way that will point the way home for them all.

Bo breaks the gap of silence. "Well, I *am* angry, Caro. I've been lied to." Bo sounds as if he's getting to his feet as he speaks. "You're *sick*, I keep telling myself, but I'm goddamn furious anyway."

"He's not my brother."

"Sure."

"He's not."

"Go see somebody, Caro. A therapist."

"I didn't lie about *that* part; I did fuck my therapist. My last two, in fact."

"Caro, please . . . get the hell out of here." Bo sounds disgusted and weary and forlorn.

"Benj is my ex-husband."

"You're lying. Even Dickie told me. He's your brother."

"Dickie *thinks* he's my brother. I was still living with Benjamin when Dickie and I met. I introduced him as my brother.

Benj and I quietly divorced right away, and soon after that, I married old Dickie." By the sound of her voice, Caro is feeling cocky. A kitchen chair scrapes across the linoleum. "Find me a drink and I'll tell you a story."

"Just the story, Caro."

I picture the two of them in a stare-down. At the window, I shiver from the shards of cold air that shatter the warmth surrounding the woodstove.

"Start," Bo says.

"Can't you at least sit down?"

"Start."

"I don't *owe* you this story. Just thought you might enjoy it."

"You owe me. Start."

"I don't owe you cow cum. You were never in love with me. You loved yourself around me, and around Dickie. Don't act like you have the monopoly on pure feeling here, Bo. You don't. You were enjoying your John Wayne image. *And,* in the beginning, you fucked a rich man's wife practically in front of his face. That usually gets the most jaded men aroused."

"Caro, I'm warning you . . . I've just about had it."

"You're too curious to kick me out without hearing the rest of my story. Get me a drink."

"I know the rest of your story. You dumped dirt-poor Benjamin and hooked rich Dickie. Not such an original plot."

Now crammed tight into the sofa corner farthest from the kitchen in my attempt to hear without the guilt of overtly eavesdropping, I wonder why Caro is driven to explain herself to Bo. She does only what benefits her and has never shown the need to bare her soul or her history. In my anxiety I push back my cuticles with a thumbnail as I imagine Bo and Caro glaring at each other across my kitchen.

"Here's the thing," Caro finally says. "I don't want Dickie to know Benj is my ex-husband. I need your promise that you won't tell him."

"I promise nothing."

"I'll back Crybaby Ranch in return for that and for your promise that you won't let Benj know about you and me."

"Your extramarital affairs aren't going to shock an old ex like Benj. Not one dumped the same way."

"Benj was not dumped."

"I don't get you."

"Benj and I agreed that I would marry Dickie for a couple years. In fact, Benj just parted from his last wife."

My heart sinks for Bo. Silence in the kitchen again. I know Caro is sitting in Bo's usual seat. From the sound of Bo's voice, I picture him leaning his hips against the sink. Arms tightly folded, to guess by his defensive tone.

"*Rich* wife?" Bo asks. He's figured something out. I'm not caught up. I feel left out suddenly, as if part of the story were scribbled on a napkin and shoved mutely across the table for Bo's eyes only.

"Right. Very rich. Almost as rich as Dickie."

"And Benjamin got a hefty settlement."

"Right, again."

Bo asks, "And now?"

"Now it's my turn."

Another silence. I feel as if I'm weighed down with emotion, emotion rightfully belonging to Bo. And Bo, knowing I'm in the living room feeling his weighted sadness, his own mind unencumbered with emotion, can dart ahead, flashing light into the dusky seams of Caro's life.

"So Benj has come to Wyoming to try to convince you to divorce Dickie."

"God. I thought you were with me here." Caro sighs dramatically. "Benj doesn't *have* to convince me. That was our plan. Marry poor, divorce rich, and do it in two years or less. We're a bit off schedule. It'll be three years in April."

I let out an audible gasp. The sofa springs screech as I lurch to my knees and face the kitchen door in my shock. An arrangement. I hate her. I hate her. The screwdriver is lying beside me and I pick it up. I'll take it back in to Bo. I'll offer to help cover up the bloody evidence. The horror of that image shocks me, and I toss the screwdriver to the other side of the sofa.

"And me?" Bo asks. "What role was I assigned in your scam?"

I hear him getting a glass, running the water faucet. He has needed to turn his back to her. But did Bo forget? The drain pipe has been removed. I listen for splashing on the floor, though thankfully only hear water go into a glass. Does Bo want what most men would: to hear that he bummed up the works? That Caro unexpectedly fell hard for him and neither man can compare? Flashes of Caro and Benj, stripped of their snowmobile suits, would intrude on such hopes. Besides, Caro has admitted that she's only telling him the truth because she wants something from him. She needs Bo's cooperation in keeping Benj's true identity from Dickie, and she needs her romantic games with Bo kept from Benj.

Caro must realize that Bo hopes their earlier affair and

friendship were important to her in some way. She scrapes her chair across the floor. I hear her take steps toward the back door, halt there, and let Bo's need for an answer stretch.

Does Caro know she is playing a dangerous game? The last three years of effort could be sucked down a hole with one slip from one lover.

Way out here in the other room, I feel Bo waiting. Caro has to answer. But how? She can't dismiss Bo and she can't give him any leverage either.

"Bo," she begins, "I don't know. You thought I was better than I really was. I guess I enjoyed that. I know I can't bribe you with backing Crybaby Ranch, and I know that played no part in our times together. But it's just that . . . Benj may as well be my brother: We are kin under it all. I don't like myself as well with him as I have with you, but Benj and I share a lot of history together. He knows who I really am. There's relief in that."

"What about Dickie?" Bo has turned to face Caro again sometime during her answer; his voice carries into the living room clearly, and he sounds strong again.

"Dickie." Caro emits a soft snort. "I'll have to stay with him another year now—or give this deal up altogether. He'll think I'm leaving him for you, and I won't get one red cent." Caro pauses, then drawls out, "So, my beautiful cowboy, you have branded your mark on my life after all. I gambled something for you. Cheered?" she asks almost playfully.

I hear no response from Bo.

Caro continues. "I signed a prenuptial. That's the only condition under which I lose entirely—leaving old Dickie for love or lust of another man. That's why he's so liberal with me, you see. Knows I won't stray *all* that far. He likes to watch, old Dickie does. All the while holding tight to the leash."

How can I find this more sickening than even incest? I ask myself.

"Maybe he'd like to watch you with your brother." Bo sounds repulsed.

Caro barks a short laugh. "That would spruce up an old routine. Unless you blow it up in our faces."

What's Bo going to do? I feel him computing his response.

In a moment he says, "Get out of this valley, don't return, and I won't have the chance."

"Sweetie, you forget." I hear Caro lean against my back door. "You used me as much as I used you. Didn't I provide plenty of excuses to play and not do your work? Isn't that what you needed? Most importantly, didn't I come in handy with your neighbor in there?"

My breathing halts.

"You lied to her, too," Bo says. "She's been a good friend to you."

"Yeah, well. We do what we have to when times are tough. I'd feel worse about it all, but I was used by her as well."

I'm back on my knees again. What the hell does she mean?

Bo says, "I don't follow."

"We're all working our own stuff here. Suzannah was happy to use me to stall whatever was brewing between the two of you—if she was honest about it. You stopped sleeping with me when she moved in." Caro laughs. "But then you got cold feet, didn't you? I've seen a lot of you lately; soon you'd become available to me again. I was looking forward to it."

"You don't know what you're talking about."

"I know exactly what I'm talking about. Now you know my story, and it really isn't all that different from yours and Suzannah's, is it?"

Bo doesn't answer.

Did Caro shrug resignedly? Did she smile at Bo sadly? All I hear is the storm door bounce shut. Then car tires crunch gravel and snow.

I fall with exhaustion to the sofa cushions and bury my face in the maroon serape that's fallen in a heap from the back. Caro's story *is* different from mine and from Bo's. But I have to admit she's right in recognizing a similar pattern. The difference is like the difference between me momentarily flashing rage with a screwdriver in my hand and me carrying out premeditated murder. Still, I feel guilty, I feel used, and I feel in need of a shower. I have been unconsciously in cahoots with her—for her benefit and for my own.

Bo has slung himself over the back of a kitchen chair, head hanging and arms braced low on the seat, when I come into the kitchen behind him. I put my arms around his chest and lay my face against his back. He straightens upward, turns, and holds on to me tightly. His chest throbs with heat and dampness. If he weren't so much bigger than me, I'd rock him.

"I'm too goddamn embarrassed to even look at you."

I pull back and face him. "Don't be. Honest people don't expect dishonesty in others."

"According to Caro, I'm not all that honest. She's right."

"People without morals always like to believe everyone else shares their value system. But I guess she's got my number, too." I'm not at all ready to say anything decent about Caro. I feel tainted by her accusation and angry at her, too.

Bo drops his arms from around me and walks to the kitchen window, keeping his back to me. I begin to pull out lunch stuff from the refrigerator. Leftover roast beef, mustard, horseradish sauce. I don't know what else to do, and it seems Bo has been doing this for me since I arrived here ten months ago, as injured and lost as he looks now.

"Sit," I order him.

Bo minds, and I begin to carve the cold roast into thin slivers. He rests his elbows on the table and leans his forehead on the heels of his palms. "I feel like shit."

He falls silent and I continue to carve the roast. Then Bo says, "At first, I don't know. . . . Caro helped remind me I was an artist. Nobody around here saw me that way. I found it irresistible."

I open a bottle of beer and set it before him, then get the dill pickles out and a bag of potato chips. A sudden thought strikes. Doesn't Caro still need Bo in her life to fool Dickie a while longer? Didn't she practically spell that out?

"I've been so stupid. I've gone against everything I believed in." Bo watches my hands plaster horseradish sauce on a piece of bread. "Right when I meet you. The worst and the best crashing together . . . practically in the same damn week."

"It happens like that for some reason," I say, arrested by the thought. I halt my work and think out loud. "When an opening occurs in a life, both the good and the bad can rush right in." Tessa could probably explain it astrologically. I go to the stove to get the salt and recall all the stories I've heard about how people turn their lives around, become model citizens, and then the cops arrest them for a crime from their past, or a life-threatening accident or illness occurs. Smack on the heels of the good they've just done.

Bo is chipping at the beer label with his thumbnail. "I've lost my instincts. She took me totally by surprise. All along, I never guessed." He speaks as if he were replaying the scene with Caro in his mind and not registering a word I just said. "I've never gone after another man's woman in my life. I was just waiting for you," he accuses.

"There are other ways to wait for a woman. I wasn't ready."

"Are you ready now?"

"Ready?"

"For me."

I glance down to my lunch plate, then look up and say with certainty, "I'm ready."

Bo sets his beer bottle aside and zeros in on my eyes.

Before he can speak, I say, "You need to take time to sort out this deal with Caro. Don't use what we've got between us to distract yourself from that job."

Bo nods. He pushes away from the table and stands. "The best and worst—it's enough to make a grown man head home and . . . I don't know."

"Get drunk?"

"Cry, I think."

twenty

On the chairlift, Bo and I dangle high over snowy slopes, mountain ranges rippling far into the distance, the sky blue as ice. We are traveling on a double lift to the top of Apres Vous in Teton Village, so there is time for sightseeing and reverie. Bo and I hold hands. This is our first day together after spending two weeks apart.

Three ingredients make up the formula for fire: fuel, oxygen, and heat. Remove one of them, the fire is out. I worried about this, about how much a role Caro played in the attraction between Bo and me.

Triangles are inflammable.

Often I am struck with the image of Bo flung over the back of my kitchen chair as Caro's Buick glided past the kitchen window that day, the wind kicked out of him. I found Bo's deeply felt response to the scene with Caro reassuring after Erik's inability to engage in heated emotion.

I twist slightly in the lift and scan the valley floor behind me. Is Caro preparing to leave someone? If so, who will she leave, Benj or Dickie?

Triangles help people engage with one another without needing to come any closer than the third side allows. I know, because Caro was right. I used the device myself for this exact reason. Perhaps we all did.

When I straighten up in my seat, Bo wordlessly points to the slope directly below us where a moose nibbles stems in a clump of aspen. Skiers careen past on each side, unaware of an animal that could stomp the powder out of them.

I smile at Bo. He'd planned to put a woodstove in his studio today so he could start work in there, but he called me instead. He may not follow through on his intentions very well in some areas of his life, but he followed through with me. He has used the past couple weeks to address his issues with Caro before phoning me as he'd promised he would. He said that he'd moved past his anger with Caro, that it wasn't so difficult once he understood who she was, what her goals were. He says he carries as much blame as anyone. Just a bad deal all around.

Bo smiles back to me now and lifts my hand. As slowly and deliciously as if it were my dress and beneath it my lacy slip, Bo removes my ski glove, then my ski-glove liner. It's both silly and erotic, and we acknowledge that with a long, silky stare that erupts in laughter, but that does not halt his heated romancing of my fingers. He pushes up the cuff of my down jacket and exposes my wrist to the snap of cold air. We're probably imitating some Edith Wharton novel or old Bette Davis movie; our laughter acknowledges that, too. Still, this is our own movie, and though the temperature is only eight degrees outside, with a wind chill of minus thirty, my wrist throbs with heat.

Suddenly, I look down and see the disembarking ramp glide past my ski boots.

"Bo, watch out." I make an abrupt decision and leap out of the chair to the packed snow five or six feet below me. I land on my skis, then lose balance and fall on my butt. I'm okay. I know that right away. But what prompted me to do this crazy thing? I'm not the type to leap out into the air, not knowing where I'll land or how. Bo has that kind of confidence and courage. This is exactly what Bo would do. Where is he?

First, I scoot out of the path of oncoming skiers disembarking the proper way on the ramp behind me. I look overhead, and spot Bo still riding the chair. The cable climbs higher, then turns. I see he is headed toward a safety net, a huge blue plastic net. The net drapes the end of the cable just before it takes the empty chairs back down to base. Bo looks wrong up there. He sits primly face forward, legs dangling, and he knows what is coming up. A shrill alarm screeches overhead.

I burst into a kind of nervous laughter. That should be me up there. I am the one that would normally choose to stay put and become entangled by the safety net, triggering alarms and halting the lift for everyone down the line. The attendant, who is sunning himself, jumps up and runs into the hut. The screeching comes to a halt. I watch Bo wrestle with the blue netting. All the people sitting in the stopped lift behind the off ramp watch him also. He has to remove his skis, poking his arms and legs through the holes of the net to get to them, then struggle with the net for capture of his poles. He does all this with patient resignation.

He finally disentangles himself and steps down off the ledge to walk toward me. I am fighting hysterical laughter and losing the battle. I get control of myself. Then the picture of him dangling helplessly from the cable above and heading for the ignominy of the net wipes out my resolve.

Bo takes one look at me collapsed on the ground in a heap of hilarity and says, "Shit." He starts for the slope, hollering over his shoulder that he'll meet me down below. I know he just wants to get away from everyone's staring. The chair still hasn't begun moving.

The lift operator calls, "Hey, you. You hurt or what?" I realize he has been waiting for me to show I can get myself off the ground. Great. I've been laughing so hard, projecting embarrassment onto Bo, I didn't catch on that I, too, was creating a problem. I get upright on my skis and yell back that I'm fine, check my bindings, and push off.

By the time I meet up with Bo at the bottom of Apres Vous, I am finished laughing and Bo is ready to start. He pulls my glove liner and glove out of his inside pocket. "Better keep these beauties covered whenever I'm near heavy machinery," he says, as he puts the liner back on my chilled red hand. "Sexy fingers make me stupid."

By the time Bo pulls into the drive next to my cabin, I am limp from the fullness of our day. Still, I want more. Skiing saps my physical energy while it invigorates the rest of me.

"What do you say we shower and meet here again in a little while?" Bo says.

I feel playful. "Meet here in the driveway?"

"Had another spot in mind." Bo reaches his arms across

to me, forgetting his seat belt, and for a moment his wrestling
with it recalls to my mind the net fiasco, but I keep myself in
line. Once unhooked he looks up and catches a lingering glint
of humor in my eyes.

Bo turns off the ignition and opens his car door.

"What?" I ask.

"Showers can wait. You'll just stand under the hot water
replaying the image of me entangled in that blue net like a
tuna."

"No, I won't," I lie. "Really."

I'm ready for what I think is coming next, but we are building up to something important, Bo and I; I feel its hot breath
fogging my heart. Sometimes it feels so big, I am frightened.
Making love with Bo will add up to more than a night's exchange of pleasure; the commitment of my body to him represents a vast promise of my spirit. I swear I could share a bed
with a stranger more easily just now.

Bo gets out of the Suburban and comes around to my door,
where I sit like a zombie thinking, Now? Right now? I try to
remember which pair of underpants I put on this morning
so I won't become shocked at the sudden sight of them. At
the same time I feel inclined to whip them off so eagerly they
will be nothing but a blur to either of us. Oh, God, I need to
focus.

Bo sets his foot in my opened car door. "Suzannah, here's
how I see it." He leans in closer, crosses his forearms on his
knee. "We got everything going for us but the physical thing.
We're like a table with one leg short, you know? We're wob-
bling, Zann."

"You think?"

"I think we had a bad start, and we're bound to be a little leery of starting off wrong again, but . . . I say let's not wait any longer." He holds out his hand.

I start to shake it, but that's not what he intended.

He turns his palm upward and pulls me gently out of the car.

In the mudroom, Bo takes off his Sorel Pacs and his ski pants. He is wearing jeans beneath them, whereas I have on only insulated ski bibs and beneath those the mysterious panties. Black silk? Could I have had such foresight? Oh, please, oh, please, not the stretchy cotton things, not the faded, threadbare ones that feel so good when I am skiing. Or not the joke panties Tam gave me. I love to ski in those, too, but they're orange and have SPERM WARFARE printed across them. I turn and raise my arms to hang my down jacket on the hook, and Bo comes from behind me, hooks my coat for me, slips his hands beneath my bib straps, and kisses the back of my neck.

He says, "Your hair smells like snow and pine trees." He moves his face around to the other side of my neck. "Like watermelon and Christmas."

It's been so long for me. I haven't shared my body with a man for almost a year. . . . Well, since Bo and I . . . Oh, never mind. I tip my head down so Bo has access to the best parts of my neck. It's all coming back to me, the way it works if you just let it. I turn in Bo's arms and face him. We rub noses, then lightly brush our lips together side to side. Bo kisses the corners of my mouth. He drops small kisses along my bottom lip until I relax my mouth. Then he opens his and we come together. We kiss deep, briny kisses, oceanic kisses, treasure-chest kisses, lost-at-sea kisses, woman-overboard kisses. Bo's chest thuds against my chest, he feels damp beneath his collar where my hands hold him, and I am grateful he is so moved by me.

Once we pull apart I hear his rough-edged breath, as if it's been cut with pinking shears, in my ear. Then he takes my hand and leads me to my bedroom. I start on the panties again, then switch to the sheets. When did I last change them? If my pillowcases smell like dirty hair, I'll die. Shut up, shut up.

Bo pulls me into the room, closes the door behind me and he turns the big old skeleton key, which has been stuck in the keyhole since I bought the place. Teasing me for my earlier reluctance, he holds the key up, smiles, and tucks it into his back Levi's pocket, before swooping down into another kiss with me.

As in a slow-motion waltz, we inch toward my bed. I hear the swish of my ski bibs against his Levi's. I hear us breathing. I hear my heart, his heart. Thoughts have thankfully stopped and I give in to the petals of desire opening within me as Bo lays me down on the bed, slips down the straps of my bibs, eases my turtleneck off, and stretches out beside me.

Bo's kisses begin below my ear, ripple across my shoulder, and move down my arm, down the inside of my elbow, on down to my wrist. He kisses the heel of my palm and uncurls my fingers to kiss me all the way to the tips.

Lying in the center of my palm is the door key.

I lifted it from his back pocket. I don't know why.

Bo sees the key, an inch from his nose, and freezes.

"Zann . . ." He gives up and drops his face down onto the sheet. He rolls his forehead side to side.

I keep meaning to say, Never mind the key. Kiss me more. But the words don't quite make it out. I am almost as surprised as he is to see the key lying in my palm. My instincts are still a puzzle to me; I don't understand their code; I don't have a reason to trust them. As if I'm reaching for a faceted garnet instead of the silver-wrapped onyx I meant to use, my actions sprout from some hidden, silent place that doesn't explain itself till later. An alarm just hums inside me now, as if its battery is not fully charged for a decisive alert.

"Zann," Bo muffles into the bed again. Finally, he raises his face and looks at me. "I suppose we have to talk now." He shakes his head again. "I got to tell you, Zann, I'm not much for talking right now. We've been talking since you moved here."

Before I can respond, the telephone rings. Bo irritably picks up the receiver and hands it to me. I would have let it ring; I don't want to talk to anybody.

"Hello," I say into the phone.

"Let me talk to him," she says back.

Caro has uncanny timing. And nerve.

I hand the phone to Bo, refusing to meet his questioning look. Now I know why I have the key in my hand—I can easily let myself out the bedroom door while Bo talks with his girlfriend.

I wrestle my turtleneck back over my head as I walk into the kitchen. He is not finished with her and I am not finished with myself. And we better Mother, may I three steps back to handholding until we are. I wait on the bench for Bo, sitting with my back against the wall, my hands folded on top of the table. I stare at the geranium on the windowsill and its reflection in the dark glass behind.

She's still here; I feel her. Still a part of my relationship with

Bo; still the third side of the triangle. I was wrong to believe she left without trace.

I hear the bedroom door open. Bo leans against the kitchen doorway, slightly behind me, so that I have to crane my neck if I want to look at him. But I don't want to look at him.

"Sorry, Zann. That shouldn't have happened."

"Which part?" I ask, feeling sarcastic as well as foolish. I've got a cartoon drawing in my head of me tousle headed in bed beside Bo with my shirt off, bare breasts throbbing, while sketched in the next panel he talks on the phone to Caro. She is drawn with towering hair and haughty nostrils, one hand spinning her diamond ear stud.

"Zann," he says, "give me a chance here. It's not like I'm sleeping with Caro. She just keeps calling me with new jobs." I glance at him. He runs his fingers through his hair, then says, "Want to ski up to watch the moon? We do better outside. We can talk when we get there."

I agree. I long for darkness to hide me while I hear what else Bo has to say. His words about Caro have taken me by surprise; my feelings toward them confuse me. We layer gear back on in the mudroom. Bo keeps his cross-country skis in his truck; mine are stuck in the snow beside my back door. Once we are outside, I close the door and reach for my skis. Bo comes up behind me and slips his hands inside the deep pockets on each side of my hip-length Windbreaker. I feel the pressure and warmth of his bare fingers low on my pelvis. I lean my back against him.

He holds me for a while, his cheek beside my ear. "Zann, let's fix this."

I believe that Bo knows me and cares for me enough to do

what is necessary to fix this. I turn my face so we can kiss. Then move away and pull my skis out of the snow, because I also believe that Bo keeps approaching me from behind for some reason I haven't figured out yet; perhaps neither has he.

The Suburban's interior light casts squares of yellow on the snow when Bo opens the rear door and reaches for his skis. Like his downhill skis, his cross-country skis have straw and alfalfa stuck in their bindings from the floor of the truck. He intended all winter to install his ski rack, but never got around to it. There are so many things he hasn't gotten around to in the time I've known him. There's no new sculpture or progress on his artists' retreat. These intentions he allows to slide past him as unheeding as he did the ski ramp this afternoon. Is it really like the aunts said? Does he have to make a big mess first in order to get motivated into action?

I watch him shake his cross-country boots upside down.

"The last straw," I say, plucking a piece from his shoe string.

It occurs to me that if I am the one physically holding off, it is in response to my sense of Bo's own reluctance. He is not any more ready than I was a few months back. Why would he accept jobs from Caro unless it was to give himself time? Leaning on my poles as I insert my boot tip into the binding on my ski, I stop and look at Bo.

"What are you scared of?"

He answers without hesitation. "You're going to change my life."

"We'll change each other. Is that so bad?"

"Let's ski."

The snowy hills gleam against the dark sky. The crescent

moon is a mere thread. Or a wick, perhaps, drawing today's sunlight from within the crystal points of the snowflakes. Earlier, just past sunset as Bo and I were driving back from the village, the Sleeping Indian glowed with a reflected light that seemed to come from deep within itself rather than the setting sun. It kindled the eastern horizon, a benign illumination guarding the valley, like a nightlight in a child's room.

Now warm winds blow from the southwest, pushing up the temperature, and I think of the last chinook in the spring when Bo and I first made love. I stop and yank off the fleece pullover from beneath my Windbreaker, tie it around my waist, and put my jacket back on. Once at our lookout point, we sit on Bo's down vest, with skis and poles stuck upright in the snow beside us. I lean against Bo's chest with a leg of his on each side of me. We are close and alone above the world, accompanied only by the crescent moon and Venus, the planet Native Americans call White Star Woman. Maybe Bo and I will make love after all tonight, in the snow, the chinook winds wrapping our bare limbs, White Star Woman guiding our coming together.

Bo is right. We can work this out better in the outdoors. But he must understand that he has to be clear with me. I can't be manipulated into demonstrating his own emotions. I'm still porous enough from living like that with Erik and my mother that I pick up signals directed my way without my own awareness. I picture the key laying in my palm like a message to me.

"Talk to me, Bo."

"Caro refuses to be dumped—she said so."

"You've been seeing her and talking to her all this time?"

"I've been trying *not* to all this time. It's eerie. She acts as if that conversation in your kitchen didn't take place. She phones constantly."

"You're still scouting livestock for her?"

"I keep telling her to find somebody else."

I am silent. Is this *Fatal Attraction* without the knife, as Bo once called it? Or is this Bo failing to act on his intentions again?

"Why do you think she's acting this way?" I ask.

"If she stops seeing me, Dickie will direct his suspicions toward her brother—I mean, Benj." Bo rests his chin on top of my head. "Hell, I should have told Caro that I'm in love with you. That would have stopped her. I could have told Dickie, too."

A cool pink rage rises from my pelvis. By the time it reaches my chin, I'm on my feet, snapped into my skis, and hissing downslope. Bo does not follow or call after me.

I cannot explain this anger. It burns through me, sizzles pathways sharp as the tracks my skis cut into the softening snow. I reach my cabin, kick out of my skis, and open the back door enough to slip my arm inside and grab my backpack off the hook. I throw myself into my car and head down the driveway.

I believed we both understood the meaning of the connection between us and that we were just biding time till everything played itself out. Till we both grew strong enough to handle what would be a demanding love affair. And then he says, "I should have told Caro I'm in love with you." Of course, he should have told Caro—if he wanted Caro out of his life. And first he should have told me—if he wanted me in his life.

How could I have figured it so wrong?

I drive to the end of the dirt road and hit the highway.

Where the hell am I going? I turn toward Dubois instead of Jackson. I drive fast and angrily, but am alone on the road, so I can get away with it.

Far into the distance I see the first lights. A bar, of course— this is Wyoming. I pull in anyway, though I've never been to a bar alone. But I am not alone. Beside me, like a full-blown entity, is my anger. It just balloons up around me till I feel my air nearly cut off. I wish I could chop it into small manageable pieces, to sort and label; instead, I feel like I should pull out a chair for it as I sit at a small round table one step above the dance floor and order a bottle of Moosehead and a glass.

A small group of musicians play. A few people slow dance. I create chains of wet circles with my sweaty beer glass on the varnished tabletop and try to keep my lips from moving as I scream inside my head, How could he say that to me? How could he speak of love for me with her name wrapped around it, like mud packed around fresh trout?

The waitress brings me another bottle of Moosehead. I don't remember ordering this. When I reach for my backpack to pay her, she mumbles something I can't hear since I am sitting close to the sound system.

I feel thick with anger at Bo and at myself. I knew somewhere inside that the mop-up with Caro was not complete, but I ignored the knowledge. Like Erik, I act one way and feel another. I passionately kiss Bo, while hiding an escape key in my curled fingers. But Bo has been hiding Caro.

I reach for the second bottle of beer and pour half of it into my glass, counseling myself not to drink more so I can drive home safely. Now that I have surfaced to my surroundings, I notice a tingling at the nape of my neck. Without lifting my eyes, I all at once feel self-conscious, as if I am being talked about or watched. I take mental inventory. Cross-country ski boots, bibs—that's not unusual around here. Hair wildly spread across my shoulders, uncombed since morning—that's not unusual around here. So what's the deal?

Finally, I look up. The entire band is swiveled my way, singing Roy Orbison's "Pretty Woman." I turn my head. The bar is two-thirds full, some couples, mostly men, and many are watching for my reaction with slight smiles on their faces. I have missed something big here.

I give my attention to the band. The lead singer is a gorgeous, long-haired blond. Twentysomething, I'd guess. He nods and smiles to me, then ends the song, calls for a break, and heads for my table.

"I'm Deak." He smiles and gives me a chance to tell my name, which I let pass. "Can I sit a minute?"

I shrug. He pulls out a chair and sits. In my head I am putting together the second bottle of beer with the song and the stares.

"I'm thinking this isn't what you had in mind, coming here tonight, but life is circular, you know?" Deak grins. "Full of curves." He leans toward me. "I'll back off if you want."

"No," I say. "It's okay." The distraction of him is a relief. He's pretty, in a masculine way. Turquoise eyes, wavy hair to his shoulders. Looks strong, probably from carrying musical equipment place to place. There is something playful and nice about him. Something clean and straightforward. Young though. Is he going to take a closer look any minute and realize I'm older than he is by a decade or two?

"Can you tell me your name?"

Seems I can. "Suzannah." Seems a smile loosens itself.

"I mean it. You are beautiful." Did he say that once before and I didn't hear? I smile in response and look around the room again. Eyes are still watching us; one set is familiar. It takes me a moment to attach a name. Mick Farlow, Bo's lawyer friend. I haven't encountered him since the barbecue. At the memory, I look again at the table and make chain links with my glass.

"The bastard isn't worth it," Deak says.

I look up at him.

"Give me a shot. I'll be gone singing in some other smoky bar in a few weeks, and by then the son of a bitch will have had some time to set his priorities straight."

"It's not my style," I say. The idea has appeal though, and I laugh a bit to think of being involved in a romance that simple. Not a romance simple enough to fix with a little dash of jealousy, but one that lasts till the lover moves on to some other smoky bar. At the moment that suits me. Brief and uncomplicated. Fun and fast moving. I have been primed for romance since I understood the one with Erik was all in my head.

Deak tells me his group, Your Sister's Cherry, has one more set to play. Then the motel restaurant next door is fixing the band steaks for a late dinner. He'd like it very much if I would join them.

I can't believe I heard the name of his group right. I look toward the bandstand and read the name on one of the drums.

Yep.

I decide two things: One, I will not look shocked and ask about this name. And two, I'll go to dinner. I'll go because I need a rest from myself and because I don't want to go home yet and don't know where else to go. Besides, Bo and I never got around to eating tonight.

I say to Deak, "I would like that." And he orders a third Moosehead for me to sip during the next set.

I am starving. I eat the entire T-bone draped over the sides of my plate. The five guys in the band are hilarious and revved. They don't intend to sleep till the sun comes up. The plan is to drive to Willow Hot Springs after dinner, soak, and smoke a little marijuana. I am invited to join them, along with two other women (who call themselves "girls") who come from the band's hometown, Louisville. Since I grew up across the river in Cincinnati and spent the first couple years there while married to Erik, we might have some places in common.

"Have you ever played the White Horse Inn?" I say.

"The White Horse?" Deak says.

"Right across the Ohio River next to the bridge on the Kentucky side."

"That was torn down; there's a circular high-rise with a revolving restaurant on top now. Not our kind of music."

The bass player says, "My parents used to talk about the White Horse. It's been gone twelve, fifteen years." I think his name is Tom, could be Ron. There's a Don here, too, and an Andy. I'll get them straight later. The girls are Delta and Sandy. Think beach.

Now that I've advertised my age, I may as well come fully out with it. "When I was in high school, it was the place to go for dinner dates."

At least they know Roy Orbison.

twenty-one

Driving home, all I think about is a hot shower to rinse off whatever organisms are mighty enough to survive winter in a Wyoming hot springs. Then I will burrow deep into my down comforter for the night's sleep I missed out on. Though I am tired, I feel rather pleased with myself. I carry a warm glow from my audacious skinny-dipping with a group of musicians who were strangers to me yesterday. I pull into my drive, get out of the car, and stretch at the new day before opening my cabin door.

"What are you doing here?" I blurt. Bo sits at my kitchen table. His Suburban isn't parked in my drive; he must have skied over from his place. "You can't just walk into my cabin whenever you want."

"Since when?" Bo sits up straighter. "Hey." His features harden. "Don't walk in here"—he checks the time with a flick of his eyes to the wall clock—"at *eight* in the morning and accuse *me* of a crime."

I feel like I took him by surprise as much as he surprised me. Maybe he fell asleep at the table.

Bo's eyes get fierce. "You didn't come home, goddamn you."

"That's not your affair." I turn my back on him and walk into the mudroom.

"That's just what I'm talking about," he says, scraping back his chair and following me. "Your *affair*. With a—"

"Go home, Bo."

"A little guitar-plucking shit with hair to his shoulders." Outrage tightens Bo's vocal cords and his voice rises at the end. I'm convinced he fell asleep and is working himself up to reclaim anger that mounted throughout the night while waiting for me to come home. I hold the picture of him pacing and checking the clock till dawn.

I hang up my jacket and, ignoring Bo, head back into the kitchen. He halts me with a hand on my shoulder.

"You *slept* with him." Bo's face flips from anger to injury. "How could you do that?"

I look at his hand on my shoulder much the same way I looked at the slime I brought up from the bottom of Willow Hot Springs on my toe somewhere around four o'clock this morning.

"Why, Suzannah?" Bo dips his face downward to recover himself, then lifts it and tries again, softer this time. "Suzannah, why would you do that?"

I continue to ignore him and bend down and pull off my cross-country boots, tie their laces together, and move away, back into the mudroom, to hang them above the dryer. I rather enjoy Bo's mistaken notion that I slept with Deak. I want to ask how he knows I've been with someone, but I'd have to break my facade of indifference.

"Some dumb-ass kid." Bo gets himself stoked up. "Sleeping with some druggie musician just to—I don't know—get me moving."

I swing around to face him. "Was that my job? To get you moving?" I yell, "Damn you."

I fill with fury. All the years with my mother and Erik and here I am again dealing with yet another person who refuses to be accountable. Same dance, different partners. It's like being with someone who needs emotional potty-training, always wading through unaddressed matters.

"This is it, neighbor. You can stay put running errands for Caro and stalling Crybaby Ranch and letting your grandfather insult the heart of your life all you want, but—"

"I've never let him insult you."

I'm stopped. "I'm talking about your sculpture." We stare at each other. Bo's immediate assumption that I am the heart of his life stirs me. But I can't afford to halt my life in hope that he'll grab hold of his. It's too easy for me to live for other people; I must make the choice to move on.

"Bo." I feel ready to cry. "Bo," I begin again. "I can't be with you. You're not living fully enough for me."

"What the hell are you talking about?"

"You're too content to follow low ground. Like a shallow stream, you just wander where it's easiest. You don't need to stand up and declare yourself and maybe that works for you. Maybe that's your family's way. Your mother doesn't declare herself. Nobody knows who she is. Your grandfather doesn't admit who he is either. And your father—you've never even tried to find out who he is."

"If this has something to do with you shacking up in a sleazy motel room, I'd like to know what." Bo turns away from me, starts making fresh coffee, as if this were any old morning, as if we were just discussing today's skiing conditions.

But I can't stop. The flow of words triggers my thought, instead of the other way around, and I won't know what I'm thinking without voicing my ideas as I hear them unfold.

"Your grandfather dishonors his own creativity, as well as yours. If you let him continue doing that to you, you will get stuck doing the same kind of artwork all your life. Like him you will never move on. You will build the same pieces over and over. And like him you will condemn anyone who does grow in their creativity. What kind of artist retreat will you offer then?"

I take a deep breath. Bo has halted his coffee making and turned to me. I wipe my eyes and shake my head.

"But nobody in your family has taught you to how to stand up for yourself or even suggested to you before that this might be a good thing for you. I think you've gotten some other message about getting along with everybody, not rocking the boat. You've accomplished a lot so far, Bo, but none of it—Crybaby Ranch, your art, your self-worth—will benefit by stopping now. And it seems to me that you have stopped."

Bo shoves the bag of coffee beans away and angrily approaches me standing beside the table. "After Farlow called I came over here and waited for you. I sat here all night *knowing* what you were doing." Bo thumps the tabletop. "You weren't

alone with him, Zannah. I was there with you the whole time."
Bo looks like he could cry himself.

I sit in defeat on the edge of a chair. Bo has finally given up the idea that we'll drink coffee together at the end of this, but he hasn't given up his position of most injured party. He's trying to win something; he's not trying to understand anything. I don't know if he can hear me right now, but I still have things I need to say, to make the feelings clear to myself and to know I've acted responsibly and honestly with him.

"Bo, I fell in love with you as a courageous, creative man taking charge of his life and sculpting it as carefully and soulfully as any piece of art submitted to a gallery. But that's not the man I skied away from last night." I rise from the edge of the chair. "Last night I saw a man who feels indecisive about his future with me, a man not ready to declare himself as an artist or to stand up for his morals with Caro or his self-esteem with anybody. I saw a scared man, a lazy man. And I left."

I go back into the mudroom, grab a clean towel from the shelf over the washer, and tell Bo I'm taking a shower. "I want you to leave."

It's silent in the kitchen. Then I hear Bo come to me as I reach for the bathroom doorknob.

"Look at me," he says, cupping my chin as I begin to turn away from him. He waits until I drag my eyes to his. "I'm your future, Zannah."

I feel a buildup of emotion that is gathering in dammed pools behind my eyes.

Bo releases his hold on my chin and I open the bathroom door.

I turn on the shower, but wait listening at the door, still dressed until I hear Bo leave.

"Zannah," Bo said to me in bed last night, "I want to hold you close, spend the night with my hand on your bare hip."

Then Caro phoned.

Was that really just hours ago?

After a shower and a long midday nap, I drive to the bar. I stand a moment inside the entrance. Right off, I spot Bo, spun around on a stool, his back against the counter and his boots stuck in the aisle. Deak whispers into the microphone, "Suzannah, Suzannah." My name echoes softly throughout the room. "Suzannah, Suzannah." Some people cheer when they follow Deak's gaze and find me here again tonight. I smile broadly at our romance groupies. Deak begins to play "Pretty Woman."

As I walk past Bo, he says loud enough for only me to hear, "Hey, Zannah, want to dance?"

I'm surprised to discover Bo has such a nasty streak. I refuse to look at him. I step over his boots and move toward the music. I sit at the table Deak said he would save. How does the band do this every night? I slept till late afternoon and still I am tired. Thank God I didn't have to work today.

Half a dozen songs later, Bo approaches and leans one-handed on my table, the narrow neck of a Beck's Dark hanging from a circle of forefinger and thumb at his side.

"What the fuck's going on, Zannah? You want me jealous? I'm jealous. Now get rid of the little squirt."

From behind Bo, after signaling his band to continue on without him, Deak has approached. He says now, "You must be Bo. Suzannah told me you're neighbors."

Bo does not move, nor does he speak; he raises his eyebrows at me in accusation, as though I had betrayed an intimate secret: neighbors.

"I'm Deak, Suzannah's . . ." Bo lifts his weight from the table, carefully straightens, and slowly turns toward Deak, challenging him to finish this sentence. Deak smiles into my eyes. "Little squirt," he finishes and offers his right hand to Bo.

"I'll shake to that," Bo says.

Deak returns to the microphone, and Bo drops into a chair. "Shit," Bo says, "he's a decent kid."

Bo never got around to installing a separate meter for my cabin so I could pay my own electric bill. He joked that we would always be wired together. So I say now, "Bo, nothing is different. We're still wired together and you're still welcome at the neighborhood potlucks." I want Bo to experience the inanity of his reaction to Deak so soon after continuing his flirty relationship with Caro.

"You kicked me out."

"I was angry. My boiling point is lower in the mountains."

"I'm not coming back till you dump him."

"So long, then."

Bo is not entirely sober. I should have realized that earlier. He tosses down the rest of his beer, bangs his bottle on the table, and stands. He looks down at me a long moment. For the first time, I see in him a strong resemblance to his grandfather. As Bo walks away, through the bar and out the doors, I recall a time O.C. was visiting the ranch and a veterinary supply salesman drove up and, mistaking him for a ranch hand, said, "Sir, excuse me. Who is your superior?" O.C. spit to the side of himself and said, "The son of a bitch hasn't been born yet." Bo could have said just those words as he stood staring down at me. As far I am concerned, he would be perfectly correct. No one is superior to Bo. If a competition were involved, the matter would be settled.

But Deak is like a cool float in the hotel pool after emerging from the turbulence of the ocean. I imagine I will surrender easily to swimming short laps with him, touching the finite boundaries of our brief future together.

twenty-two

I told Tessa about Deak approaching me in the bar. "I felt so unaware of myself and my surroundings that night, I could have been drooling for all I know. And if I was, Deak was overtly enchanted by it. How do you figure? I'm much older than he is."

"But you look really young," Tessa said. "And you're full of vitality."

I rolled my eyes at her. "You're full of something else. Come on, what's the deal? You hear about younger guys with older women a lot lately."

Tessa said, "Okay then, consider dysfunctional young men as the deepest blessing of middle-aged women and enjoy him."

And I do.

Most nights, Deak and I carry food and drink to his motel room after the final set. We throw back the covers to expose the white expanse of laundered sheets and lay out our food as if we were picnicking on snow. Prop up our pillows and stretch out on the bed. Shoes fly across the room first, next socks, Levi's, and shirts.

The lack of decoration in this motel room puts me in touch with the impersonal places I've kept within myself. Those universal shrines of femininity at which I haven't yet left personal tokens of favor.

My body had been the climbing post of the toddler Beckett, my lap his nesting box. But these leaps of intimacy were claimed without the prerequisite experiences of birth and recognized motherhood, because Delinda was expected any day to claim her child. In the same way sex with Erik was artificially accelerated to parental lovemaking without the leisure and uncertainty of new romance. As if after a proficiency test, the professor registered me in the advanced class.

"A match flame of a romance," Tessa prescribed many months ago, "something you can blow out at will."

It's odd to be mature enough to recognize I am filling in the blanks of my youth, yet still enjoying the process with naive abandon. I bodysurf waves of desire as Deak's mouth opens and nears my breast. I glimpse the edge of a tooth between his lips and feel a surge as the glint of light bounces off it. His touch is all I imagined, my response more than I expected. I am absorbed by this huge physical rush, this pooled awareness of the two of us. The word *desire* repeats itself over and over in my mind, undulating around my head as if it were writhing on a water bed. It's such a sweet word. I am tugged deeper and deeper into its sibilance.

After we eat and make love, I lie in bed and stare at a black-

and-white framed photograph of a moose standing in leafless aspens. Snow hock-high, no shadows, no apparent source of light. At first I didn't like the motel room, how it exhibits a lack of personal taste—anybody's. Now I feel grateful for the way the walls recede from consciousness, even the way TV noises from other rooms seep into our space. It's like eating at a fast-food chain: There is no flavor to object to in this room.

Only years from now am I likely to fully understand the meaning of this brief romance. I am not meant now to do more than drink deeply, swallow whole, laugh, and sleep afterward. I am certain I provide something for Deak as well; after all, he pursued me. And as much as I need his exuberant pursuance, I believe he has needed to win me over. So I give myself to him knowing I am salve to some unseen injury, even while the exercise of my giving is cure to me.

We play doctor.

As Deak sleeps I rise gently from the bed and gather the used plastic forks, the containers, and empty soda bottles. I'm often surprised at Deak's wisdom. He writes most of the group's music, a poet alert to the world around him. Yesterday we spotted an old dried nest beneath the eaves of the bar. Deak pointed to it. "A piñata of wasps," he said. Hummingbirds, he tells me, make a sound as if they were blowing kisses.

As the earth's frost line drives deeper and deeper toward its center at winter's end, and its skin layers with snow and ice and fragrances remain dormant, my body thaws, core outward. My skin melts beneath Deak's skiing fingers and the fragrances of my hair and body steam.

The planet winters and my body summers.

It's written in the small print of our contract that this romance ends with the gig. Yet my experience is larger than my previous assumptions about temporary romance. Larger, too, than an outlet for lust, a good break from the final dreary years with my ex-husband, or even a distraction from the loss of my mother—all remarks made by my coworkers as more and more people spot me sitting at the band's table during sets this past month.

"Thought I'd drop by and check out your new boyfriend."

Though I am completely taken by surprise to hear Caro's voice beneath the band's music, I don't react at all. She stands behind my right shoulder.

"May I sit?"

Without turning to look at her, I push out the chair across from me with my foot.

Standing beside the chair facing Deak, she removes her gloves and coat as languidly as if she were doing a striptease for the band.

"Yum," Caro says once she finally sits down. "They all look juicy as chicken legs. Which one's yours?"

"None of them are mine. I date the lead singer."

"Can I have him when you're done?" She grins. "Just gnaw him down to the bone and toss him my way." She signals the waitress and orders a Scotch, then says, "Just kidding. Three men—I couldn't handle."

"You mean four, don't you?"

"Whatever. Two men are ideal. They balance each other."

"So who are you cutting out?" I think I know the answer, but it wouldn't hurt to hear it from her that Bo is out of her life. I take a sip of beer.

"Benj."

"Benj?" My beer goes down the wrong way. I inhale some of it and cough. I repeat hoarsely, "Benj?"

"He's a loser."

"No. Bo is. I mean, I figured by your standards you would think . . ."

"Bo's going places. If he'd only listen to me. I've got these people back home in Oklahoma who want his sculpture. They're building practically a damn plantation house, with gardens and terraces that go down to the river."

Caro's drink arrives. She shovels items from her deep leather shoulder bag onto the table until she finds a pink plastic tampon holder, one of those that used to come free in the economy-sized box. She pulls its two ends apart and separates a hundred-dollar bill from a roll of others.

"Anyway," she says, dropping her change into her purse bottom, "these people have seen my photos of Bo's work and want a few pieces for the terraces—his new work is stunning. But Bo is so prickly with me lately. I can't get a deal going with him." She scoops handfuls of stuff back into her soft, pouchy bag. Her final load includes a pair of purple silk underpants. "I was hoping you'd have some ideas." She takes a sip of her drink and looks expectantly over the top of her glass.

My head is tipped as I listen to Caro talk—a robin listening for a worm. Her purposes are always self-serving. I say, "He and I haven't seen each other for several weeks."

"Oh, right. That's one reason I'm here. I have orders to tell you that I know Bo is in love with you . . . cha-cha-cha. If I fulfill this little duty, Bo will not tell Dickie. Our deal."

Caro takes another sip, then looks around. Her gaze ends

with the band. "God, your singer really is darling. I know you won't tell me how he is in bed."

"You know me pretty well."

"I know you can help me out with Bo, if you want."

"Me?" I've got the fingers of both hands splayed across my chest. Is she a lunatic? "Caro, I don't think so."

"Listen, Bo can get all the work he wants. These people have houses all over the world. And friends. He just needs to be spurred." Caro pokes at her ice cubes with a coral-painted fingernail. "That's the difference between Bo and Dickie. Bo has trouble getting started with work. Dickie can't stop. Dickie needs to be lassoed and dragged in the dirt every once in a while just to get his attention. But with Bo you have to keep your rowels spinning."

"Rowels?"

"Little pinwheel deals? On the spurs?"

I tip my chin up as I catch on. I am dying to hear about Bo's new work, but I'm afraid my need to know is too apparent. To cover up I say, "And Dickie dragged in the dirt?"

"That's how I get his attention. For instance, I'll tell Dickie about Benj."

"You will? Everything?"

"He'll love it. He comes out the winner."

"You're kidding."

"If I don't get a ring out of it, I'll eat that mangy vest you're wearing."

I look down. I'm wearing an old wool vest with four odd pockets across the front that Deak passed on to me because I took such a fancy to it, like O.C.'s beat-up hat.

"We'll probably go someplace for a second honeymoon."

"And Bo? How's he feel about this?" I just need to say his name.

"You two will end up together," Caro flutters her fingers dismissively at Deak. "Eventually. But Dickie doesn't need to find out."

"Find out. He has known about you and Bo for months."

"Find out that there's *no* me and Bo."

"You want Dickie to think . . . ?"

"I see why you hooked up with a kid." Caro arches her eyebrows. "Just your mental pace. Yes, I want Dickie to think Bo and I are still an item."

"But why?" I hope I'm not shouting.

"Never mind. It works for us. All I ask is that you don't set Dickie straight. I mean, go ahead and deny it. He'll just think you're stupid or something." Another finger flutter. "Just don't give me away. Oh, hell, you never would. You're as bad as Bo. Two of a kind."

As bad as Bo. Two of a kind. Caro thinks she's insulted me. Isn't it just like her to ask for a favor and try to insult me at the same time? Oh, boy, and she's not leaving Dickie. She's not leaving Jackson Hole, and she's not going back to Oklahoma. Just to be sure I'm stuck with her for life, I ask, "You're not leaving Dickie? Not ever?"

"How could I do better than Dickie?"

While Deak sleeps in the motel room, I run hot water into the tub, spilling a capful of his shampoo in to make bubbles. Earlier, about three a.m., Deak and I skied. Just the two of us silently swishing the unplowed road to Jenny Lake at the base of the Tetons. Most of our times together are in the middle of the night when Deak's work is done and his energy high.

I squeeze the water out of my washcloth above my stomach and watch it make rivers down my skin, then dip the cloth to soak up more water. I'm not entirely clear why I'm not bored out of my mind after six weeks with Deak. Instead, I glow. I chime. I can't wipe the grin off my face. Deak is good for me. Maybe Deak is me. Some young and playful maleness I'm only now allowing expression. Maybe I am Deak's mature female self, accepting, approving. And maybe I've just been hanging around Tessa too long to come up with such theories.

Part of me finds relief in the distraction of Deak; part of me feels a building anxiety about not calling home to check on my mother. I don't work with my beads and have little time for the solitude I've come to treasure. One of these days I am going to miss my self.

Soon birds will begin to stir in this last hour of darkness. I yank on the plug chain, stand, and reach for a towel. Like punctuation throughout my days and my nights, I think of Bo. As I tuck myself into my side of the motel bed, I recall the truck grinding up the ranch road, past my cabin, yesterday. Its bed was loaded down with peeled logs. Bo is beginning work on Crybaby Ranch.

As Deak shifts position and groans into deeper sleep, I pick through the magazines on the floor beside the bed and browse an article in *Outside* comparing river sandals. Maybe I'll buy a pair for the summer. I hear they are easy to stand in for long hours at the bookstore. Deak burrows deeper into the covers; his head disappears.

I lift Deak's wrist, lying alongside my hip, and look at his watch. Almost noon. I sit up higher on my pillows, bend my knees and prop the magazine against them for some intentional reading on hiking trails in Hawaii.

Deak shifts beneath the covers. He is lying on his stomach halfway down the bed like a dog might. Now I feel his breath between my legs. Now his tongue.

This makes me think of an old cartoon in which a bride-to-be was addressing envelopes for her wedding invitations while propped up on the sofa just as I am in bed. When she needed an envelope licked, she lowered it between her legs for her future husband to include in his work.

I have no envelopes for Deak to lick and wouldn't want to distract him from his main project if I did, but I continue reading.

In Hawaii you can hike cloud forests, wet, tree-covered slopes. Colorfully feathered birds flit among exotic varieties of moist, broad-leafed plants, like darts of light, like quick tongues. Deep into the dark foliage a distant waterfall crashes to earth from a high, craggy cliff. As you walk closer the force of its gushing vibrates the soles of your feet, travels up your thighs, and reverberates inside you as if your skin covers a drum. A throbbing drum.

Abruptly, I throw the magazine in the air and scoot down lower on the bed.

The band rehearses for another hour this afternoon; then Deak and I will drive into town for an early dinner. Meanwhile, I sit at the bar sipping apple juice while Delta sits next to me talking about her work as a florist back in Louisville. She says someday she and Don, the bass player, are going back to Kentucky to get married and open their own flower shop. I had hoped to write in my journal during the wait; instead I am hearing so many details about flower arranging, I feel as if I'm being trained as a future employee. As O.C. said about one of the aunts: "She talks so much she gets chin splints."

"Always use odd numbers of flowers when they're the same kind or color," Delta says.

I check the Bud Dry clock above the bar. STAGGER UP FOR ANOTHER. How can the company's conscience allow that kind of promotion? Beyond Delta two construction workers tell a third about the house they're working on. "You could set up six yurts in the living room."

"Darker colors below and bigger blossoms below. Little blossoms or buds at the top, along with your lighter shades." Delta's hands describe a bouffant spray that she imagines takes up the width of the bar top.

On the other side of me, at the end of the bar, two old ranchers are sitting with beers, talking about a friend hospitalized down in Denver. "They cut into him and found something the size of a melon in there."

"It's all them doughnuts Harold ate ever morning. You know he had himself two, three ever'day over at the Sip 'N' Dunk. What they found in there was a dough ball."

"Sixty years of eating them doughnuts sure would make a good-sized dough ball. He don't weigh but a hundred and ninety or so now."

"Must have been the dough ball. He sure weighed more than that before he headed to Denver."

"Lots of greens in the vase," says Delta, "then stick in flowers. Flowers should be, oh, about two and a half times taller than the container."

"I better hold back on the doughnuts myself. I don't need *me* no dough ball."

"You want your roses to bloom, take the guard petals off. And always make fresh cuts on the stems."

Finally, Deak finishes with the group. We push through the gloom of the bar and climb into my Subaru. Soon we are acting giddy as schoolkids released into sunshine. Deak is slumped low in the passenger seat as we approach a full view of the Tetons. "They're big," he says.

"Yep," I agree. "And majestic. That's what they could have named them instead of the Tetons. The Majestics."

Deak says, "That's already been taken. It's the name of a rock group."

"That's what this is, a rock group."

We laugh.

I'm tired of always smelling cigarette smoke in my clothes and my hair; I roll down the window partway in hopes of getting rid of it. As a matter of fact, I'm tired of the bar. Period. The smells, the aimlessness of the people, the stupid talk. That reminds me of my afternoon eavesdropping, and I tell Deak about the dough ball.

Dirty piles of snow are exposed along the roadside like winter's discarded long underwear. Like diapers sopping up the runoff. The thaw begins.

Though skiing felt like trying to maneuver in mashed potatoes, I toured alone to the hot springs this morning and spotted the first signs of spring. Spotty patches of snow and brown melted areas made the slopes beside the trail look like the rumps of Appaloosa ponies. Swans floated like feathered chunks of ice between the snowy banks of a pond.

I start to tell Deak, but I see that he's fallen asleep.

A cliff rose several stories high beside the pond, and a ram, curled horns sketching commas in the stretch of blue sky behind him, surveyed the rocky drop below. I stabbed my poles into the snow, stopping to watch the bighorn, and suddenly we locked eyes. His awareness of me was a vibrating line of attention between us. I felt as though I was in the presence of a good listener, one whose full reception of me mirrored back a greater actuality of myself, as when I'm talking to Bo. The ram and I stared at each other long moments. I felt like Bambi in the presence of the Great Stag of the Forest: "He stopped and looked at me."

While I drive I recall the applause of the river rock as snowmelt rushed shallowly in the creek bed. A flock of geese flew over, sounding like a pack of bloodhounds treeing the sun. Spring, by Rocky Mountain standards, is almost here.

"It's time you call Bo."

"What? My God, I thought you were sleeping." I don't know what made me jump the most: the sound of Deak's voice or the sound of Bo's name.

"I'm leaving in a couple days now."

"I know."

"Well, you better patch things up with him before I go."

"Why would I do that?"

"I mean it, Suzannah. You miss him, don't you?"

"I like being with you."

"I know that. But call him."

NIGHT MAIL

MAY 15–21

When robins are incubating eggs and Canada geese reach
their peak of hatching, the first arrow leaf balsamroot and
Nelson's larkspur bloom. You can start looking for morels when
cottonwoods start to green. Cow moose are giving birth to calves
when common snipe are incubating eggs. Ground squirrels are
giving birth, young badgers can be seen near den entrances.
Calliope hummingbirds are mating. Goshawks are laying
eggs, red-tailed hawk eggs are hatching, and mourning cloak
butterflies are relatively more numerous.

For Everything There Is a Season
—Frank C. Craighead, Jr.

twenty-three

This morning another truck loaded with logs chugged past my cabin. I felt an urge to chase after it, barking gleefully at its rear tires like an excited dog. Just a short hike along the butte, through the sage and aspens, I can see stacks of new lumber glistening in view of the main ranch house and barns. Often during the past two weeks, since my farewell dinner with Deak, I sat high on a slope and watched smoke curl out of Bo's studio chimney down below, as if I were reading a coded message from the Vatican. Except this smoke doesn't announce the naming of a pope, but rather announces the presence of an artist at work. Something has shifted with Bo, and I long to participate in the pump of energy I feel emanating from him now.

I haven't acted on my promise to Deak that I would call Bo. An innocence resides in men—men like Deak and Bo anyway—that is both endearing and irksome. Relationships are hardly ever as simple as they'd like to believe. But it is true that with Deak, pleasure rippled through the shallow waters of my body but did not reach the deep places of my heart. I miss Bo.

I have enjoyed my time alone. I've resumed my schedule, caught up on my life, and read new spring releases, which I TROUT from the bookstore—our shorthand for "transferring out" books off the shelves. I haven't called home yet; guilt blunts the urgency I feel to connect with my parents.

I remember Bo answers the phone as if he knows he will like whoever is calling him—not *Hello* as a question with uncertainty in his voice, like I do. Though quite late for making a call, I stand beside the phone daring myself.

I pick up the receiver and dial his number. My chest thuds raucously; if I were wearing beads, they'd rattle. The phone rings and rings again. Then Bo answers.

"Hello," he says.

I hang up. Arms weak, legs shaky.

He says *Hello*, and I am undone.

Twenty, maybe thirty seconds pass. I'm still standing next to the phone, vibrating with the sound of him in my ear. The phone rings.

"Hello?"

The caller hangs up.

Tears come to my eyes. I picture him standing like me, staring at the phone, a smile spreading across his face. Between us the knowledge of our phone calls zips back and forth, dazzling the night with sparks. I'm unwilling to leave the vicinity of the telephone, to move away from this power spot, where we have just connected so well.

After a few minutes it occurs to me that Bo can't be absolutely certain that I phoned him first. I grab my coat. I want him to know he was right. I run out the door, my head down, fingering buttonholes for my coat buttons, and plow into a canvas jacket.

"Hey." He catches me with both arms.

"Bo." I move deeper into the circle of his arms. "Bo, I've missed you."

"Not half as much as I've missed you, Zann."

"Could we argue about that tonight?" I say. All the lost pieces of myself and all the newly found ones snuggle into place inside me and call it home. My face is pushing into the warmth of his neck when the muffled ring of my phone interrupts. Who else but Bo would call me this late? I feel a sense of alarm.

Bo's jaw muscles tighten. "Deak?"

"Oh, no. We stopped seeing each other." The phone still rings, five rings, six. Abruptly, I break away from Bo and dash through the mudroom. I have a terrible image of my mother falling into Bessie Creek. Her balance has gone all to hell this past year. "Bo," I holler over my shoulder, "come in. It must be an emergency."

I answer breathlessly, "Hello?"

"Am I all right?"

That voice. "Momma." Though my mother's well-being leapt immediately to mind when the phone rang, I didn't expect her on the other end of the line. "Momma, it's me, Suzannah." I haven't heard her voice over the phone late at night for years. And then she was drinking and smoking. Last I heard she had forgotten what to do with a cigarette.

She asks, "Do you know me?" She sounds small and faint, like a lost child with alarm causing a wide place in her eyes. News stories of Alzheimer's patients wandering away from home crowd my thoughts. But no, she must be home, calling from the kitchen phone where my number is on memory dial. How else could she have reached me? It's my father, then. He must be hurt.

"Momma, I know you. And you're just fine." But she's not fine. Somehow she is alone in the middle of the night. I check the kitchen clock and add two hours: one in the morning on the East Coast.

Bo holds my hand in both of his and watches my eyes.

"Momma," I say as calmly as I can, "where is Daddy?"

"I can't find my . . . you know."

"Momma, holler, 'Addie.' Like this." I yell my father's name. "Do that, Momma."

I hear her call my father's name; then she says into the phone, "Oh," as if surprised by the strength in her own voice.

A screen door bounces in the background, and my father says, "Lizzie, good God, what are you doing out of bed?" Footsteps approach nearer. "Couldn't you find me? Here, I'll take the phone. Let's tuck you in the sack."

I sense he is about to hang up and I holler, "Dad."

The line goes dead.

I can't dial fast enough. At the same time, I say to Bo, "Everything's fine, I guess. I just have to check." While I wait for the call to go through and my dad to answer, I explain to Bo what seemed to have happened. He removes his coat and sits on the edge of the kitchen table. He takes my free hand back in both of his and holds it in the gap between his legs.

My father's surprised voice answers the phone.

"Dad, it's Suzannah. That was me on the line earlier. Mom called somehow. She couldn't find you."

"I fell asleep on the porch. I'm just beat. The orange trees are blooming. . . . Come here, Lizzie. Stay with me. . . . The whole world smells like your momma's shoulders used to. Isn't that right, Lizzie? We're getting goofy down here, Suzannah. We're running out of steam."

"I'll come down." I've never heard my father sound overwhelmed before. I feel panicky, like I need to keep him on the line while at the same time head for the airport.

"Yes, do that. Your mother would like to see you real soon."

"Day after tomorrow. They'll need notice at work."

"You hear that, Elizabeth Taylor? Your little girl is coming. We get tired of eating alone, don't we, Lizzie? One more night and Suzannah will join us." I know how he feels. I count the nights I have to eat dinner alone with Mom when he goes on one of his trips, though I've never had to count higher than seven.

When at last I hang up, I feel both exhausted and anxious to start leaving. I say to Bo, "He needs me." Though in his typical manner Dad attributed his need to Mom, instead of himself. I look at Bo. That's what I've been accusing him of doing—dumping his unclaimed emotions on me. Instead of feeling irritated by that as usual, I feel competent to deal with it. In a way it makes Bo more familiar. And I'll just learn to hand his stuff back. I say to him, "I have to get down there right away."

"I'm coming with you."

"But you and I are a mess," I wail. "We have so much to clear up. My parents are a mess. I'm a mess."

"We can't wait on this, Zannah."

"But we don't know what's going on with us."

"We know exactly what's going on with us. Besides, I'm in remission on putting things off, Zann. I don't want to do that." Bo cups the side of my head and looks me in the eyes. "We'll sit on the plane and neck and argue until we see ocean below our wings. I'll come with you to Florida to meet your parents. Then later you'll come with me to Ireland to meet my father."

That sounds wonderful, and I give a laugh from the pure joy of it. Then I cry.

Bo releases me reluctantly when I pull away to get a Kleenex from the bathroom.

My father will not rejoice over Bo coming with me. I can't even picture his response. I blow my nose. He was always rude to my boyfriends and not very chummy with Erik. I splash handfuls of warm water over my face. Suddenly I register the rest of what Bo said. I step out of the bathroom. "You know who your father is?"

"I know how to find him."

"We have a lot of catching up to do." I return to the bathroom and dry my face with the hand towel.

One night this past week, I dreamed I walked in a meadow where a poppy grew all alone. I picked the flower and skies darkened and the whole earth shuddered. Sounds of the planet breaking up roared around me. Shaken, I woke. I feared that if I took what I wanted the world would shudder to an end.

"Okay." I return to the kitchen and to Bo's arms. "Let's go to Florida together." Bo and I hold each other.

Somewhere inside a voice exults, "It begins, it begins."

Bo smoothes back all the fine hairs from around my face. "I'll help you pack. Where are your suitcases?"

"Under the bed." I lead the way to my bedroom; I open a drawer and begin making little piles of panties and bras and socks. I try to picture Bo in Florida with me.

My mother, if she were well, would adore Bo. She would monopolize the conversation. She would drink too much and show a bit of extra thigh while crossing her legs in the hope that I might report later that Bo had said, "Your mother sure has good legs for a woman her age." Despite all that, Bo would be charmed. People were always charmed.

I feel a bit crazy, thinking about my mother and wondering how much worse she has gotten since I saw her last. And all the while my heart tries to catch up to its abrupt fullness with the presence of Bo. My brain is working like a Hitchcock movie in which the camera swings suddenly to the commonplace as a reprieve from tension buildup. Abruptly, I open my closet door and get into a welcome snit about what to wear on the plane.

I tuck my pants into my cowboy boots and button a big, warm nubby shirt over my turtleneck and belt the whole business with wide leather. I pose for Bo. "Do I look like a Cossack?" My father's term for my fashion sense.

Bo is dusting off my suitcases with a dirty sock he also found under my bed. "No," he says, checking me out. "You look more like a hassock."

Laughter quickens my body, head to foot, like fast wet licks. I have missed how Bo sneaks inside my head with humor and triggers a coupling between us. He's quite knowing of that trigger's location and sensitivity.

We stand grinning on opposite sides of my bed. Bo's eyes seem to adore me for accepting his joke. So many times we have stood, kitchen linoleum spread like a patterned sheet between us, and reached across it with our words and laughter like a conjugal embrace.

"Meet you halfway," I say and nod toward my bed.

We begin our lovemaking with laughter, and later, much later, we end with soft, exhausted smiles. I feel as though Bo's hands have redesigned my body, that alterations occurred beneath his touch. My nipples elongated, moisture gathered, lips swelled. I am more beautiful now.

Bo lies flat on his back beside me, staring up at the ceiling. He says, "This is the thing I've been suspecting."

"What's that?"

"That falling in love makes a person disappear."

"You feel gone?" I'm surprised. "I feel so here."

"I got so here that I fizzed up and am gone."

I shift up on an elbow and look at him. "Is that bad?"

"I can't tell yet if it's bad, it feels too good."

I start to laugh and soon Bo joins me.

He turns sideways and looks at me. "I wouldn't go through this for anybody but you."

"I feel like you're equating love with a root canal."

"A root canal with laughing gas," Bo says.

twenty-four

"Darling Suzannah."

"There's our dear girl."

Oh, not the aunts in the bookstore, not today. I'm frazzled, trying to get my projects done so I can leave for Florida early tomorrow morning.

"We're terribly sorry to hear about your mother, dear. Bo told us everything." Violet pats my shoulder.

"This is a sad time for your family," Maizie says.

"Thank you." I smile and turn slightly so I can still slip a book from the pile in my arms into the M-N-O-P row of natural history authors.

"We did hear some good news, though." Violet smiles coyly and plucks the top book off my listing stack.

"What's that?"

"Why, the plans you and Bo have for marriage." Violet bends down to place the book on a lower shelf while she speaks, so I am left staring at her curved back.

"What?"

Maizie says, "See, sister, it didn't work. I told you she wouldn't fall for it."

Violet apparently feels it is safe to stand upright again. She scans my face, looking apologetic.

"Fall for what?" I wonder if I have ever spoken to the aunts except in the form of questions. Often with a startled look on my face, as I have now.

Violet says, "Sister and I can't get a thing out of Bo, and we thought we'd try you."

Maizie shifted her embossed leather purse to her other shoulder. "Can't you just give us the teeniest hint?"

"Sister and I always wanted a daughter, but we couldn't bring ourselves to upset Pop again. His ears turned purple when sister surprised him with Bo." Violet lifts three more books out of my arms and scans the shelves for the proper place to put them.

Maizie watches my face.

"Oh," I say stunned. "Oh."

"Yes," Maizie says. "Bo believed we should all tell each other the truth. Though Pop covered his ears and said he wouldn't talk about the foolishness, we just kept it up till he gave in." Maizie continues talking while Violet roams the shelves placing books she lifts from my arms. "We just hope you'll love our Bartholomew," she says, then ducks beneath Violet's arm to finish, "and come be our little girl. Don't we, sister?"

Violet says, "We would be honored if you'd consider joining our family."

"Is this a proposal?" I joke. Being someone's little girl sounds appealing right now.

"Well, I guess it is," Violet says.

"I guess it is," Maizie agrees.

The two sisters nod to each other. "It is," they say.

"There is no other family I'd enjoy more," I say. "But," I hurry to add, "Bo and I need lots of discussion before making any plans. It will be a long time."

"Oh, darling, don't let talk hold you up," Violet says. She lifts the remaining four books out of my arms and proceeds to find their placement. "Men are frightened of talk."

"My, yes," Maizie agrees. "If the military used women's words instead of guns, we'd have ourselves armies of men cowering in their foxholes."

"Sister, it's not fashionable to talk like that anymore. We women are supposed to show kindness, now that our superiority is out in the open." Violet dusts off her hands. "Now I've finished my job. I think we need to let Suzannah get back to work." She leans over and kisses me on the cheek. "You and Bo have as much pleasure as you can manage on your trip to Florida."

"Yes. Sister and I will be thinking of the two of you." Maizie hugs me.

From the shop doorway, Violet calls back, "I shelved your books by title, Suzannah, dear. Hope that helps."

I groan and turn toward the shelves to look for a dozen misplaced books.

Though it's her day off, Tessa pops into the bookstore. She has some news.

"You won't believe what the universe has sent me. He's a

triple Sag—all in the twelfth house. Physically gorgeous. But this is a person so leery of commitment he refuses to use turn signals when he's driving. Should I ask him out, if he doesn't call soon?"

I say, using a lazy Mae West voice, "Tell him to put a pickle in his pocket and come see you sometime."

Tessa laughs. I tell her about Florida.

She says, "Luck to us both. Stories when you get home." A quick kiss and a strong hug and she's gone.

I forgot how I hate leaving on trips. I always look forward to them until they get close. Then I wonder why anyone would try to stuff her life into a suitcase and leave such nice people. I check my watch; it's way past lunchtime, but I have a stack of SPOs—special orders—I want to clean up.

"My boy's been looking kind of gant."

I jump under my clothes and turn from the microfiche I'm scanning, toward the surprise of O.C.'s voice. "Oh." I smile as if he drops in to see me at work every day. *"Gant?"*

"Lost himself some weight."

"Oh," I say again. Does he mean *gaunt?*

"Well?" O.C. demands, leaning with both hands on his ski pole for support.

"You want me to fatten him up?" I hope no one is listening to this exchange. I'm afraid to look.

"Wouldn't hurt none." Like an owl, O.C. turns his head in a half circle without moving his shoulders, checking out the bookstore. "The girls tell me I'll scare you off if I say what I think about all these books and the people that waste good time reading and writing them. So you just tell your folks I'm sorry to hear about their hard times."

"Well, thank you."

O.C. nods. Then as if an afterthought and not the reason he came, he says, "I sent them girls to find out some things and all they do is come home with some wee notions about working in this store someday. Say they learned how."

I say, "No plans for now."

"Well, it's okay by me if you want to go ahead with some."

"Thank you," I say. "I'll let you know."

O.C. nods again. "Me and my boy are making new creations full-time now. Maybe we'll work up something together for your yard."

"That would be nice," I say, and though I can't picture how that would turn out, I'm pleased about this truce between Bo and O.C.

"You come back home real soon."

A crack forms between the earth and sky and the yolky glow of sun spreads brokenly beneath low, thick clouds. We load our suitcases into Bo's Suburban. In the bare cottonwoods above us, three ravens sit big as Labrador puppies.

As we drive to the airport, the sky brightens. A rounded cloud, hanging low, floats along the ridge of a butte like a benign whale swallowing up scrub pine and boulders as it moves past. I hear myself transferring my thoughts to Florida, conjuring beach images in the clouds, the same way I set my watch to a different time zone, in preparation for the change. The two places are so different. Wyoming is made up of spires: the Tetons, the slender, tapering pines, antlers, prairie grasses. Florida shapes resemble fans: palm fronds, the crescent ripples of a wave, scallop shells, fish fins, the curve of beach itself.

On the plane from Jackson to Salt Lake City, Bo and I sip coffee and read the old magazines I stuffed into my backpack in hopes of catching up with them. I notice Bo chose an old issue of *Time*.

I say, "I wonder how many men would pick up the special women's issue of *Time* and read it like you're doing." I sound full of admiration.

With feigned surprise, Bo flips to the cover. "I thought this was the swimsuit issue."

I'm not used to laughing before breakfast. But no use putting off any fun. It's barely eight o'clock now, and we have three more planes to catch before we finally land at six o'clock this evening in West Palm Beach. Then we rent a car for the drive up the coast, another hour. Dad was surprisingly gracious about Bo coming along. "Never been to Florida, eh?" he said last night on the phone. "Guess I'll have to show him how we fish the big water."

The Dallas-to-Atlanta run is the longest leg of the trip. A man sitting across the aisle from me has his boarding pass stuck under the latch holding the table up against the seatback in front of him, as if a train conductor will soon come along and punch his ticket. And the lady two rows in front of him has her special-meal sticker stuck to her hair. It's a pink Post-it that is supposed to be on top of her seat back.

Last night, Bo took me to the barn he uses as a studio and showed me his new work. Spirit Posts, he called them. Tall as I am, these figures were made of thick, rectangular metal tubing. Head shapes were cut out and designs etched into the metal bodies. One post sprouted horns wrapped in long streamers of red trade cloth with feathers. Spikes haloed the head of another with extravagant details cut and bent into the metal body. Horsehair hung down the shoulders in beaded strands on my favorite and each of them sat on an old cultivator disk. That place behind the bridge of my nose stung and made my eyes water when I saw them. They stirred me deeply. If I could see one of these Spirit Posts every day, I might not forget my interdependence with all living things.

I ask Bo now, "How did you get started working again?"

He looks past me, sitting in the middle seat, and out the plane window for a long moment. "I felt like such a goddamn coward."

An attendant interrupts to ask for our drink orders and puts our trays down, laying a napkin and bag of peanuts on each one. I order Bloody Mary mix without the vodka. Bo gets the same.

"A coward?"

"I didn't have the courage to get on with my art, and I threw up roadblocks when it came to you. I never even asked who my real mother was. I spent forty years just glancing off my life." An arm reaches across to set down our two glasses of juice. "I said to myself that if I couldn't grab ahold of these things, I would start to die. I'd start leaking."

"Leaking what?"

"Life force or energy or whatever your friend Tessa might call it. I'd leak until I got so weak that problems would gang up on me and illnesses would cut me down. Soon I'd have so few resources, I would have every reason in the world not to do anything."

I sip my juice and think about the enormity of Bo's experience. I try on the new idea he has suggested. "Like there is a balance of something similar to red and white corpuscles in the activity of life. Is that what you mean? A kind of immune system in the energy field?"

"I don't know. Maybe." He looks past me, out the window again. "I just figured it was like when I was a kid on the playground and got scared on top of the high slide. If I backed down the steps, I wouldn't grow up like the rest of the guys. I'd be left behind, still scared."

"And they'd make fun of you."

"In this case I'd have plenty of company. A lot of people don't follow their dreams. But you'd go on without me."

My heart soars when I hear these words. We kiss softly, barely touching, our heads lying back against the airplane seats.

"Don't cry," Bo whispers. He smiles. "The stewardess will blame me." He wipes his thumb under each of my eyes. "She'll think I stole your peanuts."

The man sitting behind the lady with the Post-it in her hair tries to pluck it off. His hand surreptitiously moves closer; his arm shoots out and back in false starts before he gives up.

Something that's been helpful to me comes to mind. "Your friend Mick Farlow told a story at your barbecue last fall. Maybe you've heard it. He said in boot camp he was taught to think FIDO: Fuck it, drive on. I use it now when I get stuck. The idea is to just keep the flow going."

My mind imagines five years down the road when I might rant to Bo about how tired I am that he just fucks it and drives on whenever we have trouble. I look out the window and smile to myself. I hope I have that problem.

Bo says, "What are you thinking?"

I say, "Maybe one of the best deals in life is getting the problems you love to solve."

"Maybe."

"You promised we'd get to argue on the plane," I tease. "You keep agreeing with me."

The man ahead leans up in his seat, preparing to make a surprise charge on the pink Post-it. I alert Bo to the drama. Slowly, the man aims his index finger and thumb toward the bobbing sticker. He's practically there. He's so close. Abruptly, the lady swings her head to the side, and the man jumps in surprise.

Bo and I laugh.

As we talk more, I realize Bo has given a lot of thought to who I am, who he is and how our differences will come together. He says to me now, "Not everybody thinks life is to be lived the *right* way, like you do."

"Of course they do. People try to live the most right way they can," I say. "And if they are not successful, they feel horrible about it."

"That's how *you* run *your* life. And why, incidentally, you grind your teeth in your sleep."

"I do not." I have to do something so unglamorous our first two nights together?

"You're hard on yourself, Zann."

It's true. I've always carried a kind of pride about being conscientious. I want to get it . . . right.

He says, "My point is that this isn't the goal of everyone. This is a personality thing. It's . . . maybe it's a spiritual thing, with you."

In order to appear openminded I ask, "What other goal is as valid?"

"Mine's not a bad one."

"You have a goal?" This is a relief.

"Experiencing. Being. Being here."

"This sounds like a great excuse to do nothing." Please, I'm so happy. Don't tell me you are a shapeless mass of urges, heading nowhere. Arguing involves more danger than I meant to gamble.

Way at the end of the aisle, the attendants begin to hand out meals. The pink Post-it has now fallen between the lady's back and her seat, out of reach even for the plucky man behind her.

"Being alert is hard work . . . if hard work is what you ad-mire. I haven't always been good at being alert. Sometimes I drink a lot of beer . . . just to give myself a vacation." Bo watches the progress of the meal cart. "But that's my motivation—being alert—and it just seems to me that you ought to know that not everyone is motivated by the same thing you are—being *right*."

Inside myself, I feel as if my soul just turned sideways be-hind my eyes. The view is sharply altered. If not everyone is consciously or unconsciously trying to live the *right* way, then I'm an oddity. And not even a superior oddity. I'm just en-cased in one more restricted perspective, just another follower of rigid law. I didn't mean this. I meant to sweep widely for my beliefs, deal from a panorama of truths.

Bo just wants to be awake.

"I have a friend, Joe Budds, who was gored almost fatally by a Brahma bull years ago," Bo says. "It was during the Stam-pede, the rodeo in Calgary. I was an outrider in the chuck wagon races and got to him first. Joe had stopped breathing. I leaned down to start blowing into his mouth, and Joe's eyes flew open and he whispered, 'Shit. We're wasting our time with a bunch of ideas.' Before he lost consciousness again he said, 'Just live it, buddy.' "

"Rodeo religion," I say. "Cowboy nihilism."

Bo says, "You're missing the point, Zann."

"The point is," I say, "that there is no point."

"Right," Bo agrees. "A natural state of living takes over during heightened pain or fear, even joy, and it isn't dependent on any theories—right ones included. It just is what it is."

No one has ever engaged in argument like this with me before, and I have longed for it. "You mean *reason* has less to do with *being* than I think it does."

"I'm talking about a quality of attention. Whereas you are talking about a quality of *in*tention. I recognize your high morality and I admire it, but I'm suggesting you don't judge me with the same harshness you judge yourself. We have different motivations."

I'm pretty pleased to discover Bo *has* a motivation. Underlying that is this lump in my throat, and I don't think it has to do with Bo's tone of voice, which is gentle but pointed. I suspect Bo is right, yet I thought we were assigned the job of becoming one with the highest idea of perfection we could conceive. I am jolted considerably to learn this may not be true.

I feel choked up and my eyes burn with the need to cry. I've never before had anyone recognize me so succinctly. Neither have I ever felt so naked, even to myself. Two teardrops break the dam of my lower lashes, yet I burst out laughing because I feel so understood.

Bo holds me as close as seat belts and armrests and lack of privacy allow. "I admire you, Zannah. You live carefully and tenderly."

On the final leg of the trip, Atlanta to West Palm, we watch the sun sink. A narrow strip of light beneath the clouds tints the sky the colors of Florida's many fruits: strawberry, melon, lime, and just before dark, the rind of grapefruit.

twenty-five

My mother likes Bo better than me. We just arrived last night, yet already she is whispering in his ear, asking him when I'm going to leave. Bo says, "Not for a while." And my mother makes a face.

Mostly, she sits quietly, passive and pleasant. Her fingers move in a slow, continuous busyness of touching each other or the edges of things around her. Mom has given me a gift several times today. The same gift. She gets up and opens the cupboard where she used to keep her cigarettes; she reaches inside, finds a book of matches, and presents them to me with a shy smile. I feel she is giving me something she once held dear.

Mom goes with all her questions to Bo now instead of Dad. Dad is putting on a show of being jealous, though he is clearly enjoying the reprieve. When Mom gives me the matches again, Dad says, "She wants us to blow ourselves up, Suzannah, and leave her alone with Bo."

We all laugh.

Mom says, "You're silly."

She refers to Dad and Bo now as her *husbands*, when she can find the word. But neither of them should feel too special. I took her grocery shopping at Publix with me earlier today, and every time she spotted a man down an aisle, she took off after him and asked, "Are you my husband?" She feels much more secure with a man than with a woman and becomes noticeably anxious when she is alone with me. Her eyes have become a cloudy blue. I don't think they have lost color, just intent. It's almost as if she looks at me through an unkept aquarium.

She doesn't play cards anymore. The deck sits on the coffee table in four tidy piles, an ace showing on the top of each, as if she finally won a game and wasn't going to chance again the disorder of failing.

This afternoon Bo and I walk the banks of Bessie Creek holding hands.

"Most people probably chop out these trees for a view of the water," Bo says. "It's nice your Dad has kept them."

"The mangroves are protected by law. Only specially licensed workers can cut them. Though people sneak out at night and chop them back all the time."

Bo pushes aside a fern with fronds taller than he is to get closer to the water's edge. "It's probably a good fish hatchery down in there." Bo looks down among the arched props of the mangroves, extending into the brackish water.

"It's perfect. That's the main reason for the law."

I turn toward a rustle in the palmettos and spot my mother. I'm surprised to see her outside on her own. Then, inwardly, I groan. She is wearing a favorite outfit: a dirty white terry cloth sun suit and a plastic shower cap that sits low on her forehead and puffs high over her ears. Bo and I walk her back toward the house. A year ago she'd rather be shot than seen like this, but Bo escorts her as if they were heading for the dance floor at a fancy-dress ball.

Now that I have been around a few days, I see that my father is managing as well as always, and is as determined as always to handle Mom's care alone. But he desperately needed a break. Having Bo here allows my father to pretend it is his duty to entertain Bo and boat him around the intercoastal waterway. Every day, Dad looks more rested. However, Mom becomes more agitated with others in the house. The length of our visit will be determined by the balance of the good we do my father versus the harm we do my mother.

Early this morning, Bo and Dad left for a fishing trip on the *Lady Stuart*, they have been gone all day, and won't return home until after Mom's bedtime. I help her undress, prompting each move. One soft moccasin slips off one foot. She studiously ponders what to do next and looks to me for guidance. I help slip off the other one. I must lie in the dark with her until she sleeps. She is restless tonight. Up on one elbow, she asks me again where her *you know* is. She becomes belligerent about Dad's absence, but can't find the words to express herself.

I try an old trick of hers, one she used getting me to sleep. I sit on the edge of her bed and slowly trace her eyebrows with one finger. And I sing.

When my dad comes in to wake me and take my place in his bed next to Mom's, I realize I have been dreaming that my mother reverted to a little person. In my dream it made sense to me that since she is regressing mentally, her body will become smaller, too, and that will make her easier to care for. I thought perhaps she'd like to lay on a blanket on the floor like babies do. Then, in my dream, I glimpsed my mother's vaginal area, labia with pubic hair, suddenly explode off from this small being and lie beside her on the blanket. Somehow I did not find the sight gory. Beside it, as well, was a piece of the back of her head, and from this, I averted my eyes.

I feel certain my dream contains clues about my mother's condition. But I never could decipher dreams. I'll give this one to Tessa when I see her.

Bo calls dreams night mail. I like that. Once I dreamed of drunk people and woke up the next morning feeling slightly hungover. Beckett told me when I last called that he dreamed I painted myself with war paint before I sat down to design jewelry. I like that, too.

As usual since Mom's illness, I am enveloped in pastry wrap, buffered, smiling, unshockable. Suzannah *en croute*. But I am aware, too, of a sodden center, enlarging as my time here goes by, gaining heaviness, solidity. Puzzled each time, I never remember this sensation from one visit to the next and spend the first few days wondering what is physically wrong with me. My father's sodden center is causing him chest pains of late. Stress, his doctor says.

Before breakfast this morning, I ask Bo how the fishing trip went. He says he enjoyed it.

"Get along with my dad okay?"

"He's great. I like him. Had his hands on my fishing pole

more than his own, but even so we caught a hell of a lot of fish."

"That's my dad. You have to ditch him, if you can. As a kid I'd sneak off to the other side of the *Lady Stuart* and fish where he couldn't find me."

Once we are all seated for breakfast, I keep glancing at my mother beside me at the table. Something is different, but I can't tell what. Maybe I'm too close to her. I push back my chair. "Anybody want more coffee?" I raise my eyebrows at Bo with exaggeration. We've been whispering about my Dad's horrible, weak coffee.

"I've had plenty, thanks," Bo says politely and gives me a look over the rim of his cup.

Having a coconspirator in my father's house offers more comfort than I would have guessed.

From the kitchen counter I wait for my mother to lift her head. She's especially quiet this morning. She chews on a card from the deck lying on the coffee table.

"Momma? You want more coffee?" I hold the pot up in the air. Mom doesn't respond. Usually she looks to my dad for her answers. But Dad and Bo are leaving the table. They have decided to go out and tinker with the dory's motor. The screen door slaps behind them. My mother lifts her head to watch the men cross the yard.

"Momma?" I set the coffeepot back. I need to double-check what I think I have seen. She lowers the card she is chewing and looks at me. Her face looks slightly lopsided. I can't swear it, but it appears that her left eye sags. I could convince myself that it didn't, if I wanted to. Her mouth on that side droops, too, just a bit. Yes, now I'm sure of it.

I pull out the chair next to her and turn it to face her. "Momma? You having a hard time this morning?"

It seems imperative that someone know what has happened to her. I think of her experiencing a stroke all alone in her bed. All alone in her head. Somewhere inside her, she knows an earthquake, a body quake, has left damage. Someone else needs to know it with her. Someone must witness for her and acknowledge what she is unable to witness and acknowledge for herself.

I smooth her cheeks and her hair. Later, I will decide whether to tell Dad. I suspect nothing can be done. My father dressed her this morning and didn't notice anything—perhaps he can't let himself notice any further damage.

"Momma?" I turn her chair so we face each other. The card is the ace of spades, and the black ink has transferred to her lips and teeth. For the first time, she looks demented to me. I fight tears. I take her hands into both of mine. They feel chilled; blue veins show through pale, translucent skin.

She lifts her head, looks me in the eyes, and begins murmuring. I can barely hear her. I bend closer until we are nose to nose. When she stops, she looks expectantly at me, and though I haven't detected the sense of a single word, I murmur back to her.

"I know, Momma. I see what a bad time you had. Life is getting harder for you."

Like we once did sitting on the porch glider watching the moon grace Bessie Creek, we both talk at once. Though now we aren't using words, just quiet murmuring sounds, like the slow-moving creek itself as it flows through the props of the mangroves.

When I spot Bo and Dad crunching across the stiff Florida grass, toward the house, I say one last thing to my mother.

"Whatever you decide is okay with me. I understand. I'll help Daddy. When you've had enough, you can do what you need to do." And now without worrying that I will confuse her, I can once again tell her what a wonderful mother she has been to me. I can pour out my love and gratitude.

Like two African lovebirds, our noses touching, our four hands nesting in my mother's lap, we make sounds to each other, quiet, private sounds. I put my arms around Mom and hold her close. Over her shoulder, I watch Bo and my father nearing us, Bessie Creek glinting sunlight behind them.

All at once, I realize that I have learned the most about gaining independence and strength through dependent and weak people. Erik and my mother. In my heart, I thank them. I remember a long-ago talk with Bo when I wondered why the strong must be in service to the weak. I think now I know the answer. It is in gratitude for the lessons they teach.

My father bursts into the house, his noisy energy bringing my mother's quiet murmurs to a halt. "Telling secrets, you two? None of that." My mother looks up at him. "Lizzie, you think it's Halloween, blacking your teeth like that? Look at you."

Bo comes to stand beside me. He rests his hands on my shoulders. And I think to myself once more, It begins, it begins.

Photo by Robert Caston, 2006

Tina Welling lives and writes in Jackson Hole, Wyoming. Her essays have been published in magazines and several anthologies. *Crybaby Ranch* is her first novel.

You can reach her at www.tinawelling.com

CRYBABY RANCH

Tina Welling

This Conversation Guide is intended to enrich the
individual reading experience, as well as encourage us
to explore these topics together—because books,
and life, are meant for sharing.

A CONVERSATION
WITH TINA WELLING

Q. Was there a particular image or idea that triggered the writing of Crybaby Ranch?

A. An image that supplied a lot of energy for writing this story occurred during an intense point in my mother's fatal illness. I witnessed my parents holding each other's hands and looking into each other's eyes. My father said to my mother, "We are partners, aren't we?" Though the scene lasted only a moment, I was seared with a profound awareness of what it means to commit to another person. They were nearing their fiftieth anniversary. I used this scene in the book to help Suzannah describe to Bo what kind of marriage she wanted.

The idea of life partners intrigues me. Though I have been married to the same man for decades now, I think of us as having five or six different marriages within the one. Partners don't always grow at similar rates or in compatible ways, so when there is a bond of deep love, this calls for adjustments instead of separation. But a relationship involves an exchange between two people, and in some cases, the exchange stops or only flows one way, as in the case of Suzannah and Erik at the novel's opening. I don't believe that every marriage should continue until parted by death, but I do believe that a committed partnership acts on many energetic levels, some very mysterious.

Q. Did you hope to send any messages through the story of Suzannah?

A. Perhaps a little confirmation for women in particular toward the idea of discovering their true selves, and a couple signposts that I have discovered during my own process of what Jung calls "individuation." One signpost is to follow what you love, as Suzannah does in moving to Jackson Hole, getting a job at a bookstore, honoring her love of beadwork. A relationship with the natural world is very healing, as is learning to enjoy solitude. Yet perhaps the most powerful and direct path is the creative one. Engaging creative energy is a sure way to awaken the unconscious and enliven ourselves. Suzannah's love for creating her beaded jewelry both arouses her evolution toward independence and supports her through the difficulties that journey provokes.

Q. Did you know the ending of Crybaby Ranch *before arriving at that point in writing it?*

A. No, but sometime early on I knew the final words: "It begins, it begins." I was so happy knowing that; it carried me through the years of writing with a bit of confidence that I would complete this project and create a story that measured up to the spiritual meaning those words held for me.

Q. So the whole story was not in mind before you began writing it?

A. No, not at all. I began the novel with a sense of magnetism between Suzannah and Bo, along with that image I mentioned earlier of my parents acknowledging their partnership. Then I just had some fun moving the story along. Then I had some trouble moving the story along, back and forth—fun and trouble—until it began to come together. After that, it was rewrite after rewrite with spaces in between for clarity to make an appearance . . . if it was going to. This book spent a lot of time sitting about. Yet each time I picked it up again, I felt a strong energy for making it work. So I would engage in yet another rewrite.

Q. Love for the natural world plays a role in your novel. Suzannah finds solace and pleasure in the outdoors. Do you?

A. Once I was a dependent, indecisive person who never strayed far from my husband and children or the places I was expected to be. Then slowly I began to wander farther and farther up the mountain canyons. First just short walks; then I packed my lunch and spent entire days on solo hikes into the Tetons. I was scared some of the time and exhilarated all the time. The love of the natural world became another relationship for me. And this relationship supported a whole new sense of who I was and whom I could become. As it turned out, I felt happy with my own company and I became confident that I could take care of myself.

Q. Is there a joining of biography with imagination in the novel?

A. Yes. And that's a good way to put it. It's a joining—a mating, a kind of love affair, even a sexuality—of actual life and the creative arts. Like real-life conception, these two qualities—my experience and my imagination—bonded and produced (in a whole lot longer than nine months!) a novel. Some parts of the story concerning Suzannah and her mother, Lizzie, came from journal entries I made while caring for my own mother as she suffered from Alzheimer's. But with time and dozens of rewrites, this biographical piece blended with fiction and became a universal story about any mother who suffers and any daughter who loves her mother. Suzannah is not me; Lizzie is not my mother. Yet, because of my experience, there is an emotional reality to this relationship in the book.

One of the things I love most about creative writing is how this blend works. It entertains me enormously to discover that I have created some character that I know nothing about at the moment, only to realize later that he or she has evolved from a past seedling. Even those crazy aunts kind of emerged from this silly routine my sister, Gayle, and I drop into sometimes when we realize we have done something nutty. We might be out on her boat and hear something fall into the water, and one of us will say in our particular dialogue voice, "Sister? Was that our house key you dropped in the water?" And the other will answer in the same tone, "Of course not, sister. That was just your lunch."

But at the same time such disclosures are dangerous to make since people then tend to jump to the conclusion that a novel is entirely true, a thinly disguised memoir, which creates an immense disservice to any work of art. Fiction, like painting or dance, is an artist's interpretive vision of life: the choices available, the working out of cause and effect, the meaning, the interconnection of it all. People who have little experience of the power of creative energy often assume there isn't such a thing and their understanding of the process is limited.

Q. What is the most difficult part for you about writing a novel? What is the most pleasant?

A. In my experience, writing a novel is a long, long process that takes me years to complete, and during that time, I don't know if I am writing something that connects me to real life in a deeply intimate way or detaches me from real life in a way that threatens my mental health. Or at least that is how it has felt in the past. With the publication of

Crybaby Ranch, my confidence in how I work has increased, and I may find this mystery solved or at least more comfortable. I fall in love with the process, the characters, the story, and even myself because of the enlivening force of creative energy. But then I wonder if I'm in some dreamworld in which no one but me finds value. In that case, those growing stacks of papers on my desk and those tiny notes that litter my car, kitchen, and business, like confetti, only attest to a kind of insanity. Then again it may be a novel, and those papers are proof that it's evolving toward completion. It may be that all novelists flirt with schizophrenia, though I suspect that this is something that self-heals with experience. I remember the first novel I wrote (which resides in my bottom desk drawer) was such an intense process that I feared I was going to meet my characters on the street. Now I succeed more often in seeing my work as my work, rather than my life. Perhaps it is necessary in the beginning of all passions—whether a relationship, a skill, an art, or an idea—for us to briefly loosen our boundaries and merge with it in order to fully experience it. Honeymoons aren't necessarily just applicable to marriages.

All of the above could also apply to what is pleasant about writing a novel. My life feels dense and textured with the fullness of experience. Writing for me brings the unconscious into the conscious. So I can enjoy discovering the first sage buttercup of springtime on the mountain behind my house and, when I return home, enjoy the discovery in another way through writing about it. Often that second experience lifts from my awareness other qualities of the experience that I wasn't conscious of at the time. And it pins down the fullness of the event for me: my fingers touching the glossy petals, the aroma of wet earth as the snow melts into it, my eyes squinting in the sunlight, my pup, Zöe, nosing the blossom. These flowers are only the size of a dime and are a wondrous surprise in the patchy snow. Writing for me enlarges my life and deepens it as well. Reading also accomplishes this for me, so I am very grateful to be involved in the whole exchange of writing and reading.

Q. Would you describe your workplace and writing schedule?

A. My workplace is a small log cabin, an old one, moved in from the elk refuge outside Jackson Hole and attached to my home. Just one room with an ancient woodstove (there is also electric heat), windows on three sides, lots of bookshelves. One wall supports a long rustic-looking counter the previous owner put in. I use the counter for crafts on one end and for manuscript sorting on the other. My desk sits facing all the windows and the stove, and in a corner, I've placed a wicker settee to read and knit, and beneath one window, I've created a small area for meditation. I feel lucky and grateful every time I walk into this cabin.

My schedule is a mere theory—a rumor I pass among my friends, a vague intention, a wispy wish. In my imagination I write in the mornings, hike or ski in the afternoons. But in reality I don't actually get out of my pajamas till lunchtime, and though I've been writing, who can take anything seriously that is done wearing pajamas? Then there is my resort shop, which I work at half the week, morning and afternoon (though not in my pajamas). I close the shop for two months after ski season and another two months after the summer season; during those times I can give myself over completely to my phantom writing schedule.

All in all, like most writers who also hold day jobs, I often feel a bit schizophrenic (there's that word again) trying to juggle two callings—my business and my passion. And two worlds—one of reality and one of imagination.

Actually, I love my life. The time I spend in my shop dealing with visitors from around the world balances perfectly with the time I spend in solitude writing. And I especially love the ledger work, where there is no doubt about where to place the decimal points, whereas in my writing life I can spend an hour deciding about punctuation in a single sentence.

Q. How did you arrive at this point in your writing career?

A. Much like a new driver learning a stick shift: starts and stops, starts and stops, jolting down the long road. Since I have envied those writers who begin their careers as toddlers, I have racked my brain to come up with a story from my childhood that shows without a doubt that I was always meant to be a writer. This is the best I could find. When I was seven years old, I had a favorite spot behind the sofa, and lying on my stomach, I would write and read. I remember announcing to my parents after crawling out of that place one day that I was going to grow up and write stories.

That was the end of that for a couple decades, until I announced to my husband, as I sat on the front side of the sofa—as a grown-up should—that I would like to write. But we had little children, and though I promised myself every time I put them down for a nap that I would use that time to write, invariably I would nap myself. This went on until the boys entered school. Then I got a position to write commercials at the local radio station. From there I began writing poetry, but every poem—just like a radio commercial—could be read in thirty seconds . . . flat.

But that was my beginning. I fell in love with how I felt when I wrote something—a good commercial, a poem, an essay. *Crybaby Ranch* is my first published novel; before this, I published essays in national magazines and several anthologies, and led writing workshops for the Jackson Hole Writers Conference and other organizations. I have always loved reading novels, so it was only a matter of time before I tried to write one. I have two training novels that will never be published. Yet they taught me things I needed to know about the craft of writing and the management of creative energy.

Q. And your next project?

A. Another novel. I am hooked on the process of developing characters that meet life challenges, fail and succeed, and along the way teach me things I need to know. I am especially entranced by relationships. My next novel is about a marriage, a good marriage. Nevertheless, the wife arrives at the need to take a sabbatical from the marriage. I want to address some universal dreams women have about mating for life and how those dreams so often oppose reality. I was raised on the Cinderella story, as are many women in our culture, and such fairy tales set us up for some disappointment. And yet marriage and partnering is still something many of us yearn to have in our life. I like to write about problems I don't know the solutions to so that instead of that old adage that suggests you write about what you know, I choose to write about what I love and want to know more about. Writing is how I educate myself.

QUESTIONS
FOR DISCUSSION

1. Suzannah leaves Erik when she realizes he is no longer invested in keeping the marriage alive. Do you think women tend to hang on to relationships long past the point of reviving them? And do you think Suzannah should have stayed longer or left sooner?

2. Suzannah wants more from her relationship with Bo as a result of her marriage to Erik. Do you think she has the right to expect this? And do you think their relationship lasts past the point in which the story ends?

3. How do you feel when Suzannah begins a temporary relationship with Deak and what do you think she gains from the experience?

4. Do you know anyone as zany as Bo's aunts?

5. Bo's grandfather, O.C., is prejudicial in a way others of his generation are. How do you handle a situation when an otherwise respected person makes prejudicial or inflammatory remarks in your presence?

6. Suzannah leaves home for Jackson Hole, Wyoming, the place she can imagine herself living alone happily. Where would you go? What qualities would you need such a place to hold?

7. Every character in *Crybaby Ranch* evolves toward a fuller, larger self except for Suzannah's mother, Lizzie, whose Alzheimer's disease contracts her sense of self. Perhaps the character who grows the most throughout the story is Bo. Discuss Bo's process of change from a heavy-drinking cowboy to a productive artist.

8. Do you have someone as self-centered as Caro in your life? If you do, how do you deal with that person?

9. What role does the natural world play in your life? Like Suzannah, do you choose to spend time with nature when you need comfort, or to celebrate your solitude, or to enjoy another person, get inspiration, exercise, or relax?

10. Creativity is found in business, parenting, housekeeping, cooking, crafts, music, and art. What changes have a creative pursuit, such as Suzannah's beadwork, made in your life?